Blood Kin

Mary Saxon Wilburn

PublishAmerica
Baltimore

First printing

At the specific preference of the author, PublishAmerica allowed this work to remain exactly as the author intended, verbatim, without editorial input.

ISBN: 1-4137-7296-X
PUBLISHED BY PUBLISHAMERICA, LLLP
www.publishamerica.com
Baltimore

Printed in the United States of America

For Brenda —

Enjoy a cool read

Mary Saxon Wilburn

Dedication

To my wonderful, delightful sons,
Dennis and Michael Mong

Acknowledgments

I am deeply grateful to Larry Johnson, columnist; Janice Duncan, teacher; Barbara Billert, teacher; Janet Walker McDaniel, author; and to Wylly Vaughn and Norma Saxon, mystery fans; for your proofreading, your criticisms, and your editorial comments. Your help has been invaluable.

Much gratitude too, to Harris Green, Sonya Smith, and Jane Milligan, members of the Henry County Writers Guild, for being part of the process that breathed life into Cassie Ryder, and to Joy Padgett, Eleanor Hoomes, Paul Bowdre, Allison Payne, Claire Baker and Wayne Parker, members of the West Georgia Writers Guild, Inc., for your pointed critiques of the work.

Thanks also to Allene Groote and Grace Taylor, for your comments and advice while I wandered through the plotting maze in the early stages of the story.

And as always, thanks to my husband, Larry Wilburn, who gives me all the support and latitude any writer could desire, and who drives me endless miles to do research for verisimilitude.

Special thanks to Larry Young, photographer and friend, for the cover photo.

One

Cherry Lake, Sunday evening, January 12, 1985

Olivia Howe snored deeply in her booze induced sleep as a wintery afternoon sun pressed toward the horizon. She hadn't seen the snow clouds or sensed the approaching blizzard as it swept into the southern Appalachians, leaving the remote little towns and hamlets of Cherry Lake, Hartsville, and Murphree as still and quiet as death.

She didn't hear the furtive footsteps creeping along the hall and up the stairs. She didn't hear the first muffled sounds of movement overhead as the prowler rooted through boxes and trunks in the rooms high above her head. At last she opened her bleary eyes and wondered what had aroused her.

Something was stirring around in her attic. She had sealed up all the outside openings, she thought, in order to keep squirrels and field mice and the like from stealing in, as they always tried to do in the winter.

"I'll fix you," she whispered to her unidentified quarry. Stealthy as a mouse she took the broom from the pantry then slipped up the stairs and down the hall, around to where the attic door, usually held closed from the outside by a crossbar, stood slightly ajar. If she ever wondered why it was open, the fuzzy consequence of drink soon took away the question.

Up she crept, one cautious step at a time, until her eyes were level with the attic floor. Someone was there! Someone was bending over the old trunk, lifting out her keepsakes, handling her souvenirs and reading her papers! In an instant she was up the remaining stairs, brandishing the broom over the head of the intruder.

"What do you think you're doing up here? Those are my private things you're meddling with!"

The smirking intruder held up a piece of yellowed paper, a ghoulish grin now replacing the smirk. "I think this is mine. It's time the piper gets his pay."

Olivia brought the broom down toward the head of the meddler, but did not hit her target. Before the blow landed, the strong, supple form moved in under the weapon and shoved the woman backward.

Olivia staggered back into a pair of old andirons, crying out as her ankle twisted and she was thrown to the floor, screaming in agony as her thigh bone cracked.

The offender leapt across the writhing body and fled down the stairs, slamming shut the door at the bottom. Quick as a flash the crossbar fell into place as Olivia cried out, "I've told them about you!"

Shouts for help and cries of pain that came from the attic went unheeded as the stealthy figure left the house by the back door, barely dislodging the blankets Olivia had placed there to stop the draft, and slipped away unnoticed into the deepening twilight.

The injured woman tried to stand but the pain threw her again to the floor. At last she was able to crawl, dragging her broken leg, to the top of the stairs. At the top, trying desperately to find a way to get down the stairs, she ventured one wrong move and lost her grip. Head over heels she tumbled down, landing in a heap at the foot of the steps, wedged against the door. In pain and shock she slipped from consciousness. A small trickle of blood leaked from her ear down through a strand of lank grey hair and formed a small puddle on the floor.

The temperature outside dropped quickly. Heavy oak embers in the fireplace burned low and turned to ash. No one would come to light the furnace. The injured woman's body temperature sank lower and lower, and soon all signs of life were gone.

The pure white snow fell softly for a while. Then came the wind that lashed through the mountains, whipping the snow into a fury of white, flying harder and harder, thicker and thicker. Soon the world outside the silent house was frosted over like a village portrayed by Currier and Ives as Olivia Howe came to the bitter end of her sadly wasted life.

Death moved on up the mountain to the snowbound hamlet of Hartsville to claim its next victim.

Two

Hartsville, Tuesday, January 14, 1985

The body of the boy in the ditch was frozen solid now. He had vaguely known what hit him, but still it had taken him by surprise. His last muddled thought was: *This must be part of the play, but I don't remember this scene!*

Meg Dothard's cat crept outside through the kitty port in the outside utility room door, pausing to sniff the frosted air. Her whiskers reached forward, seeking the source of whatever provocative smell it was that seasoned the morning. Flesh. Blood.

She looked at the spot on the top step where her bowl usually sat, where ordinarily she found food associated with that smell, and her furry brow furrowed. She saw no bowl nor steps, only a vast whiteness extending to the limits of her vision with humps and hollows in a parody of the familiar variety of objects that should be there. Only one patch of color, far out beside the road, broke the white monotony, and from that patch came the aroma that so enticed her.

Out of sorts at having no dazzling sunlight or multitextured world to greet her, Raucous thought long and seriously before stepping gingerly out into the snow. She quickly leapt across the soft, icy torment of wind-whipped snow, intent only on reaching her prey. Touching her nose to the frozen redness, she was oblivious to all else until a sudden icy clump of snow struck her in the face and a harsh human voice from somewhere nearby shouted at her. "Scat! Get away from there!" Another frosty spray hit her and, hissing fiercely, Raucous turned tail to the wind, the warmth of Meg Dothard's kitchen her immediate destination.

Meg Dothard was sleeping late. She'd stayed up half the night waiting for the sound of Ben's footsteps, and it was not until 2:00 A.M. that she had turned out the lights and gone to bed. Well, no more. She couldn't, wouldn't, spend another night like last night, waiting for that boy to show up. Not only did he not show up, he hadn't even bothered to call. It wasn't the first time she'd had this particular disappointment, but it would be the last, she determined. She'd just have to let him go. Accept the fact that he was growing up, and that she was losing her little boy to his own adulthood.

Meg threw back the covers and pushed her feet into deep furry slippers. From the chair back she grabbed a huge quilted robe and wiggled her arms into it, tying it around her on her way to answer the interminable yowling at her utility room door. She wished sometimes that Raucous had adopted someone else, or at least that she could have been a full grown, therefore well mannered cat. *Half-grown kittens could be almost as trying as half grown humans*, she thought.

Raucous was in the kitchen almost before the door was open. Pushing through the first opening her nose would fit into, she sprang past Meg like a cat electrified, with billions of hairs standing straight out and a tail like a bottle brush. "Well, really!" chided Meg, already warming the milk for the white coated animal with one dark-tipped whisker.

Meg stared at that whisker. *Funny, I never noticed that before*, she thought. As she moved toward the cat to examine it closer, she heard the sound of boots clumping up her front steps and a fist pounding at her door.

"Meg. It's me, Perry Gillis. May Nathan and I talk to you a minute? Meg! Open up! I'm freezing out here!"

"Doesn't anybody realize it's too cold to be out and too early to be up?" Meg muttered as she set the milk down for Raucous.

When she opened the door for Deputy Perry Gillis of the Hart County Sheriff's Department, he pushed in as if at home, and might as well have been for all the social graces Meg wasted on him.

"What in the world has got into you?" she asked, almost closing the door in the face of Nathan Cole, shivering in his sweater sleeves. Meg stared open mouthed and then shook her head sadly, as if Nathan were some pitiable numbskull with not enough sense to come in out of the rain, much less enough to know how to dress for a snowstorm. She gave Nathan a last pitying look while turning to the kitchen to make coffee.

Deputy Gillis was close behind her. Nathan stayed in the living room, laying a fire and lighting the gas jet in the fireplace.

"Planning to stay awhile?" Meg called out from the kitchen.

Nathan turned from the fireplace and spoke as gently as his chattering teeth would allow. "Meg, you're going to have more company over the next few hours than you really want. Sorry. There is no way to stop the curious or the media. If there is a difference," he added. Nathan Cole was the publisher, editor, and in snow storms and other perilous times, delivery boy for the Hartsville Weekly Courier.

Meg set the tray with their cups down firmly, knowing in her bones that she wasn't going to like what was coming.

"Gillis, what's he talking about? What's happened?"

Gillis knew any attempt to soften the news would be wasted on Meg. "When Nathan came to deliver your paper this morning, Meg, he found a body in your ditch."

"He found a what?" She stiffened, not prepared for the chill that ran through her, but she batted not an eye. The hand that poured the coffee shook only slightly, creating a soft *clink* between cup and pot as Perry continued.

"Young man, can't say how old just now." Seeing her frightened eyes he added quickly, "It's not Ben. The body is pretty well frozen, been there awhile. You hear anything last night?"

13

Meg relaxed a little, hearing it was not her Ben, and thought back to the night before, how earnestly she had listened for any unusual sound. She had heard limbs creaking in the cold, she had heard the fire sputter and die, she had heard a car or two. Were there two, or only one? She couldn't recall. There was one sound a little like the sound of a backfire, but she wasn't going to mention that to Gillis—he would right away swear it was a gunshot and she knew the difference—but none of the cars had brought her the person she was waiting to see.

"Nothing unusual," she said. "Is it anybody from around here?"

"I don't recognize him. That doesn't mean he hasn't been here, with all the tourists coming through to see the foliage the last two or three months and me living out on the edge of town like I do. He may have been here for a while. Or he may be one of the actors arriving early for the Shakespeare Festival. I'll go up to the hotel a little later, after the coroner comes, and see if anybody there might know something. Which reminds me, may I use your phone?"

Meg indicated the corner table where the instrument rested, and Gillis picked up the receiver. He laid it back down with a look of resignation on his face. "The coroner may be later than I thought. Your phone's out. I'll go back to the station and try from there. If my phone's out I'll try to radio through." He reached for his coat.

"You'll have a cup of this coffee first, getting me out of bed so early and letting me make it."

"You weren't in bed. You were feeding that cat. Ha! You should have seen him run when I threw that snow on him."

"He's a her," said Meg, "and her name is Raucous. And why were you throwing snowballs at my cat in her own yard?"

"He, rather she, was about to mess up the evidence out there," said Gillis, thinking that the cat's name would be an apt nickname for Meg, too. Meg and Raucous. They seemed to belong together.

"Well…" Meg's voice faded. She had few pleasures these days, but bantering with Nate, and sometimes Gillis, was the foremost of those she did have.

"You can have coffee anyway. If that man is frozen, he'll keep," she said, looking toward Nathan's shirt sleeves, as if she thought perhaps he might not keep.

"I put my coat over him. Don't guess he needs keeping warm, but, I don't know, you just always cover the face of a dead person." His voice trailed off as he went into a volley of sneezes.

"It's your face that gets covered next, then. How do you ever manage to run the newspaper single handed, not having any more sense than you do?" Meg teased.

Nathan grinned. Who could argue with the logic of Meg Dothard?

Gillis intervened. "Meg, how about coming out and having a look? You may recognize him. Maybe Ben would have known him."

"Is he that young, do you think? Ben has lots of friends, in and out of the hotel." She hadn't wanted Ben to work at the hotel particularly, would rather he had wanted to be an engineer or something, but Ben had ideas of becoming a chef or hotel manager and though it might take him away from Hartsville she couldn't complain about that. It was a better life than any of the manual jobs available in this small mountain village.

She poured each of them a cup of coffee and excused herself to get dressed properly, running a brush through the curly tangles of black hair, now showing a sprinkling of white. Her round face, still shiny with night cream, she left to fend for itself until after the men were out of her way. In the living room again she reached into the coat closet and handed Nathan an old pea coat that Jack had left there years ago, then headed out into the whiteness following close behind him and Gillis.

Nate lifted up the coat that he had used to cover the boy's face then stood aside, allowing Meg a clear look at the lifeless body. Nathan too looked at the poor young man's form, and what could be seen of his face above the snow, but Gillis watched Meg as her face whitened, clouded momentarily, then became mask-like while some unidentifiable emotion smoldered behind her deep brown eyes.

"Wish I could show you his face front on, but we better not move him just yet. What do you think, Meg?"

"He looks familiar in a way. Maybe I've seen him around town somewhere. But I don't know his name." Her mouth shut in a grim line as she turned back to the house.

The men watched her go, then followed her quietly inside. They exchanged a glance, and Nathan said, "I'll stay here, if Meg doesn't mind, in case something comes up. Have to stay on top of the news, you know."

"Yeah, okay," said Gillis, relieved. Nate was quick to realize that Meg didn't need to be left alone. "I'll go radio Murphree and get some people in here and see if those people up Mountain Road want to come down to the hotel till this storm is over. Then I'll come back to make sure you don't start inventing news stories, Nate."

"Thanks, Nathan," Meg said, not the least bit fooled by his claims of news-gathering. "I appreciate you staying here. I don't want to go through this, but I know it's got to be done." She looked at Gillis. "Just tell them to hurry, hear?"

They watched the door close behind him as if he were never coming back. "How about some breakfast?" she said to Nathan, not waiting for an answer.

The aroma of bacon frying and pancakes browning soon reached his nose, and he sat down to such a breakfast as he hadn't had in years.

As they ate, he brought Meg up to date on the morning's events. "I got up early, and when I saw what the weather was like I knew my delivery boy wouldn't be able to make it today, so I dressed in the warmest clothes I own, could barely move for all the trappings, and headed out. Thought I'd bring you your paper first, since you're usually up before the chickens, and then work my way on up the mountain and maybe get to Cassie's in time for one of her muffins and a cup of herbal tea, but I do believe I'd rather eat right here with you. Especially with snow laying three or four feet deep up that mountain, probably."

Cassie. Cassie Ryder. What was her real first name, he wondered. Cassandra? Cassiopeia? She was in many ways a mystery to him. For all the work they did together at the paper, he never seemed to be able to see beyond the walls she kept around herself. Ever since she had come back to Hartsville after her husband's death, she was almost like a closed and shuttered house, with the woman who lived there stepping outside and closing the door behind her when she talked to people. At least, to men. Oh, she was full of life, always interesting to talk to, curious about almost everything, but you never felt like you really knew her. She was, he concluded, just a mystery.

"How much would you say our record snowfall was?" Meg asked, bringing his thoughts back to her table.

"No idea, but we don't usually get more than six or eight inches at a time." He glanced out the window and saw that snow was starting to fly again, small flakes, like the cinnamon-sugar on the oatmeal muffins that Cassie, as his part-time reporter, often brought into the office. "Maybe the snow plow will be able to get through from Murphree and clear all this out before too long," he added.

He basked in satisfaction, knowing that through his own curiosity and interviewing skills and Cassie's weekly stories, along with the input from the AP and a few local contributors and stringers, he had the news of all Hartsville and beyond at his fingertips. His was the only newspaper in town, so he had no competition. He knew his fellow villagers and their habits. Well, not quite all about them. No one would ever know for sure what went on behind the closed doors of Hartsville.

Take Meg Dothard, for instance. She had lived here all her life, but since Jack Dothard, her poor excuse for a husband, had just disappeared, she had become more and more distant. She hadn't reported him missing, leading the villagers to believe she knew where he was. She had just clammed up about him, and built her life around Ben, their son. It seemed that Cassie Ryder was the only woman friend Meg had kept.

He sopped up some syrup on a fork full of pancake and ate it. Bringing himself back to the present, he went on with his narrative, as much to hear himself talk as to keep Meg's mind occupied.

"Anyway, when I got down here, I saw something lying in the ditch. I didn't know what it was until I was right up on it. I thought about coming and telling you right away, but then I thought, no, better go get Deputy Gillis. So I did." He took a long draft from his coffee cup and set it down with finality.

"I guess that was for the best. I'll sure be glad when this day is over, though."

Meg was quiet, much too quiet for Nathan Cole's comfort. He wanted to keep her talking, or at least keep her mind occupied. "Speaking of Cassie, I hope those people who live up that road are going to be all right. Maybe they'll all come down to the hotel like folks around here usually do in these situations."

"They probably will, at least if they're smart. I just hope that Ike Farabaugh up there knows he has to let them stay at the hotel till the weather clears. He hasn't been here during a bad spell before, not that I remember."

"Well, Gillis will let them know, I'm sure. He's pretty much on the ball, it seems."

Deputy Perry Gillis, left to maintain law and order on his own for the first time in his brief career, made his way through the deepening snow back to the Sheriff's Department. As he slogged through the snow and ice, he went over the morning's events, getting them in order for his report. He couldn't hold back a chuckle as he remembered watching Nate start out so confidently this morning from the newspaper office across the street, then some time later the door of his own office flying open and Nathan rushing in, wide-eyed and arms everywhere.

"Come on," Nate had commanded, dragging Perry out into the snow, giving him just enough time to grab his coat and enforcing the conviction that this was not a pleasure jaunt. Nate wasn't taking him rabbit hunting.

As they walked, Nate had lagged behind, gasping with the effort of his first trip to Meg's, then the hike back to fetch Gillis, and now the return to Meg's house. When they reached the ditch where the body lay, there was Raucous, sniffing and scratching at the redness in the snow. Throwing that snow at her had sent her scampering as the two men watched, until she disappeared through the pet port in Meg's outer utility room door.

Waiting for Nathan to catch up, Gillis had called out, "Come on, Nate. We're not out here for a stroll!"

With the cat banished from the scene, Gillis had made a cautious, cursory evaluation of the scene of death, then Nathan had dropped his coat over the snow sprinkled, icy mound and they had moved on up the lane and around to Meg's front door.

Now, back at the station with a fresh pot of coffee brewing, Gillis picked up the telephone and was relieved to hear a dial tone. He punched in the number for the Corona Hotel. As it rang, he stood at the window watching the snow flying, heavy and fierce. He waited, pacing, for someone to reach the phone at the other end. After a while, looking out the window, he rang off and began flipping switches on the radio.

The Corona Hotel stood like a matriarch near the place where the mountain began to rise, at the top of Main Street, just before it became Mountain Road, grey stone turrets and towers marking each angle of its structure. The hotel's statistics were etched on a tall marble pillar in the hotel foyer, and its sofas and tables were worthy of the marble halls they adorned.

Most of the hotel was closed up in winter, but a small staff stayed on in case a guest happened by, and to watch over the plumbing and wiring and the appliances, but mostly to watch over the antiques in the lobby. If the winter staff slept cold but elegantly in the forbidden beds of elaborate guest rooms, rather than in their own mediocre backstairs accommodations, who was to blame them or complain?

Thus it was that Evelyn and Ike Farabaugh didn't hear the phone ringing and didn't answer Gillis' call.

The hotel was cold. No fire had been laid in the lobby, no gas burned in the furnace. Evelyn Farabaugh lay with her eyes closed, awake but very still, so as not to awaken Ike. She knew he was there, his thin frame lying straight as a snake beside her.

That's what he reminded her of. A grass snake. Furtive. Sly. But no, not exactly like a snake. A snake has a spine. Ike didn't seem to have any backbone, not compared to Jamey, anyway. Jamey. If only he wasn't so young! Still, she was the same amount younger than Ike. She wasn't wanting to leave Ike and the life she had, she just needed some younger friends, people her own age, she told herself. Oh, well. She'd just wait and see how things went.

She eased her plump body a bit, sinking down again into the soft bed, brushing bleached blond hair out of her face. She felt tense and, as was her way when her thoughts were not happy ones, she sucked at her bottom lip.

Ike Farabaugh awoke, shivered, and began his day with ill-concealed anger at his new hired help. "The last thing I told Jamey yesterday was to light the furnace. I had a feeling we were in for some rough weather, and the electric lines would go down. This place just isn't prepared for it. Striking a match for a pilot light isn't too much to ask, is it?"

Evelyn rolled over under the warm blankets and tried to sink back to sleep. Ike was having none of it. "Evelyn? You awake? I was saying I told that boy to light the furnace before he went to bed last night. Wonder why he didn't?"

"Maybe he did. Maybe it went out overnight."

"Or maybe your young idol is what went out. Maybe he went out with a girl his own age and didn't come in last night, and wasn't here to strike a match."

She ignored the insinuation and his suspicions. Heaven knew she was used to them by now. "I told you a month ago that gas logs in a few fireplaces weren't going to keep us warm all winter. We may be in the sunny south, but we still get some cold weather in winter. If you hadn't waited so late to light the furnace, you wouldn't have this problem now."

Ike jerked the door open. "Well, you just lie there in your nice warm bed and let me go see what's happening down there. But I'm telling you now, when I see that layabout, I...." The rest of his words were lost on Evelyn as the door closed behind him. The sound of his muttering receded with his footsteps as Evelyn tried to drift again into lush and lusty dreams.

Ike blundered down the hallway pulling his clothes about him as he went. In the cellar he found just what he had anticipated; there was no flame, no pilot light, and no Jamey.

Evelyn, meanwhile, snuggled under the blankets, but something in her mind kept nagging her and she was unable to go back to sleep. At last she got it. Something wasn't right about that furnace not being lit. In the short time he had been here Jamey had always made sure everything was done last thing before he went to bed at night. Something was wrong.

She lay for a while, thinking, trying to penetrate the fog in her mind brought on by last night's sleeping pill, then muttered to herself, "Oh, yes. He probably didn't feel cold at all last night. Oh well. Got to enjoy life while you can." A smirk crossed her lips, then she shrugged, dismissing whatever thought had provoked it.

She stirred, stretched and yawned, and pushed her feet out onto the cold floor, seeking the warm fuzzy slippers. The flimsy lingerie she chose to sleep in left her arms and shoulders exposed to the wintery air. She pulled the blanket around her as she rose, and managed to put on a pair of wool slacks and a sweater while still wrapped within the blanket's folds. She arrived in the chilly lobby just in time to hear the last ring of the telephone as Gillis rang off.

Gillis poured himself a cup of the strong black coffee. This storm wasn't done with them yet, it seemed. The woods between the long tortuous layers of roadway snaking up the mountain began to echo with loud cracks as limbs, under the weight of too much snow and ice, left their appointed trunks and plunged down the hillsides, taking with them the phone and electric lines that hadn't already been pulled loose from the houses. A loud explosive crack turned his thoughts sharply to Cassie, her neighbor Jesse Lankford, Doc Abbott and his paramour Miss Nell Meade, and the others up on the mountainside, but he forced his attention back to his immediate purpose.

Perhaps if he tried the hotel again. He lifted the receiver once more but this time he heard nothing but his own breathing. The explosion he had heard must have come from the transmission tower far up the mountain.

He replaced the phone in its cradle and walked back to the window, looking again at the car in his parking lot, wondering who it belonged to. He'd check its registration later. He could only hope that things were all right up the mountain until he could get to the hotel and remind the Farabaughs that the Corona, with its auxiliary electrical power supply, would serve as a storm shelter for the local residents who were without utilities because of this unexpected blizzard.

They had some winter staff still there, he knew, and the stranded residents would surely pitch in. He didn't know how many people would come down off the mountain to the hotel, but he was certain the Shakespearean troupe would need better quarters than the ragged little trailers out at the edge of town where they were now staying. Some of the local villagers would go to the hotel too, of course.

As these thoughts passed through his mind, the close trimmed hairs on the back of his neck stood up, not entirely from the cold air he had just come through. This sense of urgency he felt was almost as powerful as fear. But, he chided himself, it was not fear. It was just that this was his first winter in Hartsville as Deputy Sheriff, and the first case he must handle alone, without the assurance that Sheriff Thacker was as close as the telephone. Sheriff Thacker was on leave at his coastal home, and it might be several days before Gillis could reach him or before Thacker might be able to get back. Gillis would wait and see how things developed before he disturbed his superior. This just might be his means of getting that much needed promotion. No, he was not afraid, but he felt in his bones there was more trouble to come.

Thank goodness he had already radioed Dr. Duggal MeHarg, the coroner, in Murphree, who said he would arrive as soon as he could get adequate transportation. Gillis made a few notes, then looked up the road toward the hotel for a few minutes as he shrugged into his coat. May as well go on back to Meg's, he thought, and try to decide what to do with the corpse.

It couldn't stay in the ditch, although if the practical truth were told, it would be better preserved there than any other place he could think of. Also, the scene of the crime would be better preserved for the Coroner than if they moved the body.

And how would they move it, anyway? Who would move it? He knew the answer to that without asking. He would move it, maybe he and Nathan. Nate was a good sport most of the time, but he was a little beside himself today.

Thinking of the hot breakfast Nate was probably enjoying at Meg's table at this minute caused Gillis's stomach to rumble. He closed the door behind him and headed out into the cold, a tarp for the corpse over one arm and his other parka hooked over his finger for Nate to wear.

He would have to get up to the hotel sometime soon, but that could wait a bit.

Up the mountain, at the top of Mountain Road, Jesse Lankford had been up for hours. He had watched the arrival of the morning—and such a morning it was! His fireplace was simmering deep in the warmth of crackling hardwood. Tea steeped and brewed in a pot on a tray at his elbow, strong, rich Earl Grey tea. He savored its aroma, then poured it into a cup already primed with warm milk. His eyes had never seemed to leave the pages he was reading for the second or third time.

Why had he been such a coward and put off reading this letter when it first arrived, last Friday? He could already have gone down to Cherry Lake to take care of things. He had read the one from his estate managers in England when it came on Thursday because those letters usually brought his funds for the coming quarter, but seeing who this second letter was from, he had expected it to be the usual litany of loneliness and disappointment and had decided it could wait.

Now it was impossible for him to leave. He had already turned on his scanner, and learned that the roads were closed in all directions out of the mountains. He could ski out, break in those skis he'd bought twelve years ago and never used, but he wasn't sure he could even find the right direction. Even though Cherry Lake lay at the bottom of this mountain, it was still forty miles east. Too great a risk of running into trouble himself, not knowing the terrain any better than he did.

He laid the letter down and sipped from his cup of tea—the great comforter of Englishmen everywhere. He wanted to distance himself from the letter and the possible message behind its arrival, and come back later with a different perspective, but he reached for the phone and, at the dial tone, punched in a number.

There was no sound of ringing at the other end. He dialed two or three others with the same result. As the same sudden explosive crack that Gillis heard echoed through the woods, his line went dead before the second ring. A frown formed deep lines between his dark brows as he gazed at the useless instrument.

He needed to get out, give himself room to think. Slipping into his coat and boots, he turned off the kettle and lights, looking out the window toward Cassie's house across the road and a little way down. Small icy snowflakes peppered down across the mountains, casting her house in a white haze. He would just go and make sure she had heat and water, he thought. She was, after all, his nearest neighbor and a fellow writer of sorts, and though he found her deep honey colored hair most attractive and her hazel eyed intensity positively intriguing, she had always seemed unavailable, more than a little mysterious. He never asked why she sometimes seemed to favor her right side when she walked. To him it was just a part of what made her unique.

He often helped her with chores about the yard or house, but he sensed that she would not welcome any advances toward a personal relationship, and for that he was glad. He understood it perfectly. Though he hadn't thought it through, he kept a certain part of himself closed off from emotional involvement just as she did. He had seen enough of what that sort of thing could lead to. Maybe someday, when he was back home in England, maybe then he would be ready, but not now. *Not here*, he thought as he pulled on fur lined gloves, tucking the cuffs up under his coat sleeves. Not until he knew his aunt and young cousin down at Cherry Lake would be taken care of. He might need to just take hold and do something about their situation. Someday.

Pushing that unwelcome thought aside, he opened the door to a blast of arctic air that almost took his breath away.

Three

Cassie Ryder, awake in the cold light of morning, lay in her featherbed listening to the house freeze around her. The water heater gurgled, and she wondered if the outside pipes were frozen. The furnace ran frenetically in a vain effort to live up to what was expected of it. Her electric blanket clicked on and off, and by its sheer proximity to her skin lulled its comfortable occupant into a cozy sense of serenity.

She stirred from under the covers and looked at her watch. Seven o'clock. The paper should be here soon, but she wasn't sure she'd go out for it unless it was delivered to the door. If Nate brought it she would make him a cup of the hot herbal tea he enjoyed so much.

Wrapping herself in a fleece robe, she stood for a moment at the bedside. Would the cold weather bring the stiffness and pain back to her leg? It did sometimes, since she fell, or was pushed, off that cliff in the Arizona desert. She winced as she remembered the pain of lying for hours, her crushed leg pinned beneath a boulder, before a friend from the Hopi Reservation found her and got help. She tried the leg again. It seemed all right so far. She shuffled into slippers on her way to the bay window and looked out, and a thrill of excitement coursed through her as it always did when Mother Nature provided entertainment in the form of weather, the more exotic the better.

25

Snow was always the high point of any year, and this looked as if it was going to be a good year indeed.

From her window looking down the mountain she could see where the road turned as it wound downhill to the village but now she saw not the road itself, only the deep heavy snow, already glazing over with ice, and the falling flakes changing to sleet, spreading ice across the mountain like frosting on her orange muffins. From all across the mountainside came the sharp retort of breaking limbs.

In the other direction she could see smoke rising from Jesse Lankford's chimney and a faint glow of light behind the heavy drapes at his windows. Now, there was a strangely solitary man, but a good neighbor nonetheless. His help with heavy jobs around the place was invaluable and much appreciated, but he was never intrusive. It never occurred to her to wonder why he was in this country, and she didn't now. Her only thought at this moment was that he, like herself, should be preparing for a potential power loss.

Knowing that at any time one of those falling limbs might take the power lines down with it, Cassie nudged the thermostat up, breathing a silent prayer of relief that she had kept her gas range and space heaters in good working order. She hadn't needed them in the six years since she had come back to Hartsville, but she had known enough hardship in her years as a nurse among the Hopi to remind her to keep prepared for emergencies.

It was still hard for her to accept the fact that Matt had been dead more than six years now, leaving her widowed while still in her twenties. Matt had loved snow. This blizzard would have been so exciting to him. For the millionth time, in her mind, she apologized to him for not having kept the promise she had made at his grave side, the promise to solve the mystery of his death. She had tried and thought she was getting close, but her search had caused an awful lot of trouble for her missionary parents on the reservation, and almost led to her own death as well, and who would be the better off for that? She had come very close to being killed in that fall before she agreed, at her father's insistence, to give up her search and return to Hartsville.

Pulling herself away from those thoughts, she started a full pot of coffee to dripping. While it brewed, she put on warm, soft brown corduroy slacks and a pale cream sweater, pleased that she could still wear the size ten clothing she'd worn on the reservation six years ago. She fastened her hair back with a barrette. Her mother used to say her hair was an indescribable color, somewhere between ash and auburn. Whatever it was, it suited Cassie, both her coloring and her temperament—quiet, but with warm, sometimes fiery, undertones. She applied a touch of makeup and put away the cosmetics as a last gurgle from the coffee maker signaled that the brew was ready.

The stimulating jolt of that first sip warmed her as she sat down to read over yesterday's output from the word processor, the preface to the history of Hartsville she had contracted to write for the Historical Society. In it she had described the present day attractions of the tourist season which opened in the spring with the Shakespeare Festival and closed in the autumn with Oktoberfest. She would now begin the actual work of tracing the history of this, her hometown, from its birth as a spa with healing hot mineral springs to its current status as a summer tourist mecca in the foothills of this southern mountain range, and she was growing more and more eager to get on with the writing of it.

Before she had got through the first three pages though, she heard the clumping of footsteps, then a knock at her door. She hurried to open it to whatever near frozen body might be there, calling, "Who is it?" as she went.

"Frosty the snowman. Open up, there's a good girl," came Jesse's voice.

Cassie threw the door wide and stood back, arms hugged tight to her body to keep off the chill. The snowflakes melting on his dark brown hair caused it to curl more than she had seen it before, and made it look almost as dark as his deep-set eyes, as intense a brown as rich, dark chocolate. Then she thought of Matt and stepped aside for Jesse to come in.

"Good morning!" Jesse's warm smile belied the redness at the tip of his nose. "We've got snow!" he proclaimed. "How do you like it?"

"Blowing, wild and deep, maybe two, three feet of it. How do you like it?"

"I prefer it melted, but it does tend to keep me in the house, out of trouble," he said. He thought again about the letter, that the snow wasn't keeping him completely trouble free, but there was nothing he could do about it now. He couldn't make sure his aunt was all right, but at least he could make sure his neighbors here were all right, starting with Cassie.

She assured him she was fine, thanking him for his concern, then said, "What is it about snow that makes people want to go out and play in it? You could have just made a phone call."

"I needed a breath of fresh air. Been in the house all weekend and just thought this would make a good change. Besides, some neighbors just make a man want to go out in the snow to check on them."

"Better come inside, then." Cassie raised an eyebrow, yielding to a tiny smile. He hadn't made any effort to come in until he was invited. "I'll pour you some coffee. Or would you prefer tea, like a normal Englishman?" She turned toward the kitchen chanting an old British chorus, just loud enough for him to hear and recognize, "Mad dogs and Englishmen go out in the noonday sun...."

"Coffee, please, perhaps with a little Irish. I've had all the tea any Englishman needs or any mad-dog could stand." Jesse grinned. "Actually, I did try to call and found your phone is out of order, as well as all the others on the mountain, apparently."

"Really?" Cassie grew more serious. "You've tried them, then?"

"Well, not all, actually. I tried to call Doctor Abbott's and a couple of others. All the same, nothing but crackles. Lines are down, you see. The load of snow and ice on the wires could have torn them loose."

"What about down in the village? Have you tried any down there?"

"No. I tried to call an aunt in another town first, but couldn't get through. Then my line went dead too. So I decided to come and see if I had been abandoned up here. I wouldn't like being snowbound all alone." She brought his coffee and offered an apology for not having any Irish whisky. He sipped the rich, fragrant Columbian brew, then continued, "The lines in the village may have survived. They're on more sheltered ground, nestled into the foot of the mountain. They might not have as much ice and certainly not as many limbs to fall on them as we do up here."

"And I suppose Doc will check on Miss Nell," she said, thinking of their nearest neighbors on up the mountain.

"Yes, I'm sure that if Miss Nell Meade has a problem, Doc Abbott will be there at her side, no matter where that portly side is situated."

"Jesse Lankford, you should be ashamed. Why should you begrudge Doctor Abbott his little pleasures? Or Miss Nell either, for that matter?"

"Little pleasures? I think he has chosen a rather largish pleasure. As for her choice of pleasure, well I'm sure I can't address that matter with any degree of authority."

"Go and wash your mind out with soap." Cassie grinned. She would not have thought the reserved Jesse Lankford capable of making suggestive remarks, based on what little she had learned of him in their few years as neighbors. But this was the 'eighties. Taboos were now a thing of the past. She turned to the stove and began pouring batter into muffin tins. Her activity at the stove allowed her to conceal whatever reaction may have expressed itself on her angular features. When the muffins were in the oven, she began stirring oatmeal into boiling water.

"Why, do you think, do we always refer to her as Miss Nell or Miss Meade? Why not just call her by her name, as we do everyone else?" Jesse asked.

"Why, because she is, or was, a school teacher. You never call a teacher or an ex-teacher by her given name, not if you want to live and thrive. Especially if she taught you in sixth grade. Nell Meade will forever be Miss Nell. It will be on her tombstone."

Jesse grew serious. "With the phone lines already down, the power lines will probably go down soon. Do you have wood for the fireplace in case you need it?"

"I have a little, and some Propane in the tank. I haven't checked it lately, but there should be plenty." She looked out the window as if to read the gauge from where she sat. "Who would have thought we'd get a storm like this, this far south?"

"It happens every fourteen or fifteen years in England," Jesse said. "Maybe it does here. too. My paternal grandparents both died in a blizzard in the Cotswolds. Both caught pneumonia from the cold and coal smoke."

"I don't imagine we'll suffer from coal smoke, but it is cold enough. What if the blizzard outlasts our supplies?"

"Perhaps we should pool our resources until this is over," he suggested.

Cassie looked at his face, searching for any sign of an ulterior motive but saw none. What he said did make sense. In the years since her return to Hartsville he had always respected her privacy and space. Deciding there was no hidden agenda involved, she said, "That sounds like a good idea to me."

She began setting the table and poured more coffee into Jesse's cup, wondering how she would react if she detected any personal intentions on his part. But with Matt's death still unsolved, she knew she would not reciprocate, no matter how attractive Jesse was.

"You get the spare room," she said, "and you also get to eat well here. If your meals at home are anything like those I've heard you order at the hotel restaurant, I may have an opportunity to expand my palate, so to speak, if this storm lasts that long."

"Oh, not at all, not at all. My meals at home often consist of only cheese, fruit, biscuits, things out of a tin. That's why I choose the things I do when I dine out. I've learned to enjoy a great variety of foods since coming to America, but I don't know how to prepare them."

"When was that? That you came here, I mean."

"Umm, maybe fifteen or sixteen years ago. I came as a tender lad of twenty, for the same reason, more or less, as Mr. Wodehouse. Are you familiar with him?"

"P. G. Wodehouse? Who isn't? So you came for the same reason, which was?"

"He's quoted as saying he came for 'writing opportunities.'" He sketched quotation marks on the air. "Worse luck, though, I didn't bring his sense of humor with me. My dull offerings have never made me wealthy, no more have they made me famous."

"Surely that isn't the only reason you came, unless, of course, you've been pretty widely published in England?"

"Well, no, there was a family matter involved," he said, directing his attention to his coffee cup.

His brow furrowed and he gazed into his cup. Cassie knew she should drop the subject, but her irrepressible curiosity won out over her good upbringing so she delved just a little further. "You still have relatives in England, then?"

He set down the cup and leaned back. "Yes, a few, I think, distant ones anyway." After a few seconds in thought, he began to tell her more about himself. "Things there began to change in 1966, when I was but seventeen years old. Both my parents were killed in an automobile accident. They were archeologists, on their way home from a dig. I was just enrolled at Cambridge, and it was decided that I should stay there until my education was finished. When that time came I was still at loose ends regarding the rest of my life." He grew quiet then, sipping his coffee.

Cassie waited in silence for him to continue as she finished putting their breakfasts on the table. She was just adding a small jar of blackberry jam when they heard the sound of a motor vehicle whining into the driveway. By the time they reached the door, Bernard Klas, blond hair spiking out from under a knitted ski cap and looking larger than ever in his down-filled jacket and ski pants, was already out of his much used Land Rover and coming up the front steps, stamping the snow off his boots as he came. It took no coaxing at all to persuade him to share the muffins and hot coffee. He helped himself to the oatmeal.

When they were all seated Cassie said, "See, I told you. Men just like to play in the snow."

Bernard chuckled, childlike. "What you say is true," he said, his speech revealing just a trace of his Austrian background. "I have been playing in the snow since I was a little boy, skiing and sledding. That is why I come to this country, to play in your snow." He bit into a fresh, butter-dripping muffin.

"You've come to the wrong part of the country, then. There is very little skiing this far south."

"Yes, this I know. I was in the state of Wyoming, then in Colorado. The mountains there are lovely and the skiing is wonderful, and those people out there, oh, my, my, my! But the cost, it is so great! Out there I could not earn enough to support my skiing. Now I work hard all summer at one of your resorts, and save my money. When I get enough money in my pocket and the summer season is over, I go to the big mountains and ski and ski. This year though, I've stayed a little late." He grinned, to show them it was not too painful an arrangement.

"So," began Jesse, "Is this trip up the mountain today in search of good skiing terrain? Going to take advantage of this fresh snow?"

31

Bernard's eyebrows twitched and his mouth fell open as he remembered his errand. "Oh, no! I am to bring all of you Mountain Road people to the hotel. It is the custom, so Mr. Ike Farabaugh tells me—and Deputy Perry Gillis told him—that when there is trouble from the weather the hotel opens its doors and offers shelter to all the local residents who want to come. He says there is no cost to you. That is taken care of by donations from the guests, and the city covers any loss. Of course, if you wish to stay here...?" He looked from one to the other.

"I do remember hearing something about that arrangement, from Doctor Abbott, I believe, at some point or another." Jesse turned to Cassie. "What do you think? Shall we go to the hotel or stay here and tough it out?"

"That's fine with me," she replied. "Besides, that will give me a chance to poke around and get some of the hotel's history. It will be sort of like a working vacation, really."

Jesse smiled at her eagerness. "Then it's settled, to the fine hotel we go."

Seeing the direction of Bernard's gaze as Jesse helped himself to the next-to-last muffin, Cassie watched the interaction of the two men, amused at Jesse's reluctance to violate good breeding by taking the last morsel from a plate. Bernard, on the other hand, showed no such inhibitions and never let it touch his plate before downing the last bite. Cassie was glad she had taken one to begin with.

Jesse kept talking throughout the little scene. "I've been giving some thought to trying my hand at fiction. Perhaps I could start work on a novel about a snow storm, where all the inhabitants go to a hotel for safety as guests of the city. They run out of food, and are eaten one by one by...."

"Some of the more indiscriminate guests?" Cassie interrupted. "A grizzly bear? The City Commissioners? Yes, you do that," Cassie laughed, her mind going to the mayor, Tal Moorehouse, or rather to the mayor's wife, Gaynell. She was not so much a grizzly as a wolverine, Cassie mused, waiting for Jesse to continue.

Bernard looked from one to the other as if he didn't quite get the gist of their conversation, then, with a nod, brought them back to the situation at hand. "They are saying that the temperature is dropping. It is going to be very cold by tonight. You are wise to leave the mountain, I think."

Jesse began clearing the table. "That means the pipes up here might freeze. If we are lucky, the electric power will stay on. If not, we will be in trouble." Sliding the last plate into the sudsy water where Cassie was washing dishes, he said, "Bernard and I will finish in here while you get some things together, Cassie. Then we'll stop by my place. Just be sure you leave the water dripping a bit here. That may help prevent broken pipes. Maybe."

Cassie packed warm slacks, sweaters and socks. She dug into the back of the closet for the warmest coat, gloves and boots she had kept from earlier days in the colder climate of the southwest and western mountains. Within a short time they had loaded her suitcases, overnight case and briefcase into the back of Bernard's battered and bruised vehicle, then gave the house a final once-over before locking the door.

"Maybe I'd better take my typewriter, if we have room?" Cassie suggested.

"We'll make room. Pack it up," said Jesse. Cassie attached the cover to the portable case in which the machine sat and the little group started out to gather any other mountain residents for the journey down to the Corona Hotel.

At Jesse's house Bernard and Cassie waited as Jesse collected the things he'd need. As they were leaving, he stopped. "Just a minute, please. I'll just pick up some correspondence from the study and be right with you." He was back in less than a minute, pushing two or three envelopes into his coat pocket.

Bernard consulted a rough map he had drawn from his own pocket. "Next we go to find Doc Abbott, then to his neighbor, Miss Meade." Doc Abbott's lawn blended into that of Nell Meade, forming a pristine, unblemished blanket of snow. When Bernard stopped the van in front of and about halfway between their two houses, both Nell and Doc came out of her house to greet them. Jesse's left eyebrow twitched wickedly at Cassie, who turned away, grinning.

The older pair readily fell in with the evacuation, or perhaps rescue, and Nell began delegating tasks to each in preparation for their departure and for their comfort once they arrived at the hotel.

If Miss Nell was retired from teaching sixth grade, she had only retired from the classroom. Her air of authority remained intact and she treated everyone as she had her pupils. "Jesse, you go and help

Doctor Abbott get his things ready. Help him with his bags. Cassie will help me here. Bernard will carry my bags." The men looked at her as children always look at school teachers, and moved off to do her bidding.

"Now, Cassie, you will find the cat carrier in the laundry room. Wipe it out, put a fresh towel in the bottom, and set it in the hall by the door. The litter box is there as well. Clean it out and put it and the new bag of litter with the cat carrier. I'm going to get ready," she said, closing the door to her bedroom behind her.

For a long moment Cassie gazed at the closed door. Did Miss Meade not want anyone to see in, or was she wary of openness in general? Cassie shrugged, putting those thoughts aside, and went in search of the feline's necessities.

Bernard, left without an immediate chore, sat in the living room staring back at an animal he presumed to be a half-starved cat. It had no extra meat on its bones. Its color was a pale tan, somewhere between straw and yellow. To say it had fur would be misleading. It sat washing the tiny crisp ripples of some sort of fiber that covered its body. When it looked up, its thin wedged face looked pinched. Pathetic, really.

When Cassie opened the cat carrier, the beast leapt down from the chair it had occupied and tried to dart past her, but she deftly scooped it up by its underbelly and deposited it in the little cage. The cat hissed when she shut the wire door.

"What was that thing I just picked up?" she asked of Bernard, who merely shrugged his shoulders.

Nell came into the hallway, calling to Bernard that her bags were ready. He rose obediently and went to fetch them. Nell looked around the hallway, observed the cat carrier sitting alone, then looked at Cassie from beneath raised eyebrows.

"And the litter box?" she asked.

Cassie smiled sweetly and walked out onto the porch to wait in the cold.

When Doc and Jesse returned, she detained Jesse by a grip on his sleeve and an almost imperceptible shake of the head. Doc, looking puzzled, went into the house as Bernard came out with Nell's bags.

The three of them were waiting in the van when Doc emerged carrying the litter box and a bag of litter, a look of total disgust on his face. Nell locked the door and followed, her lips set in a tight line, her look at Cassie on entering the van saying, *you haven't got away with this clean, my girl.*

The trip down the mountain was slow. Bernard drove the vehicle with skill, yet still at one quite sharp turn they slid into deep snow. There were moans from the occupants until Bernard, stepping out into a deep snowdrift, assured them there was no problem. He unleashed a wench from the front of the vehicle, securing the free end of the cable around a stout tree, then drew up the slack to pull them out. In very few minutes they were again on their slow and slippery way. Bernard stopped at other houses to see if the residents wanted to join them. An elderly couple were patently relieved to be rescued from what threatened to be, for them, a long, cold vigil. No one was home in some of the houses, perhaps having gone to a warmer locale for the winter. All told, they ended up a company of nine as they left the last house on Mountain Road.

It was just half past ten when they pulled up in front of the hotel. Ike Farabaugh met them. "Glad to see you made it," he said, pumping the men's hands and patting the women's shoulders. His wide smile showed large yellowing teeth but little warmth. "Come in, come in, I'll show you to your rooms. All the summer help is gone now, and my new handyman seems to be stranded somewhere by the snow. I'm being the bellboy today," he chuckled, or perhaps whinnied, and in some way reminded Cassie of Uriah Heep.

Four

Ike set their bags down at their doors, the first ones down the east wing to the right, and across the hall from each other. "If you brought any valuables, family heirlooms and such, anything you want me to lock up in the safe, bring them down when you come. I'll give you a receipt, of course. We'll be serving refreshments downstairs in just a little while. Come on down whenever you're ready," he added as he trudged back down the stairs, an unctuous smile pasted on his thin lips.

Jesse set up Cassie's typewriter on a trestle table facing the window. "You'll have a good view here," he said, seeing the snow-covered expanse of terraced lawn and beyond it a stand of white frosted pines and the icy bare limbs of oak, laurel, mountain ash and countless other varieties of plant life.

They stood together for a moment gazing out at the stark beauty before Jesse turned and moved away.

Thanking him as he turned to leave, she added, "Don't take too lightly Mr. Farabaugh's offer to lock up your valuables. I'll probably put a few pieces of jewelry in his safe. It may sound silly now but we might be thankful later."

He laughed, taking the envelopes from his pocket. Tapping them against his fingertips he said, "These are the only things I have with me that are remotely related to family heirlooms. I'll just tuck them in with my socks."

It took them no time at all to decide they could finish their unpacking later. As they were locking their doors, Ike returned, this time placing a litter box and bag of litter at the last door on the right down the hall. The smile had faded.

The innkeeper turned to Doc, who forestalled whatever Ike was about to ask him by requesting the room adjoining Nell's, separated from Jesse by one room.

Two groups of new arrivals moved into the rooms farthest to the left of the landing, most of them strangers or just acquaintances to Cassie. Jesse seemed to know many of them by name, but did not let them detain him. With his hand at Cassie's back he steered her toward the staircase that took them downstairs. The atmosphere there was almost festive now with the arrival of new lodgers.

At the foot of the stairs, Evelyn Farrabaugh stood behind a large buffet table handing out cups of hot mulled cider, coffee and cocoa. Her bottle-blonde hair was a bouffant frame for her artfully and generously made-up face. "Brunch will be ready pretty soon," she said, handing Cassie and Jesse cups of cider. "You'll love it. Ben is a wonderful cook," she smiled and stuffed a stick of gum into her mouth.

"Ike," Evelyn called as her husband started up the steps with more luggage. "Tell Wendy to come here. We need her to serve and to help Ben in the kitchen."

"Why haven't you got her here already?" Ike replied, not slowing down.

Cassie observed the two, and for a moment she wondered how they had ever met. To Evelyn she said, "I don't think I've met Wendy. Is she a new employee?"

"Sort of. She came late in the season and is staying on." She turned to the next couple offering them cups of the fragrant steaming concoction. "Would you like a hot drink, Mayor? And you, Mrs. Moorehouse?" With their cups in hand, they entered into conversation with Jesse and moved aside as Evelyn continued her commentary on Wendy.

"She's one of the acting troupe, I think. Some of them get here ahead of the others, hoping to get first choice of parts in the play. They always talk with that fake English accent," she said, smiling at the memory of past seasons. "Even the ones who came from Dallas. My sister's youngest came two years ago just to help out with wardrobe, and by the time they left she was talking like the queen. Of course, this year's bunch could all be from Buckingham Palace for all I know."

Cassie finished her drink and Evelyn refilled the cup, obviously enjoying having an audience.

"Thanks," Cassie said, sipping the spicy cider. "I didn't realize they started preparing for the festival this early."

"Oh, the play doesn't start till late April, but they come during the winter to get the costumes ready, make the sets and so on. But they play the roles and talk with those accents the whole time they're here. Have to 'stay in character,' as they say. They make a great production just out of getting ready for the big event. They are a hoot."

Cassie moved back behind the table with Evelyn in order to let a newly arrived group of cold guests gather round. Since she was now standing in a server's position, she began filling cups upon request. "Do any of them stay here at the hotel when they come?" she asked.

"Oh, no, they don't have money for that. They usually stay out at the edge of town in that little trailer park. It's a pretty run down little community and a lot of the trailers don't have power. I hear that some of them don't even have plumbing that works, either. Bernard's just now gone out there to see if any of them want to come here for a few days, just while the weather is so bad, you know."

Having freed himself from the mayor, Jesse was now beside Cassie again, listening to Evelyn's chatter. Having made sure everyone had a hot drink, Evelyn looked toward the stairs where Ike, having returned from whatever task he had been about, stood waiting for her to do some bidding of his. She moved in his direction pausing only long enough to deliver one last line. Looking slyly up at Jesse she said, "Wendy might be just what you need. She has the British accent down pat."

"Then perhaps she and Bernard will hit it off," said Jesse, dismissing yet another of Evelyn's endless attempts to pair him up with one of her acquaintances. He should perhaps tell her that he had no interest in new involvements. Not until he got back home to England. That's what he told himself, anyway.

Cassie sipped her cider and moved away to greet some of the other residents-by-chance as tantalizing aromas drifted in from the kitchen, pulling her thoughts in that direction. She strolled around the lobby admiring again the glowing grey marble floors, the elegant, arched leaded windows, the beautifully preserved life-size portraits, and landscapes done in rich oils.

Reading the inscription on the central pillar, she found that the hotel had been constructed in the year 1874. It mentioned the names of the founders of the town and the builders of the hotel. As she read the names, she realized that many of the older inhabitants, staying at the hotel right now because of the storm, might be descended from the founding fathers of the town. She might be able to learn from them a lot of the history of the hotel and possibly some colorful legends about eccentric residents of the town itself. She would also seek whatever information the hotel's records and files would yield.

Doc and Nell had come down the stairs after having gotten their quarters situated and now approached the pillar and Cassie. "Did you get your cat settled in?" Cassie asked, not sure if she was being polite or just needling Nell.

"The *cat* is named Porsche. P-o-r-s-c-h-e." Nell, nostrils flared, spelled the cat's name clearly, as if Cassie had difficulty understanding the language.

"I'd have thought P-o-r-t-i-a would have been simpler," Cassie said.

"I wasn't looking for simplicity," Nell replied.

She now turned a coy look up at Doc and explained, "I have always wanted a Porsche, the car, you know, and I knew I could never own one on my teacher's salary, so when Marlowe here presented me with my perfect, precious little kitty I just gave the name to her." She almost simpered as Doc smiled indulgently down at her.

Cassie was appalled to see her former teacher behaving like a giddy sixth grader, but had to smile at the puppy love of the mature set playing itself out between these two as they clasped hands and moved away.

A gong with a voice as deep as the ages sounded from the door of the dining room. Ike, in his taunting nasal twang, announced that brunch was served.

Cassie looked with approval at the end-to-end tables and plastic plates and flatware. With so many to feed and so few to prepare the meals, the more time saving steps taken the better. No one seemed to mind. The guests were putting the best face on being uprooted from their homes; most of them seemed to be looking forward to an adventure, to roughing it, and were more excited than critical. The gathering began to take on an almost holiday mood.

If the table setting was less than grand, the food served up by Ben Dothard took up the slack. From the hotel's winter supply of foodstuffs he had created egg and sausage casseroles, salmon croquets, hot biscuits, muffins, pancakes, orange juice, cubes of white and yellow cheese and a fruit compote, enough to feed the dozens of unexpected guests. Steaming coffee was poured, and those who had brought their flasks added to the festivities in their own small way.

Ike and Evelyn attended the buffet along one wall. A dark-haired young woman glided gracefully through the crowd, carrying carafes of coffee to the sideboard for the guests to help themselves. Jesse murmured to Cassie that this must be the dawdling Wendy. The too bright smiles on the faces of all the staff showed the strain of being called on to accommodate so many on such short notice.

Cassie was thinking she might suggest that the guests take turns helping. She turned to say as much to Jesse but he had gone to refill their coffee cups. She smiled at his long, searching look over the rim of his cup in the direction of the dark-haired Wendy, then her brow wrinkled in curiosity as he exchanged a few words with the girl before returning to his chair.

Any chance of learning what had transpired between the two was lost as Doc, seating himself at one end of the table, took advantage of this opportunity to address the company. "You know, we are following an old tradition, being here like this today. Whenever the weather causes inconvenience to the local residents, this hotel is always the shelter. Can anyone remember a worse snow storm here in this county? A worse freeze?" He beamed around the room at the silent, indifferent faces of people who could not have cared less about years gone by, intent on filling their plates and bodies with the delicious food.

Ignoring the apathy his remarks had inspired, he fell into a tale of some long past disaster and continued until Mayor Moorehouse managed to interrupt. "I remember one year, I must have been about eight or nine, it snowed the week before Christmas. My brother—he was older than me—we got a sled that Christmas. We kept that sled for four years before we got enough snow on the ground to try it out again. But when we did, oh, boy! Did we fly down that mountainside! Of course, most of those years it was pretty dry, and the sled didn't get used much, so what can you say?" He shrugged and turned back to his food.

"What about that summer the tornado hit?" interposed Nell Meade. "I think the hotel was more packed full then than ever before or since. This whole town was almost destroyed," she concluded.

"What year was that?" asked Cassie, making notes on the paper napkin in her lap, unseen by the others, she hoped.

"I don't exactly recall. Let's see, maybe fifteen, sixteen years ago? Ike, do you remember? How long was the hotel full of locals, waiting for their homes to be rebuilt or repaired?" Nell asked, attempting to include the host in their remembrances.

"That was before my time, Mrs. Meade. Might show up in some of the old records, though," he offered. "They seemed to write down just anything they wanted to in there."

A shiver of anticipation ran down Cassie's spine as she envisioned herself poring over those records, but she kept her excitement to herself. As they ran out of disasters to relive, the group around the table settled down and ate in companionable silence

As it turned out, this was the last really comfortable gathering they would have here.

As the guests enjoyed their meals and second cups of coffee, the dining room door opened and Meg Dothard, followed by Perry Gillis, came through, shivering with cold.

"Gracious, it's cold out there. We had to walk half way up here. The sheriff's car couldn't get through that big snowdrift where the road divides." Meg set down her burden, a pet carrier containing something that looked like a moving snow mass but sounded more like a banshee. "Where shall I put Raucous, Ike?" called Meg.

"Outside in the snow for all I care," Ike called back, then told her to leave the cage in the lobby until he had a chance to help her upstairs with it. "You'd think I'm running an animal shelter here," he grumbled, then laughed nervously as he remembered that the mayor, whose coffee he was pouring, had brought two poodles which were even now yapping it up in their room upstairs. "At least yours will be leashed, Mayor."

"Tell me a room number and I'll take her up myself," Meg offered.

"Just pick an empty one," Ike said, pouring more coffee for the mayor's wife.

Cassie rose, full to the brim with the food prepared by Meg's son. "Hi, Meg, come sit here. Ben's cooked a delicious brunch," she said, seating Meg in her vacated chair. "I'll take Raucous to the room next to mine, if that's all right, Ike?" He nodded assent, and Cassie carried the howling animal up the stairs with Gillis close behind carrying Meg's suitcase.

With the cat and the luggage stowed in the room that was to be Meg's, Cassie held the door open, preparing to leave.

"Wait a minute, just a minute please, Cassie," Gillis stammered, seeming to find something worth scowling at in the area of his feet.

Cassie turned and, seeing the tension in his face, closed the door again. "What's the matter, Gillis? Is something wrong with Meg?"

"Not exactly, but, yeah, you could say she has a problem."

"What kind of problem?" *What is wrong with this man?* she thought.

"A dead body in her ditch," sputtered Gillis, in a hurry to get the words out of his mouth as if they tasted foul. "A boy, about Ben's age."

Cassie lowered herself into the one chair in the room, searching for the right question to ask. She didn't have to search for long. Once begun, the words poured out of Gillis until she knew almost as much as he did about the body, how Nathan had found it and come for him, that none of them knew who the victim was, and that Nathan was now waiting with the corpse for the arrival of Dr. MeHarg, the coroner from Murphree, whenever that might be.

"He could come in on the snow plow, I guess. I don't know if they can take the body away with them that way or not, though. We may have to borrow Ike's freezer."

Cassie shuddered. "Meg seems to be handling it okay," she said.

"You know Meg. She may be screaming inside, but no one will ever know it. If she doesn't have an ulcer the size of Wisconsin it isn't for lack of pent-up stress."

"What are you going to do?"

"I'm not sure yet. I'll ask a few of the men to go back there with me. If two or three are there, they can take turns standing outside with the body while the others warm up inside. Then Nate can get on with his life. He isn't quite as cool about all this as Meg is."

"Do you think it's a hit-and-run?"

"I suppose. It looks like it right now, anyway."

"Are you going to tell the others?"

"Not yet. I'd rather keep it quiet until I know more and can stay here to talk to people one on one. Somebody here may be the driver of a hit-and-run vehicle. I don't want to set up a situation where a lot of talk between these people might distort information and set up a field for false or contradictory evidence. I know it will soon be common knowledge, but I'd like to keep it quiet as long as possible." He moved a little closer and placed a hand on her shoulder. "I'd also like your help. You might be able to pick up some information from the other guests here."

"Confidentiality will be no problem, of course. As for the other, I'll give it my best shot but you know my track record in investigating crime."

"Don't let that Arizona episode discourage you, Cassie. I think you might have been getting too close to a cover-up. That's why they came down on you like that." He patted her shoulder and turned, moving a step away.

"Just keep your eyes and ears open to everybody," he continued. "See if anybody mentions being out in a car last night. People are used to seeing you jotting down notes. Writers are allowed to do that. Just make a note of anything you hear about anybody being out last night, about a missing person or an accident, and especially anything about a death. Nobody here should know anything about that yet. And I've asked Meg to keep it under wraps for now, no matter what. She'll know I've asked for your help, though. Meantime, I've got to get back there. Wonder who might be able to identify the body," he mused.

"I'll do what I can," she said, thinking how fast bad news travels. Someone was sure to find out and spread the word before much more time elapsed. After a moment of introspection she stood up, ready for action.

"Jesse will probably be willing to go with you. And Doc will have to be in on it, of course," she added, smiling at the likelihood of Doctor

Abbott, the semi-retired guardian of these people's good health, ever passing up a chance to be present at either a birth or a death. Or any other event of public or personal interest.

Gillis opened the door and stepped back to let Cassie pass through.

"And keep close to Meg, too. I don't know if she's involved in this, but the fact that the body was found in her yard might mean something, or it could mean nothing. She's stoic, but if Ben is involved—and since this kid is about his age that's a good possibility—if he is involved, there's no telling what Meg might do."

Together they went downstairs and into the lobby where they found a setting quite different from the one they had left.

Bernard stood at the open front door ushering into the lobby fifteen or twenty people of varying ages and in varying sorts of apparel, each dropping a ragged knapsack or some other piece of makeshift luggage wherever it chose to fall.

Several of them were talking at once, all in their version of Shakespearean elocution, and their sentences fit together strangely, as if they had all just sprung from the early seventeenth century English countryside.

Although the Shakespeare Festival itself was several months away, the village had already begun to feel the influx of the artists. Every winter they came, some setting up residence in one or the other of the few local boarding houses, some finding lodging with one or the other of the patrons of the theater. These now entering the hotel were the ones who had rented the tiny trailers and cottages in the trailer park on the edge of town and packed themselves in like sardines.

Every year they came and, after establishing their lodging places, set right in reading lines, rehearsing for that year's chosen selection from Shakespeare. Some of them would be chosen for roles in the auditions and the rest, those who weren't chosen for speaking roles, would hide their disappointment in serving as stage hands, makeup artists, wardrobe people or understudies.

No matter where they lived or what their part in the festival was to be, they would hold together as an elite breed, a tight-knit group having very little interaction with the local population. The rare exceptions would be those who did not have private means of support, who took jobs in the village to pay their way across the stage.

Cassie, having composed herself after the shock of Gillis' news and the appearance of the new arrivals, moved behind him into the dining room. They were followed by Bernard and his group of 'mummers' who converged on the buffet, quiet but quite intent, as if they didn't want their hunger to show. Bernard was the only one of the group who seemed at ease with the situation, stopping for a word with a busy Wendy before she moved away to her next task.

Jesse was sitting to the left of Meg, now among the last of the local residents remaining in the room. On her right sat Ben, at last having his own meal after making sure he had prepared enough food for everyone else. Cassie was struck by how much he resembled his mother. Meg looked at her son fondly and often, kissing his cheek at one point. He blushed, but blessed her with a smile.

Meg's pride in her son and concern over the stress he was under showed in her face. Who wouldn't be under stress, after having to come up with a meal for all these people without warning? He had done a fine job, and she was proud of him, more than she had ever been since he decided to become a cook. Or *chef,* she reminded herself.

She looked up as Gillis and Cassie returned. Gillis stood in the doorway. "Jesse, can I talk with you for a minute, please?" he asked. Cassie stayed where she was as they talked, watching Meg and Ben who were more or less alone now in their little space at the table.

Meg leaned close to Ben as he ate and spoke in an undertone and at some length to him. Ben looked straight ahead for a moment, then nodded once, not looking at his mother. Meg placed a hand on his shoulder and said a little louder, to pacify any nearby curious listeners, that she would get Ben more coffee. He nodded again and picked up his napkin, lingering with it across his mouth.

Gillis stepped around the larger form of Jesse to speak with Meg and Ben in hushed tones. "I'll be back later in the day, Meg. You stick with Cassie, keep her out of trouble. She'll be there for you if you find you need an ear or a shoulder. I'm taking Jesse with me. Remember, keep this as quiet as you can. Don't talk about it to anybody but Cassie. And you can tell Ben if you want to, but Ben, I'll expect you to keep quiet about it, too."

"Where are you going, Gillis?" Ben asked, undaunted by his own youth or Gillis' position.

"There's something we need to look at. We won't be long."

"I'm coming too," Ben said, rising from his chair.

Gillis looked at Meg, knowing she must have already confided in Ben. He wondered if she knew more than she let on. The way she had reacted when she saw the body, that flash of naked recognition in her eyes when she saw his face, had meant something, he was sure.

He realized, though, that he might be able to get a positive identification of the body from Ben, if the boys had been acquaintances, and so he did not argue with him. He trusted the boy even though for right now he had to consider him a suspect, along with everyone else. And he didn't blame Meg for confiding in Ben. She needed to talk to someone, surely, and who better than her own son? He hoped she would take his suggestion and stick close to Cassie while they were gone. At least anything she told Cassie would be safe. The fact that a dead body had been found in her yard, hers and Ben's, did not make Gillis seriously suspect either of them of involvement. *Meg*, he thought with a smile, *if she had killed anyone, would probably have been the first to tell the police, and dare them to deny her right to do so.*

Ben would be a different story.

Five

Gillis paused in the foyer, saying to Cassie, "I'll be back as soon as I can. See what you can find out, but be careful. I don't want you to put yourself in danger, or throw a monkey wrench in my case." There was no reassuring smile, only grim determination on his face as he, Doc, Jesse, and Ben filed out the door and climbed into the Land Rover where Bernard already waited, the vehicle warmed up and ready.

Cassie turned back to the lobby to join Meg. They found a vacant sofa by one of the tall back windows and settled down in intense conversation.

Cassie's parents and grandparents had been friends of Meg's family when Cassie was a child. Both families had been among the original permanent residents of the little village, and both families had prospered. Meg was the last descendant of her family just as Cassie was of hers. When Cassie had returned to Hartsville the friendship between the two women quickly moved into a grown-up level. Each respected the independent spirit of the other. Cassie enjoyed Meg's candor while Meg knew she could trust Cassie as she could no other woman in Hartsville, if perchance she ever felt inclined to share any secrets with anyone.

They didn't hesitate now to come to the point. Cassie leaned forward, keeping her voice low. "Gillis told me what happened out your way. Must've been quite a shock for you!"

"For me? You should have seen old Raucous. That cat knew somehow that things weren't as they should be. Wonder if all cats would have known that?"

She's hiding her feelings in inane chatter about Raucous, thought Cassie. "Cats are weird," she said. "Some of them really are witchy, I think. Others are just.... "

Seeing Wendy moving in their direction, Meg laughed, drowning out the rest of Cassie's sentence, and placed a warning hand on her arm. Wendy joined them, carrying a tray laden with paper cups and a carafe of coffee, with cream and sugar in little pots.

"Hello there. My name is Wendy. You ladies like a drink?" Her broad *"a"* in ladies made Cassie think of an exciting film she had seen recently, about an Australian adventurer, but she suppressed the urge to question the girl about her background in spite of her curiosity.

That curiosity was a habit she'd have to break one day, but please, Lord, not yet. There were so many interesting people and so many exciting things to know about them! For now, though, she would have to be patient and wait for the right time.

"Thanks," Meg said, smiling up at Wendy. "I'd like a cup of coffee, how about you Cassie?" Meg helped herself to generous dollops of both sugar and cream.

"Yes, please," Cassie said, taking the cup from Wendy. "No cream or sugar, thanks," she responded to Wendy's offer. "I take it plain."

If Cassie was content to move slowly in learning about Wendy, it was not so with Meg. "My name is Meg Dothard. This is Cassie Ryder. Your accent is different. Where are your people from?" Not where are you from, but where are your people from. *That should pin down one's roots,* thought Cassie. *Leave it to Meg.*

The girl looked at her, startled eyes showing a flutter of surprise. "Oh, I've lived lots of places. Almost everywhere, actually. Europe, Canada, Australia, like that. Been lots o' places." She set the tray down and poured herself a cup of coffee, easing down into a chair placed at right angles to theirs. But she hadn't mentioned her people.

Meg persisted. "What is your last name, Wendy? I don't think we've heard."

For a few seconds the girl hesitated as if not accustomed to being questioned so openly, then murmured, "Foster. My last name is Foster." She now turned toward Cassie. "You're Cassie Ryder? I've heard about you. You're that writer lady, the one who lived with the Indians, aren't you?" She took a tiny sip from her own cup.

"In a manner of speaking, yes. I worked on the reservation for a while. How long have you been here, Wendy?"

"Oh, about a month or so. I got here right at the end of the tourist season, actually. I'd just been seeing a bit of the country, sort of."

"Have you met Jesse Lankford? He's from England," said Meg.

"No, really?" Her eyes grazed the room. "Is he here now? I'd like to meet him."

"No, he went off with the sheriff, but he'll probably be back later in the day," said Cassie, thinking back to the brief exchange between Jesse and Wendy in the dining room. "You spoke with him this morning in the dining room. But there were so many people in there you might not remember. He's lived here a long time, though. I think he came just out of college."

"University," Wendy mumbled, standing. She had caught Evelyn's stare in her direction and read in it her annoyance at Wendy's sitting and visiting. Excusing herself, she hurried away with her tray of refreshments.

"She certainly intends to keep the English persona alive. Or else she really is British. College in this country would be university in England, I suppose," mused Cassie.

"Did you get the idea she didn't want us to know about her family?" Meg asked.

Before Cassie could answer, Evelyn sat down in the chair Wendy had vacated. "I do wish that girl would make up her mind to work or else be on her way. Seems like she's mostly interested in the boys and her looks."

"Oh, she seemed all right to me," said Meg, never one to agree if she had a chance to do otherwise.

"You hire her, then," Evelyn laughed. "Actually, Ike was the one to let her stay on. Of course, I'm glad she's here now to help through this calamity," she said, sipping something amber from her cup.

"Is she a maid, a receptionist, or what?" Cassie asked.

"Ike lets her do the books, work the desk, just whatever needs to be done. If you can keep her at it. She can do anything that needs doing, I can tell you that. Smart girl."

"She works full time then?" Seeing Evelyn's questioning look at her, she hastened on, "I was just wondering if she ever gets out into the village. Why I hadn't run into her before, you know."

Evelyn relaxed. "She works pretty much as she wants to. I don't care, as long as she gets everything done that I want done, and what Ike wants done, of course."

"She must live in, then," Meg ventured, her gaze wandering around the room, feigning half-hearted interest.

"Not until just recently. I think at first she must have been staying out there with the rest of the theater people." She looked at Meg as if for validation. "In that little trailer village outside of town. You know the place I mean, where the festival people always stay. At least she was staying somewhere else. She'd come to work, then leave, until just lately."

Meg's gaze found Wendy across the room, then pulled her attention back to Evelyn just long enough to say, "She's one of them, then."

Evelyn looked at her as if she were a very dim bulb. "Well, I guess so. She sure talks like one of them, doesn't she?"

Cassie could see in Meg's face an acidic response beginning to form itself, and hastened to change the subject. "How about Bernard? Does he work here too?"

"He did during the summer, but quit when the season was over. He said he was going back to the Rockies for the skiing, but then he changed his mind and decided to stay here and work with the Shakespeare Festival this year. Said it was something he'd always wanted to do and would never get a better chance. Personally, I think he's taken an interest in Wendy."

"Where does he work now?" asked Cassie.

"He tried to come back to his job here but Ike had already hired Jamey for it, for less money. I think Bernard's been doing some repair and carpentry work for some of the people in town since he quit here. Ike lets him borrow some of his tools now and then. He likes Bernard, but he won't put Jamey out after he's already hired him."

"So did Bernard move out, then?"

"No, he still stays here sometimes. He sleeps in the staff quarters when he's here. I don't know where he goes when he isn't here. Ike will let him stay until after the festival, probably."

"Is Hartsville your home then, Evelyn? Have you and Ike always lived here?" Meg asked.

"I have. Ike used to live in Wheaton. He was a woodworker there, had his own shop I think. He's pretty good at it, too. He made a lot of our furniture when we first got married."

Her gaze drifted across the room and seeing Ike motioning to her, she excused herself. "Duty beckons. Make yourselves at home, and if you need anything be sure to let me know," she said as she stood and walked toward her scowling husband, smoothing her tight skirt over plump hips as she went.

"They don't seem like a well-matched pair, do they?" asked Cassie.

Meg didn't answer her. She just kept looking across the room toward Wendy. "I think that girl was in a car in front of my house the other day," Meg said as if to herself, gazing in the direction of Wendy and her coffee tray. "In fact, that was the same day Ben brought that poor boy there. He came in with Ben but she waited in the car. I'm pretty sure that's her."

"What poor boy? Who are you talking about?"

"That boy that is—that got—oh, you know!"

"You mean the one...*that* boy?" She let her raised eyebrows finish that question. "What's his name? Did you tell Gillis you knew him?" She was fairly certain that Meg hadn't mentioned it.

"I said he looked familiar to me, but I didn't know his name, that's all. In fact, he looked familiar that day when he was there with Ben. Ben may have known him well or hardly at all, but it's Ben's place to tell or not tell, not mine. Whatever he wants to do."

And, Cassie realized, if Ben was more than casually involved with the dead boy, Meg didn't want to muddy the waters before she learned from Ben himself what his story would be. Mothers are like that. Meg would go down to the grave with her knowledge rather than betray her son. Cassie wondered if there was more yet that Meg hadn't told. Did she suspect that Ben may have been more involved than she knew?

Her gaze again fell on Wendy, standing by the table where Ike had set up a bar, pouring red wine into a glass. She set the bottle down and instead of passing the drink to one of the guests as Cassie had expected, moved away from the table with the glass in her hand. Both of them watched her as she slipped away into the foyer, coming back in a few minutes looking fortified.

Nell's voice at their side brought them sharply around. "Well, where is that noisy animal you brought in with you?" She parked her ample bottom in the chair recently vacated by Evelyn, her green woolen suit bulging at the front and hiking well up her thighs as she sat down, stroking the hairless cat that lay in the crook of her arm.

"Are you referring to Raucous?" Meg eyes seemed to grow horns.

Nell's laughter only served to rile her more. "You couldn't have chosen a better name for her! Raucous—ha! Well named!"

Cassie laid her hand on Meg's arm. "Tell her your cat's name, Nell."

"You mean Porsche? I think that name fits her well, don't you? She's so sleek and fine."

"Tell her how you spell it—and why," Cassie teased.

Nell repeated the story of the much longed-for automobile and how she related it to the cat. "So now, when I call her Porsche, I still have my fantasy and everybody else has their stodgy idea that I named the poor animal out of Shakespeare. The reason they think that is because she is an English breed of cat, a Cornish Rex, you see. In England, *Rex* indicates royalty."

It was Meg's turn to smirk. "I don't think I ever heard of an English wreck. Was she born on the wrong side of the road, do you think?"

Before Nell could reply, a rowdy singsong chant came from behind them: "Por-sha is a wre-eck. Por-sha is a wre-eck!" They turned just in time to see a little girl about eight years of age with long dark blond braids dancing across the lobby toward her daddy, the mayor, chanting about the cat with the funny pedigree.

Nell, her face crimson with anger, rose majestically, snorting. Placing Porsche on the chair, she tugged at the legs of her panty girdle then retrieved her strange looking animal and sailed up the stairs where she would remain alone with her noble feline until Doc returned.

People were beginning to settle down in groups, some playing cards, some setting up for checkers or chess. An occasional one read in solitude. Meg leaned back on the cushions and closed her eyes.

Cassie watched Ike as he went through a well-camouflaged door at the opposite end of the lobby. That must be his office. She'd just go in there and talk with him first, while he was alone. She had to do it, and the sooner the better as he would probably be among the first to hear about the accident at Meg's. If it was an accident. If she waited until the word got out, they would all be on their guard, whether they knew anything about it or not. She tapped twice on the door then opened it and went in.

Six

Ike looked up from the ledger he had just opened, his watery eyes glinting through straggling wisps of straw-colored hair like an animal peeking through underbrush. He made a show of placing a finger where he had been reading, letting her know she was interrupting something important.

She chose not to notice. "Excuse me, don't let me interrupt you. I bet this snow was the last thing you needed right now, wasn't it? You're so kind to open the hotel to us refugees like this."

A grunted response and a nod were his only acknowledgment.

She leaned against the desk, almost sitting on the edge. "How about this storm, really? Isn't it something? Were you able to get enough supplies in yesterday before the snow started?"

Seeing she wasn't going away, he closed the book, ran his fingers through the wayward hair then clasped his hands on the ledger's cover. "We keep a pretty good supply on hand. Anyway, I always send one of the staff to do that sort of thing. Sent one of them out on an errand yesterday morning and he hasn't come back yet," he grumbled, lifting the ledger cover as if to open it again and get back to work.

"Oh? Aren't you worried about him? What's his name? Did you tell Gillis he is missing?" she asked. Perhaps she had struck a vein already. Could the dead boy be that missing employee?

"Boy named Jamey, and no, he's old enough to take care of himself. You wouldn't know him, probably, he's sort of new. He took Bernard's place when he quit just at the end of the season. I took Jamey on so I could have him trained before the season opens again in the spring." From his proprietary tone, Jamey might well have been a new fox hound.

"So why do you think he didn't come back? Could he just be still in his room? Oh, of course, you would have been looking for him there already."

"I've got more to do than traipse around looking for the hired hands," he either grinned or snarled, it was hard to say which. "He just didn't have the furnace going this morning when I got up. That's part of his job. He hasn't been seen since he left yesterday, best I can tell. Me, I don't leave this hill unless I have to. At least not in the daytime, and not very often at night. Last time must be over a week now," he said. "One night week before last, maybe. But you didn't come in here to find out about my personal life, I'm sure?" he said, opening his book again.

"You're right, I didn't. I'm sorry to have kept you, really, knowing how busy you must be now, but I wonder if you could help me?"

He again closed the ledger and laid his interlocked hands atop it, assuming a pose of exaggerated patience. "I'll do my best. What is it you need?" he asked.

"Well, I'd like to do some research for a book," she began.

A fleeting smirk said that Ike was not impressed. "Yeah? What do you write, romance novels? Children's stories? I don't know a thing about those."

"No, actually it's a short history of Hartsville and some of its more prominent citizens, for the Historical Society. They asked especially that I include the history of this hotel, since it's been here since the settlement started."

"How's it coming, are you almost finished, or just beginning?"

"I'm just beginning the research."

Ike's cold gaze slid to the side, his face half a turn away before he spoke again. "I guess who you write about would depend on your interpretation of the word prominent?"

Cassie watched him, her curiosity piqued by the sly look in his eyes. Was he afraid he wouldn't be included, or afraid that he would be?

"Well, yes, people like yourself, for instance." She watched his expression waver between pleasure and caution.

He settled for caution. "You want the people who founded the city, not newcomers like you and me." So saying, he turned back to his book.

But Cassie was not finished with him yet. "How new are you, Ike? You were here before I came." She stopped there, seeing no reason to tell him that she was not a newcomer but had, in fact, just come back to her old home.

"Exactly. You are the newest of the residents in this little gem in the hills, and I haven't been here much longer than you, so you can save yourself some work there."

"Well, okay," she said as though the news deeply disappointed her, "but I still need to know about the hotel, anyway. It's really the crowning glory of the town, don't you think? Do you happen to have the early records of its background, the early patrons and guest registers?"

Ike's face brightened, his mind taken by a new idea; perhaps he might capitalize on the free publicity, as long as he was kept out of it. "I'll look. They'll be in that storeroom somewhere," he said, indicating a door leading to a small room off the office to his left. "I'll have a look."

"I don't want to be a bother to you. May I just go in and see what all is there that might provide grist for the mill, so to speak? There are probably some pretty famous names in the earliest guest logs. I won't be interested in any actual financial information except as it relates to the hotel's history."

Ike hesitated a moment, then evidently decided there was no harm in it. He nodded toward the little room. "Yeah, go ahead. Help yourself. I keep all my business records in here anyway. I haven't had time to even go in there hardly since we took over."

That would have been more than six years ago, Cassie reasoned. You'd have thought even the most incurious person would have looked in there by now, but then, her own bookshelves contained books from her parents' years, books that she didn't remember and certainly hadn't read.

The dim bulb flickered as she touched the switch, casting eerie shadows in darkened corners. There were shelves from floor to ceiling along two walls, a few almost empty, some of them filled. The furnishings consisted of one lone table and two cane-bottomed chairs, all covered with a patina of years turned to dust.

Cassie lifted a large volume from a nearby shelf, and sneezed violently. The cover crackled with age and she had to be careful not to break the fragile binding. The crisp, yellowed page she saw was filled with an old-fashioned scrawl, a long list of names written in time-dimmed ink.

A thrill of excitement ran down her spine as she sensed the richness of an era whose history she held in her hands. She felt as if the people listed on these pages were part of her own family. She may even find the names of some of her ancestors.

Some of the shelves held old volumes of various genre, a few volumes on hotel management, some historical volumes about the two great wars, a biography or two and even a couple that were pure fiction. The higher shelves contained stacks of tall grayish-green volumes that she recognized as ledgers and registers. Cassie marked their position with a nod and returned her thoughts to the room itself. This, she decided, was going to be worthwhile. But first, she would have to do a bit of housekeeping.

Leaving the storeroom by a back door, she found herself in a short hallway. Facing her was a door with "Utility" lettered on it. She opened the door and found what she was looking for, all within the one room, even new light bulbs. As the vacuum cleaner roared to life, Ike jerked the door open.

"What the hell…oh. I thought you were Ben or Wendy, wasting time in here when they should be in the kitchen. What in the world are you doing, anyway?" His eyes swept the room, making sure nothing was broken or damaged.

"Just moving a little dust out. I don't mind. Save them the trouble. Don't let me disturb you," she said, turning to vacuum a corner, hoping to get away with the bluff. She did. Ike withdrew, shaking his head in annoyance.

Cassie spent a good half hour getting the little room presentable. After she had returned the cleaning supplies to the utility closet, she found her way back along winding hallways to another entrance to the foyer, near the dining room entrance.

She made a quick trip up to her room to fetch her pad and pencils and hurried back to the little room she was already thinking of as her office, where she began rearranging the guest registers on their shelves in chronological order, from 1874 forward. Then she started on the ledgers, their first dates starting with 1875. She wondered why there was none for 1874, but she could look into that later. Right now she only wanted to dive right into the life and times of The Corona Hotel.

She stood back and appraised her little work space with a satisfied smile. Meg would be impressed, maybe even willing to join her, she thought. And with the thought of Meg, her mind leapt back to Gillis and Jesse and the others, wondering what they would find, wondering about the sad little scene that was even now playing itself out on Meg's frozen lawn.

Seven

The snowy plain of Meg Dothard's front yard was well trampled when the van arrived with the group from the hotel. They tightened their hoods, snugged their gloves and began to emerge into the icy air where Nathan stood sentinel over the body. He had tracked out a large circle in the snow around it and was patrolling it diligently to protect the death scene from being trampled by the small crowd of red-nosed gawkers who had gathered.

These were the people who lived in the sheltered old village at the foot of the mountain, where their forebears had built homes to withstand whatever havoc the elements might wreak on them. They had little use or sympathy for the newcomers of the past thirty five years who built homes up the mountain roads. Let them run with the women for shelter at the hotel, these men would stay in their own homes, thank you, for these were also the brave souls who broached any hardship to keep track of the daily goings on around the village.

In carrying out this obligation, they now found themselves stuck here, unable to tear themselves away and go on about their business of carrying the news, because Nathan would not let them near enough to see who lay cold and dead at the roadside.

Bernard had stopped the four-wheel drive on the road beside the body, shielding the scene from some of the biting wind. Snow swirled in small flakes around the scene, feeling like tiny icicles when it touched bare skin. Gillis had brought along his Polaroid and took photos from all sides and angles before he stepped across Nate's line and knelt beside the body.

Jesse and Ben gravitated to the point where they would get the best view of the face once Gillis had cleared away enough snow and lifted the head.

The face. Jesse looked and looked at it, trying to get just the right angle. He was sure he saw something—a familiar similarity. Seeing Gillis watching him he shook his head once. "I don't know. I may have seen him around. Ben?"

Turning, he saw the boy standing rigid, staring, caught in the grip of strong emotion. His cheeks were flushed against the pallor of his face. His mouth was a thin, tight line. A wrinkled brow overshadowed pain-filled eyes, and he said nothing.

"Ben," Gillis said, "do you recognize him, son?"

Ben tore his raw eyes away from the roadside and met Gillis' kindly look. In a strangled whisper he uttered, "Yeah, it's Jamey, all right. I knew it would be. He didn't come home last night."

"Home?"

"The hotel. He shares my room."

Gillis had not yet heard about the absentee employee. "He works there?"

"Yeah. At least, he did."

Jesse placed his hand on Ben's shoulder and the boy seemed to draw strength from it, pulling himself up with firm resolve. Jesse was glad that Ben was comforted, but now he himself felt a growing emptiness in the core of his being, a gnawing suspicion and a bleak knowledge. He didn't want to have to face the next few days, but he knew he must at least begin and hope that all his fears were unfounded.

His mind framed words from an old poem, "… let the dead past buries its dead …." He forced himself back to the present and looked at the faces around him. He was in a way relieved to see the same pain in those faces that he felt within himself.

Perhaps he was just imagining things. Maybe his suspicions were groundless. Maybe this was just a fluke. Best not to jump to conclusions, he told himself.

Gillis questioned each of those at the scene, trying to learn the boy's last name, where he had lived, or next of kin. No one else from the hotel could shed any new light on the boy's identity, nor could any of the gawkers milling around the perimeter. At last the crowd grew weary with waiting and some drifted away.

Gillis asked the group from the hotel to stay with the body while he went to the station to try to radio the coroner again and find out when he might be arriving, if he was going to make it at all, before they started thinking about moving the body to a more appropriate place.

While he was gone, Bernard stood watch so Nate could go inside, to Meg's kitchen and coffee pot. The others huddled in the van in silence until Doc said, "I hope the coroner gets here soon. We don't need anybody getting frost bite."

Jesse was debating whether to ask Bernard to take their senior member back to the hotel when, as if in answer to his thought, the white hush was broken by the throbbing sounds of a helicopter as it clattered in and settled on the snow. Its arrival coincided with Gillis' return to the scene.

"Leave it to old Doctor MeHarg," said Gillis, grinning, as the short round form jumped nimbly down into the snow, bag in hand, muffled to the eyes in a scarf done up in his family plaid. "He'll always find the quickest way to get to the scene of a death."

"Vulture," muttered one of the few remaining onlookers.

Gillis stopped the small ripple of laughter with a fiery look in their direction, then strode forward as well as one can stride through drifts of snow, to clasp the mittened paw of Doctor Duggal Ewing MeHarg, possibly the only thoroughbred Scot ever to attempt to master the southern Appalachian accent, which, ironically, had filtered down from the original Scots and Irish tongues that first were brought from Britain to these mountains. "Glad to see you, sir," said Gillis, demonstrating his respect for the crowd to see.

"Now then, what have we got here?" the doctor asked, only a slight burr evident in the consonants among his broad vowels. He knelt a little distance from the body, surveying the scene before moving in closer to examine the corpse itself. His "Hmmm"s gradually diminished until only silence remained. Gillis and Jesse exchanged glances as the doctor's face changed from that of a kindly old country doctor to that of an astute scientist.

Doctor MeHarg faced Gillis. "I won't make any statement right now. I'll contact you from Murphree as soon as I have a definite conclusion." He turned to the group and said, "Let's have a hand here, gentlemen. Let's get this poor boy into the chopper." Turning back to Gillis he said, "Is any of the family here? Anyone going to accompany the body?"

After a brief silence Jesse said, "I would be honored to go with Jamey."

Ben turned a surprised but grateful look toward him, and Jesse sensed that the gratitude was for more than just the escort. Ben was thankful that he was not expected to go, to leave his work and his mother at just this time.

"You look out for your mom, Ben. She's had a shock." He gave the boy a quick hug around the shoulders as Dr. MeHarg and Bernard wrapped the body in a tarp from the chopper and respectfully laid what remained of Jamey into the hold.

Jesse drew Gillis a little away from the others and engaged him in quiet conversation. Gillis' face showed some signs of concern at first, then he nodded, and Jesse boarded the chopper, waving to Ben as he closed the door.

The little group on the ground watched as the slashing propeller tore at the air and the clumsy craft lifted off in a cloud of blowing snow. The onlookers wandered away while the few from the Corona, after making sure Meg's house was secure, loaded into the land-rover and made their way in silence the half mile or so up to the hotel.

All except Gillis. He stood watching the helicopter chug away into the icy air until it was just a speck, then ambled back to his office where he sat in silence, pondering the things he had just heard.

Eight

Cassie's mind was brought back to the present by the tension between her shoulder blades. For what seemed like hours her thoughts had been in the past century and the early days of Hartsville. Her eyes felt as if every mote of dust she had stirred up had settled under their lids. She looked at her watch. Two thirty. She needed something to drink, a break from her work.

In the lounge four elderly ladies sat, intent over a game of Canasta. They glared at her when she came in, and Cassie could only imagine their thoughts about her, this upstart who had seen fit to leave her hometown for a broader world, and then come sliding back to her parents' old home when the going got rough.

Cassie imagined them asking themselves who had given permission for this person to stay here, of all places. Why wasn't she out in the trailer village with the rest of the artistic types, or better yet, why hadn't she stayed in the house up the mountain where the rest of the hermits lived?

She liked that last thought offered up by her imagination. It perfectly described the little community up there. She and Jesse were solitary souls by nature of being writers. Doc and Nell had each other and certainly didn't need other people always in their lives just now. Others of the mountain people were public people like doctors and lawyers who came, some of them from far away, in search of just that solitude offered by the rugged mountains.

All the houses up the mountain were very private residences indeed. With that thought, Cassie imagined a new depth for the old ladies' resentments. How dare those hermits, she attributed to their thinking, have private lives they refused to share with the city fathers and mothers, and ask no advice from them?

Even Evelyn was being ignored by the card club, who had turned back to their game. Cassie strolled over to the desk where Evelyn sat reading a paperback. When Cassie got closer she saw the cover, a lurid heart in chains and a bodice ripping display in words and illustration. Evelyn looked up and closed the book as Cassie approached.

"Hi. Boy, it's boring just sitting here waiting for someone to want something. Can I get anything for you? Any little old thing at all?" she asked, laughing.

Cassie smiled, "No, I don't need a thing. You have already organized this whole episode out of its socks, Evelyn. See how calm and peaceful things are?"

"Yeah, so's a morgue. But it's not necessarily a jolly place."

Just for a moment Cassie recoiled at Evelyn's candor. How could she talk like that when there's a dead person out there in the snow? But of course, she doesn't know about it yet. Or at least, she shouldn't. This might be the very best time, then, to engage her in small talk.

"Did you have time to prepare for this yesterday before the snow started and the roads got so bad?" she asked, picking up another paperback from the desk and leafing through it. It was another torrid romance, this one with tall ships and bare chested pirates scaring the bloomers off a maiden in distress.

"Yes, I guess so. I didn't know then, though, that all this was going to happen." She waved a hand to include the lobby and its occupants. "I got my hair done in the afternoon and did a little shopping at the boutique. You have to look pretty all day in this kind of business, you know, no matter how the customers dress these days."

Cassie looked down at her own casual attire, knowing that no matter where Evelyn was she would always look like one of the girls on the covers of her paperbacks from morning till night. She thought she might have cause to wonder at just what Evelyn would be capable of. She not only didn't mind getting dressed and preened up, she thrived on it. It was her. She might get up to all sorts of mischief along those lines, but did that go along with a personality that would run over another human being? Probably not.

"Did the stores close early because of the snow, or were they open till their usual time?" How many ways could she ask one question, to lead a person to answer another one?

"I don't know. I came back here pretty early in the afternoon, around two or three I guess. It had started snowing, and I couldn't see staying out any longer. Not like some of these kids around here. Jamey was just heading out into it when I got home, he and Wendy. Not me. There's no place important enough for me to go in these mountains in a snow storm."

"Who's Jamey?" Cassie felt a small frisson and watched Evelyn's face even closer. Ike had mentioned Jamey, too, and he wasn't too pleased with him not coming home last night.

"One of our staff."

"They must not have gone far. I see they got back okay." She didn't flinch at her deliberate deception, her leading statement. "Wendy seems fine, anyway."

"I know. Wendy was here last night when I came down to get a cup of coffee." She dog-eared the page she had been reading from and laid the book aside, gazing off. "I didn't see Jamey, though. I don't know when he got home. Of course, he and Ike might have gone off somewhere a little later. Ike came upstairs pretty late. He'd had a drink or two somewhere. I didn't ask where he'd been. I know he was madder than a hornet at Jamey this morning just because the kid hadn't got the heat going on time."

That Evelyn didn't share Ike's opinion of the boy was not lost on Cassie. "Do he and Ike not get on well, then?"

"Oh, usually they do okay. Sometimes they go off together at night, drinking I suppose, I don't know what else they'd find to do around here. And sometimes they go to the auctions over in Murphree. Ike likes to see what all the tourists will buy. He gets a kick out of that." She looked at the clock behind the desk. "Goodness, how the time goes by. And by. And slowly by. Want a cup of coffee or something?"

"In a few minutes. I'm going to run upstairs first, put my notes in order. Have you seen Meg?"

"She's up there, I think. The reason I say that is, that cat's not howling anymore. She must be with it, keeping it company."

Cassie considered for a moment. "Do you think it would be all right if she brings it downstairs? It must get awfully lonesome, shut up there in that one room."

"I don't see what harm it could do. At least it would be quieter. Besides, Nell Meade brought that funny looking animal of hers down, and the mayor's wife has brought those poodles, I see." Her sidelong look in the direction of Mrs. Moorehouse and her bored looking animals clearly expressed her opinion of that arrangement.

"Ummm. Wonder how Raucous gets on with dogs."

"Frankly, the cats will be more entertaining than those two poodles, anyway," Evelyn grinned, straightening the stack of registration cards. She shuffled them as if to deal out a hand and began sorting them again. "Those two cats have more pizzazz."

Cassie nodded and turned to go upstairs. "I'll be back in a few minutes and we'll have that coffee."

A disheveled Meg holding a protesting cat answered Cassie's knock. "Come in quick, before this she-devil tears me to shreds," she said, closing the door and releasing the cat in one movement.

"Meg, you can't stay up here in this room all the time with that cat. I asked Evelyn about bringing Raucous downstairs and she said it will be okay. It's up to you, though. After all, Nell always carries her royal feline around and those poodles of the mayor's go wherever they want to."

Meg considered. "I don't know how she'd act in a strange place. She's not as predictable as those other animals. If she broke something valuable, like one of those antiques or something, I'd be in for it."

"Well, try it. You can always take her cage along, just in case. At least you'd both have a more stimulating atmosphere. She could choose the people she wanted to tear to shreds. You could help her."

Raucous, released from Meg's grasp, was pacing the floor, switching her tail at a low angle. Meg watched her. "She's trying to look like a caged tiger."

"And doing a darn good job of it." Cassie looked at her watch then headed for the door that, when unlocked, joined this room with her own. "I unlocked my side earlier in case you needed anything. Let's leave both sides unlocked. It'll be easier to talk after we're ready for bed. And, if we leave it open, Raucous can have more room when she does have to be shut up."

She went into her own room and freshened up, then tapped on the door to signal Meg, who came through carrying the pet carrier with a pacified Raucous inside.

"If I didn't know better, I'd swear that cat was smiling," Cassie said.

"What makes you think she's not? She got her way, didn't she?" Meg cast a malicious look at the cat and preceded Cassie out the door.

Downstairs again, they met Evelyn and went into the dining room, where Wendy waited with trays of sandwiches and a large tureen of French onion soup. "With such a late breakfast, I thought a light lunch would go well. Not too filling, but it will get us through till dinner." The ham-based sandwich spread was delicious, and they ate heartily in spite of their late brunch. When they were finished, they helped Wendy clear the tables, loading the dirty dishes onto a cart just outside the kitchen door before wandering off to pursue their own interests.

They returned to the lobby to check on Raucous, who was busy reaching a paw through the bars batting and scratching at the latch. Cassie stooped in front of the cage to watch, and Raucous sat down on her haunches, staring back at her with flattened ears and down turned eyes and mouth, disgust twitching in every whisker.

"I can almost hear her saying, 'Well, are you going to open this thing or not?'" Cassie said. "What do you think, Meg, shall I?"

"I guess it would be all right. We'll never have a better chance to find out how she'll behave."

Cassie opened the door, whereupon Raucous turned away and moved to the back of the cage, sat down and began to take a bath. Cassie huffed and dropped her hands to her sides in aggravation. "Wonder how you say 'bitch' in cat language?"

"Raucous," answered Meg.

Seeing the cat content, the two women returned to the lounge where they sat quietly engaged in idle chatter and thumbing through magazines until they were interrupted by a furious Nell. Her red jowls quivered with rage and indignation as she bore down upon them. "Mrs. Dothard, this is the last straw. Your animal," she spat the word out, "Your animal has upset my Porsche so badly that the poor thing has hidden from me and I can't find her. You must remove your cat from my wing of the hotel immediately. Furthermore, I insist that everyone come along and cooperate in finding my poor Porsche!"

The assembled guests, along with Ike and Evelyn, gazed at her in awe or amazement. Some of the guests rose from their chairs, ready to begin the search as they were bidden. Ike was uncertain what measures he should take and quickly surveyed the faces of the group to see where the majority of the sympathy lay. Evelyn smoothed the sides of her already taut slacks and excused herself from the room. Nell turned toward the stairs, ready to lead the hunt.

She was saved the trouble. Just behind the newel post at the bottom of the stairs huddled the cause of her distress. But for the naked look of its kinky fur, it was unrecognizable as the cat in question. A shriek rose from her throat. "Porsche! What have they done to you?"

Porsche preened as if she had seen herself in a mirror and found the prospect pleasing, as if she knew that the rich raspberry lipstick smeared around her wedge of a mouth and the midnight blue eye shadow daubed across her brow made her even more beautiful than ever.

"I hold you responsible for this," she hissed at Meg, who found it hard to heed the venomous words while trying hard not to laugh.

Nell was not finished. Forgetting that she had just blamed Meg for her cat's condition, she roared, "Who did this terrible thing? Whoever did this will pay, and pay dearly, you mark my words!" She gathered up the animal in her smothering embrace and mounted the stairs on feet of pounding wrath.

A whimpering voice was heard, partly stifled by folds of the owner's skirt, bunched up and pressed against her mouth. Amy, the mayor's daughter, sat hidden in the shadow of a grandfather clock, and she was very near to crying.

"I wanted her to look pretty, too. Miss Evelyn said I should try to be pretty. She always looks so pretty with her make-up on. That cat looked like it needed some help, too, so it could be pretty like Raucous."

Evelyn returned carrying a broken eye shadow wand and her opened tube of lipstick. If anyone had looked closely at the lipstick, they would have seen the tiny, kinky hairs from the muzzle of the adored royal feline. She had arrived just in time to hear the child's confession, and turned away but not in time to hide her smile. The mayor's wife, however, followed her with a look that bespoke badinage to come regarding her daughter's purported need of enhancement.

Meg had disappeared, and Cassie was certain that, wherever she was, she would be enjoying the latest turn of events too much to hold a sensible conversation. As the others went about their own purposes, each one smiling now, Cassie sought refuge in the little room she already thought of as her study.

She tried to concentrate but her thoughts kept wandering back to the morning when Jesse sat at her table and spoke of his past. What, really, did she know of him? She had to admit to herself that it was unusual that he, a thoroughly pleasant and cultured man, would stay here in this remote little town, hidden among floods of tourists in the summer and in near solitude in winter.

If he had an aunt in a nearby town—had he said nearby? No, only another town—why did he never go to visit her? Well, perhaps he did, he probably went lots of places Cassie didn't know about. They were neighbors, but just as he enjoyed his solitude, so did she enjoy hers. She did not monitor his comings and goings.

Anyway, she was often out with Nate or Perry, or both, working on newsworthy topics with Nate or hearing about the latest antics that introduced Perry to some of the more recalcitrant tourists. She didn't know much about Jesse's personal life, and had no reason to. Having said so to herself, and having rationalized and somewhat accepted the fact that she was, at times, altogether too curious, she restored Jesse to his usual high place in her esteem and at last returned to the research at hand.

She began by examining the old ledgers, intrigued by the prices of goods back in the last century, and the simplicity of the accounting system. Before she reached the point where she would begin making notes, Ike stuck his head in and said, "They're back, Gillis and them. I'm going to go speak to them, see what's going on. Here's the spare key to this room, come in any time you want to. Just don't ask me any questions. I don't know any answers."

And if you did, you wouldn't tell, thought Cassie. But she reshelved the ledger she had opened and locked the door behind her. Then she went to find out what Gillis had learned about the death of the young stranger.

Nine

Gillis, Doc, Bernard and Ben were taking off coats and gloves and asking for warm drinks, but Jesse wasn't with them, Cassie noted. When she and Gillis were apart from the others, he said, "Ben identified the body. He said his name was Jamey, and he was Ben's roommate here. It turns out that he worked here."

"Ike and Evelyn both mentioned a Jamey this morning. Ike was mad at him for not having the hotel warm when they woke up, but Evelyn seemed to like him okay," Cassie offered. "But where is Jesse? Didn't he come back with you?"

"He escorted the body to Murphree," explained Gillis. Cassie had drawn him into a quiet corner by a table where someone had set up an urn of hot mulled cider. "He said he hated to see that boy all alone there. He must be a real sentimentalist."

"He's a gentle man I guess, if that's what you mean," Cassie replied. "Why didn't he feel like the coroner would be an adequate escort, I wonder? Looks like he'd have taken time to come get some clothes and a tooth brush."

Gillis raised a questioning eyebrow, his tongue exploring the edge of an incisor. After a brief pause he said, "He didn't want the boy to lie out there in the snow any longer." He took a sip from his cup of cider and said, as if he wasn't sure he should, "Oh, he said he was wanting to go check on his aunt in Cherry Lake anyway, if he can get through. What do you know about her?"

"Nothing, until this morning. He only mentioned that she existed. He didn't say she lived as near as Cherry Lake."

Nathan and Meg joined them. Meg's face showed that Nathan had told her about Ben's role at the scene of death. Bernard went off in the direction of the lounge while Gillis and Nathan wandered away in subdued conversation about the morning's events, leaving Cassie, Ben and Meg with no further word about the death, whether it was accidental or otherwise.

Ben's face looked frozen. Not just cold, but set as if destined to bear forever-after the stunned look of raw pain and heartache that only the face of the young can achieve. For one unguarded moment his eyes reached out to Meg, like the arms of a small boy to his mother. The moment passed, and he drew himself upright and forced a look of confidence, or at least determination, to his face.

Meg hadn't missed the moment. Now she stood beside him, not touching him, but neither did she violate with words her son's present steps in his passage from youth to adulthood. "I hated seeing your friend like that, Ben. It must have been much worse for you. I'm sorry."

"I had to identify him," Ben said, staring into the cup of cider, "And I couldn't even tell them where to find his—you know—next of kin. He's even been helping me in the kitchen a lot! God, I just feel so.... " His voice had risen to near the breaking point and he bit back whatever word had been coming, trying hard to keep his face from crumbling.

Cassie found it necessary to either speak or break down. She spoke. "Gillis can find out about his family with no trouble. Ike probably knows, if he hired the boy. Don't you worry about it. What was his name though, Ben?" she asked.

"Jamey. Jamey...," he began then stopped. Cassie would have urged him on but she saw him staring white faced across the room. She followed his gaze. Doc and Wendy, with Bernard at her elbow, were standing more or less together. Had Ben seen something disturbing there, or had he been looking inward at his own thoughts?

The look passed, and Ben turned to give his mother a strong embrace. "I've got to get back to work, Mom. I'll see you as soon as I can, though. Send for me if you need me. I'll be in the kitchen."

"If I need you, I'll come after you, Ben. Ike Farabaugh isn't going to keep me away from my own son, no matter what the rules say."

Ben grinned. "The County Health Inspector isn't apt to come out today just to see who all is in the kitchen, anyway," he said, turning toward the door.

Cassie still watched the group across the room. Ike, seeing Ben leave, turned to Wendy and spoke to her. She nodded and followed Ben to the kitchen. She was, apparently, to replace Jamey as cook's helper.

Where were Gillis and Nathan when she—they—needed them? Or Jesse? She needed an objective mind to bounce her thoughts off of so that she could get them in order faster. Well, if Gillis and Nathan kept avoiding her, Jesse would sure have to do a lot of listening when he did get back.

Ten

Cassie felt restless. Deciding to see if she could help in the kitchen, she followed the way Ben and Wendy had gone. The doors swung shut with a soft *whish* behind her as she entered through the servers' station, which probably had at one time been a butler's pantry. She stopped there, abruptly, held by the sound of angry voices.

Ben's voice was raised only slightly but the emotion behind it was staggering. "Don't you understand, Wendy? He's dead! Has been laying out there, dead, since last night! Dr. MeHarg and Gillis said so! You were with him yesterday, now you tell me, what happened? Because if you don't tell me, I'm going to sic Gillis on you!"

"Oh, God! I don't know what happened, I tell you! He wasn't dead…. " A sob wrenched from her and the sound of falling metal clanged through the stark space. Wendy ran through the server's station, pushing Cassie aside. "Leave me alone!" she wailed, doors flying behind her as she ran toward the service stairs at the back of the hall.

Ben didn't know she had heard any of the conversation, Cassie realized. Pushing through the inner doors, she said, "What's got Wendy so upset? She almost ran over me. Should I go see about her?" Getting no immediate answer, she swept on, "Actually, I came in here to see if you want some help with cooking. It's one of the things I do best," she said, tying an apron around her middle.

Ben, with red and angry face, looked at the apron and then looked around the kitchen. "Yeah, I guess so. You can either peel vegetables or cut up the beef. I'm making a big pot of stew."

"I'll peel. You probably have a favorite way to do your stew chunks," she said, and began washing potatoes and carrots and putting them in the peeler. "This is the first time I've met Wendy. I didn't even know there was a new girl here. Of course, I haven't been here since the season closed. Funny they would hire her so near the end of summer," she ventured, hoping he would rise to the bait and tell her about the argument.

"Yeah, she did come on sort of late. Ike kept her on to help him with the bookkeeping and Evelyn wanted someone to help with the domestic work, keeping things up through the winter. She seems to do okay with both jobs."

"I heard her say she had left with Jamey yesterday afternoon but came back without him. Did you or Bernard happen to go out, by any chance? Did he come back with one of you?" It was weak, but the best she could do on short notice.

"No. I didn't go anywhere, and Bernard hasn't been staying here the last couple of days. I don't know if they met up or not. They weren't very close."

He offered no other comment, and realizing he was in no mood or emotional state to chat, she allowed him his privacy. She had questioned him enough for now. They worked side by side until the stew ingredients were ready for the pot. Then she untied her apron and hung it back on the hook. "I think I'll just go and see if Wendy is all right. Do you think she'd mind? You know her better than I do."

"Sure, go ahead. Thanks for your help. Tell Mom I'll be out soon," he said, smiling a little as he held the door for her. "Oh, and I don't know what Ike and Evelyn would think of a guest helping me in here, and Wendy not helping."

"I'll swear I never saw the place." Cassie held up her right hand to seal her oath and headed for the door through which Wendy had gone. Through it was a part of the house not open to the general public.

These rooms must be meant to house the staff. Cassie climbed the narrow staircase, stopping to listen on the first landing. Hearing nothing, she went to the second. From the hall to her left came the sound of water running.

As she stood there a door opened and Wendy emerged from what was evidently a shared bathroom, face freshly scrubbed and a towel over her arm. Her firm and forbidding expression said she did not welcome visitors right now.

Before Wendy could ask her to leave this private part of the house, Cassie said, with more solicitation in her voice than she really felt, "Are you all right? I was so worried about you! I couldn't rest until I found you. Evelyn doesn't know I'm here, or she'd probably send me back to the public part of the hotel, but I had to know you were all right." Only as she said it did she realize the effect it would have, how it set her with Wendy against the world.

Wendy looked at her for a long moment before speaking. "Sorry. You needn't worry about me. I'll cope. It was just learning about poor Jamey like that...." She turned away, trying to dismiss the uninvited guest.

Then she paused, thoughtful.

Cassie waited when Wendy stopped, waited as she watched the girl's expression change as the thoughts that passed through her mind took a different turn. Wendy faced Cassie and said, "Look, I'm sorry about that scene downstairs. It was just the shock, you know? Come on into my room for a bit if you want."

Wendy's room was sparsely furnished. Nothing of a personal nature showed itself to give Cassie any insight into the woman who occupied it. She sat in the only chair while Wendy sat at the small vanity and began putting on fresh make-up.

Cassie watched as cover stick went on at the eyes and around the mouth, and realized that there was a little more age on Wendy than she had at first thought. Instead of early to mid-twenties as she would have guessed, she must be at least into her thirties. But she was clever with her make-up and hair and if she could get away with the deception, more power to her. Perhaps she, Cassie, could learn a thing or two here.

After quickly reviewing just what information had passed between herself and Wendy, she decided that would be her best approach. "You're good with make-up. Are you with the theater troupe?"

Wendy looked at Cassie through her reflected image in the mirror, and answered, "Yes, since I'm here anyway I thought it might be amusing."

"Oh, you didn't come because of the festival then?"

Wendy opened her mouth to speak but closed it again, as if giving careful thought to what she wanted to say. She turned to face Cassie. "That too, of course. But the real reason I came is, I think the expression goes, 'to take the waters'. I have a sort of condition that causes me a good bit of pain sometimes, and when I heard about the hot mineral springs here I felt I wanted to come and try them, just to see if it might help. The theater group gives me a bit of a lift, too, of course. Takes my mind off the pain."

"I'm sorry. Have you found the baths helpful?"

"Some, but then I haven't had a lot of chances to try them yet. I haven't told Evelyn about my problem, of course. She might not want to keep me on if she thinks I'm not very well."

"I'm pretty sure Evelyn would be sympathetic. In fact, it might be best if you do tell her. She seems very kind, at heart. A romantic sort, always looking for soft gentle things in life. Try it. She won't fire you, and if you find that the idea doesn't sit well with her, then just don't mention it to her again. As long as you get your work done ...."

Wendy had listened attentively, and now nodded in agreement. "Thanks. I'll do it, first chance I get. After all this is over, of course."

"Good." Feeling bolstered by her success in clearing the first hurdle in gaining the confidence of this girl, or woman, Cassie now ventured further. "You must have got to know Jamey very well."

Wendy's eyes slid downward to the tissue she held in her hands, picking and twisting small bits off it, letting them fall to her lap. "Not really, Ben and Jamey and I would go out for a while now and then, just for a break from this. I did leave here with him yesterday, I guess you heard Ben raging about that, but we parted early in the afternoon so I could take care of some things. And he was on his way to see someone else, he said. Anyway, we didn't know each other all that well. But I'm sorry he's... he...."

"Don't upset yourself about it. I know you feel bad. Just don't let it get you down." She placed a comforting hand on Wendy's arm.

"You heard what Ben was saying. He thinks I'm responsible, somehow." Her voice quavered, as though she was about to burst into new tears.

"That was just his own grief talking, I'm sure. After all, he worked with Jamey, and even shared a room with him. He was pretty upset down there when he saw Jamey's body, especially when he had to make the identification. He's having to be a lot more grown up during all this than he ever has before, if you see what I mean. And too, there is always anger of some sort when somebody close to you dies, and that anger has to be directed at something."

Wendy was thoughtful for a moment then brightened a bit. "Yes, I do see what you mean," she said, grabbing at the wisp of comfort Cassie had offered her. "And you are probably right. I'll have to just not get upset over what he says, won't I? I mustn't let him make me feel any worse than I already do. It's just his way of coping." Her accent became more pronounced as she continued, "After all, people do die. I've known a lot of people who are already dead." She spoke as if shedding the load of guilt brought on by Ben's remarks had given her a new perspective.

She looked at her watch. "Oh, dear! I do have to get back. Evelyn will think I've deserted her."

She held the door open for Cassie to go through. Together they went downstairs, Wendy back to the kitchen, Cassie back to the lobby to muse over their conversation. The girl did seem to have a deep sense of duty.

She also seemed to have an unsettled, lonely sort of life. No wonder she had health problems, considering that she had not mentioned a family, was having to fend for herself and no one to help her, no support system, as Cassie's peers in nursing would say. But she seemed to be 'coping'—wasn't that the term Wendy used?— coping quite well at present, in spite of her hysteria at hearing about Jamey. That could be overlooked.

Perhaps what Wendy needed right now was a good friend. Cassie made up her mind to be just that. Anything she was able to learn about Wendy or any of the other Shakespeareans would be incidental, but no less important to Gillis' investigation.

In an alcove off the lobby, a group of those very thespians were huddled together reading lines to each other. Beside one of the men lay a papier-mache donkey's head. Between two of the women lay a solid white cat, all its whiskers now immaculate.

"I see we're to have *A Midsummer Night's Dream* on the marquee this year," she said to Meg who was playing Canasta with the mayor, his wife Gaynell, and Nell. Cassie pulled up a chair behind Meg and spoke at her shoulder, "Ben says he'll see you soon."

"Yes, I know. He came out for a little while. Where were you?"

"Upstairs, talking to Wendy. She seems to have a reclusive sort of life."

Meg turned questioning eyes toward her but said nothing.

"It's your turn, Meg, let's go," declared Nell.

Meg smiled benignly at her, drew a card and discarded another after laying down a book of jacks. Cassie stood to leave. "I'll be in the little room at the back of the office. I'm using it as a study, my own little office for now. There are some old books in there."

Meg nodded, not looking up. "There you go, Gaynell," she said, smiling at the player to her left, who obviously would have preferred being called Mrs. Moorehouse, or perhaps Mrs. Mayor.

Cassie could imagine the tension with which Meg was resisting Nell, and the frustration Nell must be feeling at not being able to control Meg beyond Meg's willingness to be controlled.

Cassie found Ike in her little study thumbing through the ledgers. "I thought I'd pack some of these into a box, get them out of your way. They don't have anything but figures in them. You're not interested in the finances, are you? Just the history? I thought maybe you'd like more room in here. I'll put them in the attic, or somewhere out of your way. How's that for service?"

"Fine, as long as there is nothing of importance to posterity in there," she said, a little disappointed. "But I really would like to look through them, if you don't mind, just to be sure. I might find some interesting tidbits, and of course since I'm not interested in the finances of the place, I'll skip over that. Would that be all right, do you think?"

"Well, okay then, just let me look through them first," he said, gathering up an armful and taking them to his desk.

For the next hour or so she pored over the dusty, crackling guest registers, beginning with the most recent, the listing of this past summer's guests, working her way backward. Her notes grew slowly, since she had found little of significance in the recent years. But in the log for 1967 she found the answer to her earlier question during brunch: When did the tornado strike? Listed among the guests who took refuge at the hotel at that time were Nell Meade, Doctor Marlowe Abbott, several of the older ladies who were among today's gathering, and numerous names Cassie had never heard of.

At the end of each line the words "Billed to City" were pencilled in. There was nothing in the registers regarding payment expected from these guests except for one, a Mr. Benefield, who was billed a hundred and fifty dollars for cigar burns on furniture.

The city had picked up a largish tab for that tornado, thought Cassie as she looked further and learned that many of the guests had lodged there for more than a month, while repairs were made to their own homes.

She laid that volume aside and opened the one bearing the next earlier date, then the next. Her eyes burned and the air had grown stale. Restlessness began to set in. Having no news of the dead boy and no way of hearing any was getting on her nerves. When was Jesse coming back? And when was Gillis going to have more information for them? Cassie replaced the books on the shelf, closed the door behind her and wandered back toward the lobby.

There she found that Gillis had already returned and was chatting with various of the guests. When he saw her, he drew her aside. "Have you had a chance to talk with anyone yet?"

"Yes, all of the staff and a few of the others. Haven't learned much, but I'll tell you later what I did find out."

Gillis moved away then, showing the Polaroid photographs he had taken at the scene of the death to little groups of guests that gathered around him. "Have any of you ever talked with him? I need to know all I can about him, especially where he'd lived away from the hotel, where his family is, anything like that." When the guests had all looked at the pictures and moved away shaking their heads, Gillis continued, "I'll be back later. If any of you think of anything that might be helpful, anything at all, come and talk to me."

Cassie took the pictures from his hand, slowly examining each one. She thought she might have seen the boy, probably here at the hotel when she was having dinner at one time or another, but there was nothing specific that she remembered about the occasion. She handed the photographs back.

"Sorry," she said. "He looks familiar but there are no details connecting themselves to him in my mind. But didn't Ben already identify him?"

"Yes, but some of these people might tell me something that will help answer some other questions. Sometimes people will tell you more if they think you don't know anything much to start with. Which, actually, is just the case right now. At least I might find out who knew him best. I'll be back in a little while," he said on his way out.

He picked up his hat from a silver tray on the hall table. "Keep an ear open, okay, Cassie?" He started out the door, then turned back. "Oh, and you can do one other thing for me if you will."

"What is it, Gillis?"

"There's an abandoned vehicle in my parking lot. Yeah, I know it's a strange place for a criminal to ditch a car but with the snow, and it being night, they may not have noticed that the little building next door was a jailhouse. It's registered to a Janet Wright. Ask around and see if anybody here at the hotel answers to that name, will you?"

"Of course. And meanwhile, you can check the registration on whatever cars are up here now, and see whose is missing."

"I don't know who all up here has a vehicle, but I'll find out when I get a minute. Every little bit helps."

"I might be able to find out which of the staff own automobiles."

"Don't get too obvious with it. You just listen and pick up what you can that way. I'll ask the questions. I'm licensed to ask questions," he said, "and don't look so disappointed. The things you'll be able to pick up just through talk may be more help than you think." He smiled down at her and turned toward the door.

"Of course," she said, but the glint in her eyes was no assurance that she meant it. She admonished him to be careful on the icy road as he walked across the wide snow-covered veranda, then she closed the door against the cold.

Instinctively, she straightened the tray that had moved slightly when Gillis picked up his hat. It had been placed there to cover an old burned place she had seen just after she came back to Hartsville, when she was staying at the hotel while her house repairs were being finished.

Then she remembered what she had read about Mr. Benefield. *Was this burn his doing? But probably not. He had been charged for the damage he had done, to cover the cost of repairs, and this table had obviously not been repaired.* She would probably never know, but it would make an interesting anecdote for her history.

She liked remembering those early days in Hartsville, just after she had left the reservation and sought the serenity of these mountains again. She was still consumed in her grief and bitterness over Matt's death, and still felt like a loner, a stranger, thriving on solitude. She hadn't yet solved the mystery of Matt's murder, and her failure to avenge it still haunted her at times. She refused to even think about that last confrontation with those she thought of as his killers, that fall that had left her hospitalized for weeks.

It was only a few weeks after her return here that she had been able to move into her childhood home after spending those days in the hotel. When she had visited the shops in the village, she was sometimes faced with suspicious looks, cold receptions. Gradually, though, some of the younger residents had drawn her into their midst and a few dropped in to visit her, like family, until eventually her hours of solitude, even in her remote little house up on the mountain, were at times hard won hours. She was glad those years on the reservation were over, glad that she now had a chance to live among friends and be happy again.

She felt fortunate indeed in having found a friend like Nathan who published her articles, and in having moved in across the road from a neighbor like Jesse who had introduced her to Nathan and who seemed as reclusive as she herself. Most of her activities since her return had centered around the newspaper and Nate, and sometimes Gillis.

Snapping out of her reverie, she smoothed the cloth on which the tray sat and returned to the lounge and its yawning residents. Nate was sitting at a large table with a group of men that included the mayor and members of the older male population of the town. They smoked their pipes and cigars without regard. They looked as if they had engaged in this practice on a regular basis and had no intentions of forsaking it.

Meg was just coming down the stairs. "I wondered when you were coming out," she said, taking the chair across from Cassie. "You must have found a lot of interesting things, staying in there so long at a time."

"Just dusty old books, and dusty old bits of information," Cassie replied. "Ike doesn't spend much time there, that's for sure. Of course, his own records are kept somewhere else."

If they thought they were going to have a quiet conversation they were wrong. Nell chose that moment to join them, Porsche cuddled in her arms, her little face shiny from the cold cream Nell had used to remove the make-up. Nell herself seemed to have recovered from her fury, at least for the present. "This is dreadful, just dreadful. It isn't enough that we have to leave our homes or freeze to death. Now we are surrounded by this pall of a very real death. What do you think happened? Don't you suppose it was an accident?"

"Couldn't say," said Meg, watching Wendy move about the room, drawing ever closer to where they were sitting. "All I know is...." Cassie's covert nudge interrupted whatever else Meg was about to say. In an obvious change of direction she finished weakly, "All I know is I am sort of enjoying the change of scenery, being here at the hotel. Feels sort of like I'm on vacation." But Meg's gaze rested on her hands, clenched in tight fists on her lap, belying her words.

Wendy joined them, taking the seat beside Cassie. "Did you see those horrid pictures that policeman was showing around?" Her tone begged agreement with her emotions. No one either agreed or disagreed, but waited for her to explain.

"Poor Jamey. I don't know what I'll do without him. I depended on him! And now he's got himself killed." A tear slid down her cheek. Cassie remembered the apparent acceptance Wendy had managed in their previous conversation and wondered if the tear was quite large enough to be crocodile in nature, or if she had misinterpreted Wendy's response during their earlier talk. Or maybe it was just the stages of grief repeating themselves, as they sometimes do. Perhaps Wendy was more fragile than she had appeared.

Wendy's voice quavered as she went on. "Well," she said, "We'll just have to look out for ourselves now. I don't know how I'll cope, though, with dear Jamey gone."

No one spoke for a little while, the only sound being Wendy's sniffles. Finally she wiped her face on the paper napkin she still carried from serving her last tray of beverages.

Meg said, as sweetly as she could, "Well, my dear, we can't think of ourselves at a time like this."

"Well, I have to think about myself, don't I? I have nobody else to look after me. Jamey would go and get my medicine when it got so I couldn't breathe or if I ran out of the other."

"What medicine? Why can't you breathe?" demanded Nell, apparently keeping an eye on the effectiveness of Doc's prescriptions.

"I have asthma. Cold-induced. Maybe a cat allergy, too," she said, shooting a sharp look at Porsche, who smugly closed her eyes and nestled deeper into Nell's lap. Nell's protective hand covered the animal's bald head as she returned Wendy's look in kind.

"Oh, don't blame him, the poor thing," Wendy consoled. "He doesn't know what he's doing to me."

"It isn't a he, it's a she, and she probably knows very well what she's doing to everybody," snapped Meg.

Nell's face turned a deep puce. "Come along, Porsche dear, these people don't appreciate good breeding. How could they? They've never been exposed to it before," she snarled, gathering the ungainly beast up into a quivering, awkward wrack of legs and spine, all ill-fitted together, and carried it away, muttering over her shoulder, something that could have been "witch" or perhaps something similar.

Cassie, in defense of Meg, cast a mocking barb at the retreating back, "Watch out. She bites."

To Wendy she said, "It's too bad our weather chose this particular year to go to such extremes and stir up your asthma. Are you planning to try to stay here, or will you look for a more suitable place?"

"Oh, I'll stay awhile, at least till the festival is over. I can't give in to asthma when I'm here to treat the other condition in the springs, you know," Wendy said.

"The play will take your mind off things, and if you need more medication I'm sure Doc Abbott will have some emergency supplies on hand. Just don't you worry too much, Wendy." Cassie said, thinking to detract her from her ills. "What role are you going to try for, anyway?"

"Oh, I'm sure I'll get one of the female leads. If not, I'll just help the others with their lines and accents and things like that." Wendy answered, moving away to mingle among the guests, inquiring after their needs.

"She must be short on cash, staying in a place that makes her sick when she seems to have been everywhere else in the world she wanted to go to. Guess the funds ran out, do you think?" muttered Meg.

"What I think is, that young lady needs a friend, a confidant, and I think I'll try to be it," said Cassie. There was a lot going on underneath that glossy exterior. How much of it would she be able to learn? Once again she wished that Jesse were here to engage the girl in conversation. He would know just what to ask of his fellow Brit and how to interpret her answers and spot any innuendo.

Right now she needed to talk with Nate. When she finally caught his eye, she signaled for him to meet her at the drinks table. After Wendy had served each of them a cup of coffee, Cassie moved a little further from the crowd, drawing him with her. "I need to ask you a favor, Nate, if you don't mind."

"What sort of favor? I'm not going to be a cat sitter, if that's what you want," he smiled, but the smile did not reach his eyes.

"No, no, nothing like that. In fact, you'll love this. Gillis is trying to locate the owner of a car abandoned in his parking lot. It's registered to someone named Janet Wright. He says she isn't a local, or at least he isn't familiar with the name, but she may be one of the actors that are staying here. The thing is, he wants to find her without her knowing anyone is interested in her. In case she is the driver of the car that may have hit Jamey, you see. The car was left there after dark last night, so whoever was driving it could be involved with the accident. All you need to do is get acquainted with some of the girls and learn their names and find out if this Janet Wright is among the cast or crew. Do you think you'll have time to do that?"

"Oh, I believe I can just about handle it," he leered, relieved that she hadn't asked anything of him that would tie him down. All she had asked of him was that he do the thing he had cut his journalistic teeth on anyway—behave like an investigative, albeit undercover, reporter.

The next time Cassie saw him, he was sitting with a fiery haired young woman and her dark-haired companion, all of them engaged in solemn conversation. Cassie watched for awhile, then she moved into action on the next step of the plan that was coming together in her mind.

Nathan, though to Cassie's eyes engaged in conversing with the two young women, had not missed Cassie's movements.

He was remembering how he had planned his route when he started out this morning. He had reasoned that Cassie would be late waking but still, he was sure she would have a large pot of herbal tea brewing within minutes of getting up and maybe some hot buttered English muffins or homemade bran muffins to go with it. Spending a little time with Cassie wouldn't have been a bad way to start the day, he thought, even without the tea and muffins. He hadn't any idea then that they'd be thrown together in this way, here in the hotel, before nightfall.

While his interest in Cassie was more than journalistic in nature, he was most curious about her years away from the mountains, but there seemed to be no doors to her personal world. All he had been able to learn from her on the few occasions when they had talked was that she was a widow, had lived in Arizona with her husband teaching the Hopi children how to read and write, at least until Matt was killed, that she had somehow been injured in a fall, and that she was now writing the history of Hartsville for the local Historical Society. All their other conversation had been focused on local or current issues of interest to most newspaper people.

He had often thought of doing that himself, writing a book about the city and its mineral springs which were so popular in the late nineteenth and early twentieth centuries and were still enjoyed by some, especially the tourists. In a way, he was glad it was Cassie, not he, who was doing it now. He didn't really have time for all the research, but he would offer whatever help he could. If it would help him get to know her better then they would both be well served, he mused.

"You haven't heard a word I've said," the red-haired girl beside him piped in a broad Irish accent.

"Oh, yes I have. My mind isn't always where my eyes might lead you to think, you know," Nate protested.

"Well, you could have fooled me. What was the last thing I said?"

"You started out by telling me about your growing friendship with Jamey. And I am sorry you lost a friend so early in the acquaintance. Terrible thing, to die so young." He pressed her hand, and with her free one she wiped away a tear.

Nate went on. "Then you said that you had known most of these people, the people in the troupe, only long enough to learn their names. You mentioned Kitty, Bethany here, Heather, and you're Regan, of course, and, let's see...." He didn't have to continue because she was now folded up in laughter.

"All right, All right! I believe you," she conceded. Her sorrow was eased for the moment, anyway.

Nathan was thankful for the gift he had developed in journalism school, that of being able to watch a scene and at the same time record mentally most of what was being said around him, to play back on paper later and fit into the context of what he had seen. It was this gift that brought him through many sticky situations when other people mistook his scattered attentions for lack of concentration.

Leaving Regan and Bethany with a comforting wink, he strolled away. From beside the cushion where she sat, Regan took up a small Irish harp. The notes of an old Celtic ballad sprang from beneath her fingers as they plucked the strings of the harp, as if they were the strings of Nathan's heart.

But Nathan's mind was already wondering about the poor boy who had died in Meg's ditch, cold and alone.

Eleven

At about the time the hotel guests were settling in for their late lunch, Jesse left the morgue in Murphree. Turning his collar up against the bitter cold, he walked out into the snow, walking blindly in the direction toward which Doctor MeHarg had said he would find a car rental agency.

The cold he felt was not entirely because of the weather. The cold reached deep into his heart. He knew now that the poor dead Jamey who lay in the ditch all night was the son of his Aunt Olivia, and his own young cousin. The birthmark that looked so much like a dolphin leaping across the left thigh had removed any hope that it could be any other Jamey. When had he last seen the boy? Eight, ten years ago? He remembered watching the little boy diving fearlessly into the pool at a holiday lodge where they had spent a week just before Jesse moved to Hartsville.

He had suspected at Meg's house that the dead boy was his cousin. He had seen a faint resemblance in his death mask of the young man to that younger Jamey, but had tried to hold out some small hope against it, especially in light of his Aunt Olivia's letter that he had received and read—was it only this morning? There had been no mention of Jamey.

93

He was glad now that he hadn't been able to reach Olivia by phone earlier. They had never been able to form a close bond while he lived with her and Jamey, but over the past several years since he had moved to Hartsville, they had gradually lost contact almost completely. Until he received that letter, he'd had no desire to rekindle the relationship.

He pushed on through the deserted streets, lost in his thoughts. The words of the letter had, after the fourth or fifth reading, burned themselves into his mind, but just now, with the memory of Jamey lying dead in the snow, the contents took on a clearer reality portending far reaching effects. He hoped that when he reached Olivia's house she would be able and willing to explain it all and put the matter to rest.

He reached the car rental place and found what he wanted, a four-wheel drive vehicle with a come-along. He had learned that valuable precaution from Bernard just this morning. He rented the vehicle for a week and pulled out into the street, going in the direction of Cherry Lake, where Olivia lived.

A scan of the radio dial picked up nothing that he wanted to listen to, and he soon switched it off. He could learn as much about road conditions first hand as he could learn from the radio and be better able to evaluate the conditions for himself. Besides, the silence would help him concentrate. Soon his mind was filled with memories of Olivia and Jamey, and the way things had been when he first came to live with them.

He remembered that day in July of 1966, in England, when both his parents were buried, and the funeral itself, where he first met Olivia. She had tried to comfort him as much as she could in spite of her own grief over the loss of her sister, Jesse's mother, and in the months to come he began to think of her as a sort of surrogate mother. After he finished his studies at Cambridge, he had come to Cherry Lake to stay with her for a while.

That had not lasted long. As he drove now once again toward Cherry Lake and his Aunt Olivia, he did so with a deep sense of dread.

He swept a hand across his eyes again and again, as if to clear his vision and forced his thoughts back to Hartsville. When he first moved there he had, over a very short time, made many friends, including Meg, with whom he had sensed an acute and instant bonding. He was several years her junior, but still their friendship flourished. There was a certain aloneness, a certain secrecy, about each of them, and each recognized it in the other.

She tried at first to fix him up with some of the women in the town, but he declined to pursue any of her artfully arranged liaisons, knowing that one day, sooner or later, he would be returning to England to resume his life responsibilities there. Finally, she quit trying and his life sailed along without interruption. He wrote and researched, visited with his friends and conducted by mail any business he had with the estate and its interests back in England.

Until Cassie came to town. With the unbidden thought of Cassie he realized that, finally, he had found a subject that brought him warmth rather than the chilling nothingness he had felt a few minutes before. He had wanted to know Cassie better, perhaps to know her very well indeed, but it remained only in his thoughts as he had often seen her going out with either Nate or Gillis, and sometimes both. He reasoned that those relationships must involve civic activities and a certain amount of work, but still, she never had shown any interest in getting to know him better. He supposed that their conversation this morning had been the longest one they'd ever had. And the most personal.

He pulled his mind away from her and shifted down into a lower gear, guiding the car through the snow and icy ruts along the road. He tried to imagine what might be happening back up at the hotel until at last he pulled to a stop before the tall, narrow house that had been his first home in America.

There was a silence about the house that told him, even before he reached the door, that no one was there. Although there were lights on in the surrounding houses, no light escaped around Olivia's shuttered windows, no smoke rose from the chimney, there had been no melting of the snow on the roof to indicate a fire or heat of any kind from within.

In spite of that, Jesse pounded again and again on the door of his Aunt Olivia's house, and was not surprised when he got no response. He tried peeping in at the windows, but Olivia had apparently closed all the shutters and draperies against the cold wind. Perhaps she had gone to some neighbor's house to wait out the storm in this area just as he and Cassie and the others of Hartsville, forty miles away and farther up into the mountains, had gone to the hotel.

Smoke rose from the chimneys of cottages on either side as he looked at them for some sign of occupancy. He was cold and hungry by now and was considering the feasibility of breaking and entering his aunt's house when the door to the house on his left opened and an old face wreathed in grey hair emerged.

"She home?" called a scratchy male voice.

Jesse called back, "She doesn't answer the door."

"Go around and try the back. We ain't seen her for a day or so. See if she's all right. It'll be okay if you break in. I would have already, but Alma won't let me go outside. I been coughin'...."

As if on cue a screeching came from the depths of the cottage, "Shet that door, you old fool! You'll ketch yore death, and mine too!"

The old man's head withdrew inside the house, his final "Let me know..." cut off without mercy as the door slammed and Jesse knew it was slammed by a hand other than that of the gentle 'old fool'.

Feeling justified now, he trudged around to the back, remembering that Olivia had always left a key on top of one of the rafters under the back porch roof since that occasion when she had locked herself out. He took off his glove and ran his hand along each one until his search was rewarded. He placed the cold object in the old lock and pushed the door inward a few inches until it met an obstacle on the other side. A different kind of chill ran down his spine as he pushed the opening as wide as he could, just enough for him to squeeze a hand and his head through.

He searched for the light switch beside the door, hoping that the power supply was still intact in the lower elevations around Cherry Lake. He wished he didn't have to turn on any lights, because he dreaded what he might find blocking the door. When dim light filled the gloom, he breathed a quick gasp of relief.

He was also relieved to see that the object blocking the door was not the dead or injured body he had expected but only a rolled up bundle of blankets and quilts, held in place against the door by the legs of a chair, evidently placed there to keep out the draft. It hadn't been doing much good though, as he had not felt any resistance from it until the door was open a bit. Since Cherry Lake still had electrical power though, and if he was lucky, he should be able to find a warm drink somewhere when he was through here.

More confident now he called out, "Olivia? Olivia, are you home?" There was no answer. His search through the downstairs rooms revealed nothing but the same furniture that had always been there, and possibly the same dust. He felt colder in here than he had outside. There had been no fire here for hours, maybe days. A soured smell just touched his senses, as of unwashed bodies and linens. He wondered where Olivia would have gone. Perhaps she had become ill and gone to the hospital. It would be no surprise, the way she neglected herself. He could check with the local clinic if he had no luck in the neighborhood.

It was fairly obvious she wasn't home, but just to make sure he called out to her again, knowing now there would be no answer. She could be upstairs in bed, too ill to answer, but if she was, then she would be beyond help now anyway, in this icy house. But he should go and check, he decided.

Hesitantly he climbed the stairs, harboring visions of the unpleasant things he might find. If Olivia had fallen into a drunken stupor, she could well have frozen to death by now. At her bedroom door he knocked softly, then more firmly. Getting no answer, he opened it a bit, peering into the gloom. He reached in and switched on the light. The bed was rumpled and unmade, as it always had been when he lived here. It was as if she had just gotten out of it. The other bedrooms revealed no sign of recent occupation. The bathroom door stood open, the room empty.

Jesse left the house, locked the door behind him and dropped the key into his pocket. Alma may as well be given cause to squawk, he thought, as he walked up the snow-covered path toward the jaws of the dragon next door.

The old man answered his knock from within, not opening the door. He had been watching though, for he said, "Did you find Miz Olivia all right?"

"I didn't find her at all. When did you see her last?" Jesse asked, wondering if the old crone would allow him to reply.

"Two, three days I guess," came his answer just in time to finish before the screeching voice ordered him to quit yelling through closed doors.

"Thank you, sir," Jesse said with a grim smile. "And a good day to you, madam," he muttered, turning toward his car again.

He drove on until he came to a peculiar looking structure that had once been a house, its wide front porch now enclosed to house a coffee shop. He parked the car near the door and went in.

A rank, musty smell like the smell of an old soiled carpet hung in the air. The proprietor, a tiny woman of middle age looked up from the counter top she was wiping with a dingy cloth. "I'm just about to close," she announced, looking at him with curious eyes.

He smiled at the faded woman. He remembered her well, and found she hadn't changed much since he had last seen her. "Could I just have a cup of hot coffee, please? Or tea? Won't be long."

She poured him a cup of steaming black coffee. It didn't smell fresh, and he had the impression that he may be the only customer she'd had all day. Coffee sloshed over when she set the cup in front of him. She mopped it up and waited, smiling, for conversation.

He spooned in some sugar and added cream to the brew. "I don't expect you remember me. I'm Olivia Howe's nephew. I stayed with her a few years back, when I first came to America."

"Oh, yes, I remember you now. I knew you looked familiar. You moved on over to Hartsville or somewhere, looking for a place where you could be alone to write, or think, or whatnot. Did you find it?"

He blushed and smiled tentatively at her, not sure if she was being genuinely friendly or insidiously vicious. He decided it didn't matter and erased the smile. The important thing was to learn what he could about his aunt. "I came to see about Olivia. I couldn't reach her the past few days," he said, despising the lie, "and am rather concerned about her with this weather. She hasn't ever been exactly well, I know."

"That's an understatement," she sneered. "I been worried about her and would have told somebody if anybody had asked. That boy of hers comes around every now and then. You might ask him if you can find him," she said. "Or that girl she took in. Don't know if she's still there or not."

"No one seems to be there right now. What about this girl? Do you know how I can get in touch with her? Can you give me her name, tell me where she works?"

"Olivia told me her name, but I can't recall it right now. It'll come to me. Don't think I ever heard where she works. She's a pretty girl, likes to fix herself up. Always kept her hair smooth and shiny. She don't talk to me, though, and Olivia never says much about her either. I asked once or twice, but she just said she was a *guest*," almost spitting the word out, unwittingly telling by her tone that she didn't like being left out, not knowing things. "Hasn't been in here lately, though," she concluded, making a wide sweep of the counter with the same dingy cloth.

"Well, thank you for your help," Jesse said, looking at the deepening grey sky outside and then at his watch. "I guess it's too late to expect her home this evening, but if you should hear from her, tell her I'm in town and will see her tomorrow. Will you?"

She agreed that she would, and with hungry eyes allowed her nice looking visitor to leave.

Jesse made his slow and careful way back to town through the frozen evening as the lowering sky flung out yet another layer of snow. He checked into a motel and immediately telephoned the local sheriff.

Twelve

Cassie examined her reflection in the bathroom mirror, decided her make-up was good enough, then brushed her teeth and her hair. The hotel was quiet as darkness fell and she looked forward to a good supper of Ben's hearty stew and an early night in bed. Suddenly the echoes of a crash, as of something falling, rang in her ears. Further away than the hall, it sounded. Was it in Jesse's room? Was he back? Then the sound of running footsteps in the hall faded and disappeared as she hurried to the door. She threw it open and looked up and down the passageway, but whoever had been there was already gone.

She went to Jesse's door and knocked. There was no sound from within, so she turned the knob. The door swung open and she peeked in just enough to see that, at a glance, it looked undisturbed. But no, on closer inspection inside the room she saw the source of the crash she had heard. A vase that had held a few bright red silk poppies had been knocked off the bureau and now lay in broken pieces, the poppies scattered like little pools of blood across the shiny hardwood floor.

She left the room, pulling the door shut behind her. If Jesse had left it unlocked, then shame on him. Although someone had been in there and knocked over a vase, she decided it would be too presumptuous

101

of her to lock it now. There would be a master key of course, in case he didn't have one of his own when he returned, but in the back of her mind she knew that if she locked it now she would have no chance to learn who was interested in whatever was in there. If she left it open, she might be able to catch them red-handed.

Back in her room she stood gazing out the window, sorting through the guests and staff who would possibly have any interest in what was in Jesse's room. Who would have any reason to care? She knew of no one. Unless it was one of the staff doing some housekeeping chores, and having knocked over the vase, went to get a dustpan to pick up the glass. But no, housekeeping would have brought everything they needed with them. Besides, who was there to fill that post now, in this situation?

So perhaps the intruder had gone in, not for any reason, but out of curiosity? Her mind then leapt to the child, Amy, who had boldly entered Nell's room and kidnapped her cat, then just as brazenly gone into Evelyn's room where she applied makeup to the cat's pitiful little face.

Any child who would kidnap a cat and paint it's face would not blink at looking through an adult's belongings. To such a child all adults were fair game. A child as coddled as Amy, whose father held the highest position in the town, would feel entitled to do almost anything, expecting the victim to find it no more than annoying and probably downright cute. Being cute seemed to be the driving force of the child's life, anyway.

The longer she thought the more certain she became. Why didn't the mayor or his wife or both try, at least try to discipline their daughter rather than ignore or indulge her? It was Cassie's firm belief that children needed boundaries. She thought back to the well-behaved little children she had worked with on the reservation, and the gentle guidance they received from all the adults in the community. She had never even entertained thoughts of what it would be like to have had a child of her own, hers and Matt's.

Thinking along these lines, she decided that, for the child's safety, the mayor's wife might need to be cautioned. Should she be the one to do it? As if in answer her father's old maxim, "Where you see a need, you have a responsibility," came sharply to her mind. With some reluctance and some determination she walked to the door of the mayor's suite, took a deep breath, and knocked. After a second series of raps the door opened a crack and Gaynell Moorehouse peered out, irritation showing on her brow and in her eyes.

"Yes? What do you want?" she asked, not attempting to disguise her pique at being disturbed in her own quarters.

"Mrs. Moorehouse, I'm Cassie Ryder. I'm here about your little girl. Is she here?" Cassie asked in her most polite voice, undaunted by the assumed authority of the woman within.

"Yes, I know who you are, and yes, Amy is in here with me. Why do you ask?" Her tone said that, if she could have done so without risking the loss of a potential vote for her husband, she would have told Cassie to leave and mind her own business.

"Someone just went into the room across the hall from mine, the room where Jesse Lankford is staying. When he's here, at least. I didn't see who it was, but since your little girl had gone into at least two other rooms when their occupants were out, I thought that it might have been she I heard awhile ago."

Mrs. Moorehouse stood stone still with hard eyes leveled at Cassie's face, saying nothing, leaving a silence, compelling Cassie to fill it. Cassie plunged ahead: "If it was Amy, you might want to explain to her that it could be very dangerous to go into the rooms of strangers. If someone had been in any of the rooms at the time she went in, she may have found herself in serious trouble. As it is, there is no harm done, but she probably should curb her curiosity, at least as long as she is here in the hotel."

The little girl's mother gazed at Cassie as a serpent might, wondering where she should bite her first. "When did this terrible crime occur, Miss Ryder?"

"Only a few minutes ago. I heard a crash, and there was no mistaking that the sounds came from Mr. Lankford's room. Whoever was there knocked over a vase and broke it."

"And you are very sure it was my daughter who was in there?"

"Well, no, but it's just the sort of thing a bored, precocious child might find amusing. And Amy does have a history...." Gaynell's icy voice cut off the rest of that sentence.

"Miss Ryder, you don't look like the type of person who would accuse a child of a prank just because a child is present, but my little girl is certainly not guilty in this case. She is at this moment in bed, very upset over that ridiculous cat episode, and has been there all afternoon."

Cassie's face flushed. "Are you sure? Well of course...," she stammered, then recovered her composure. She fixed a confident smile on her face.

"Forgive me, Mrs. Moorehouse. It's just that she so brazenly kidnaped the cat and I naturally thought that only a child would perform such another childish prank. And she is, after all, the only child here."

"Well, yes, dear, just go and take a pill and perhaps you'll soon feel better."

The door slammed in her face. Cassie raised her hand to knock once again, wanting to have the last word, but thought better of it and turned away, rather ashamed of herself for her premature misjudgement. When would she learn to look before she leapt?

She was not totally convinced, however, that it was a premature judgement. She was not sure at all, in spite of Mrs. Moorehouse's comments. Who else of the group that was here would have any reason at all to do such a thing? The child could easily have slipped out of the suite, out of the hotel perhaps, so quietly that her mother, if she had been involved with her own pursuits, would never have known.

In her room once again she quickly sponged her still pink face, added a little lipstick, and went back downstairs to scan the group in the lobby. Anyone who might have been roaming around the hotel in the last few minutes would not yet be playing cards or deeply involved in any activity, but the small number of people who were there, just a few of the older citizens of the town in their usual configurations, made the idea seem like an exercise in futility. She might as well forget about it.

Outside the windows the waning day had taken on a blue-grey cast and snow was flying faster and heavier. In the grand marble fireplace hardwood logs crackled and spat like irascible old miners, dead set on outlasting the elements. The exotic aroma of Ben's stew wafted in from the kitchen and fresh coffee gurgled and steamed in the urn on the drinks table. Cassie poured herself a cup and settled down with last May's issue of the Architectural Digest.

Guests soon began to drift in from various parts of the hotel, Meg among them. She had been upstairs to feed Raucous, she said, an evil smile flitting across her face. "When I left her, she was having quite a yowl through two closed doors and down the hall to that animal of Nell's. I don't know what we'll do if that keeps up. She didn't start until I put food before her, though. Maybe it's the territorial instinct."

"Let's hope so," said Cassie, turning a page. "And please don't feed her at bedtime!" Meg began leafing through a magazine, and they became one with the hush that prevailed.

Soon Nell descended the stairs in a cloud of indignation and walked over to stand in front of Meg. "That... that... beast of yours is upsetting my Porsche! If you must put out canned meat for that animal, please select one with less odor to it. I could smell it from the hall. Personally, I wouldn't dream of feeding that to Porsche. But then, she is much finer bred...," her voice trailing off.

Meg only smiled sweetly up into the angry face, her lack of response clearly conveying the premeditated, deliberate intent of her cat feeding techniques.

Wendy, hearing the commotion, moved in their direction. "Hello, then," she began in her British vernacular, "What's all this about?"

Cassie saw a sudden opportunity. "Nothing, really," she said, taking Wendy's arm and leading her a little way from the others. "Where are all the Shakespeareans today?" she asked.

"Oh, they're out in the carriage house. That's what Evelyn likes to call the old stable. They're rehearsing out there. I told them I'd be along later. Sometimes I just don't want to be 'on stage' all the time. Do you know what I mean?"

"Why, yes, I think I do. Sometimes you just want to be yourself, let your hair down. Is that it?"

"Exactly! Right now I just wish I could curl up by a nice fire and talk girl talk and drink cocoa," Wendy said.

The mellow voiced gong signaled that dinner was ready, making any further communication along those lines a waste of time and words.

"Well, right now doesn't seem a good time to do that, as we might be needed in the kitchen, but let's do it, say, after supper is finished and you and Ben are done in the kitchen? I think it would be fun," said Cassie, steering Wendy toward the dining room and thanking the unknown providence that had opened up this opportunity to learn more from the girl. "I'm likely to be in the confiding mood myself. We can use my room," she suggested.

"I know of a more private place than that. It's cozier, too," said Wendy. "Upstairs in the staff quarters there is this little sitting room overlooking the garden. It's quite shut off from the rest of the house. Must at one time have been a snug for the servants, I should think. Let's go there. We'll be able to hear anyone coming."

As if by herd instinct the guests had migrated into the dining room where Ben, who was at first perceived as Meg's son and a short order cook, had by now gained respect as a blossoming chef, a person in his own right. They moved along the buffet table with their plates and found seats. Meg came in a little later and took her place beside Cassie.

Mourning. That was the sense Cassie got of the mood of the residents in the dining room. Meg seemed even more despondent than the others.

"Bet you wish you were back with those Indians right now, don't you?" she said as they tucked into their supper.

"I do miss it sometimes. But no, I think I like my life here much more than that life, especially after Matt died. It was rewarding in its way, but now I want to feel less rewarded and more fulfilled. The only way I can do that is to indulge in some of the things I want to accomplish," she finished with a modest smile, as if there was some guilt involved in her pursuing such a course.

They continued their meal in silence, each involved with her own thoughts. After they had finished their dishes of savory stew and had extra servings of fresh baked rolls, Meg took her and Cassie's cups away and brought back both filled with steaming coffee. They sipped the rich dark liquid, looking around the room at the other diners, commenting from time to time on one or the other of them.

"Let's get out of here," said Meg, when they had finished their coffee. They refilled their cups, then strolled around the lobby, inevitably drawn to that little semiprivate alcove where the Shakespeareans, having wasted no time dawdling over after dinner coffee with the townsfolk, had encamped.

The slim, long limbed, red-haired woman sat and strummed her harp, crooning what sounded like an Irish lullaby. She was dressed in a huge woolen shawl over a long, patchwork dress, the brogans on her feet completing the ensemble.

Beside her sat a small, exotically striking girl with black hair and deep olive complexion, huddled inside a man's overcoat. She was humming in strange ethereal harmony with the harpist. Raucous lounged between the two, licking a paw and drawing it over one ear.

Cassie and Meg stood near and when the song was finished Cassie said, "That was truly beautiful! Do you mind if we stay and listen?"

"Not at all, sit if you like. It's a song about a girl whose lover has died," came the haunting reply as the goddess strummed another chord on the harp.

"Do you like Celtic music, then?" asked the dark girl, her mysterious beauty somewhat dampened by a voice that bore faint traces of the American upper Midwest, mixed with the theatrical English accent.

Regan nudged her, murmuring, "Watch it."

The dark-haired girl smiled sheepishly at Cassie and Meg. "I keep forgetting we are supposed to stay in character on stage and off until after the play. Regan has to keep reminding me. By the way," she continued, now as an English maiden, "I'm Bethany Fox. I'm going to try out for Titania, but so are all the other women here. I would settle for Hermia or Helena though, just to stay here in this lovely town. It is so... so home townish!"

Cassie introduced herself and Meg to them, then responded to the singer's comments. "Your accent was fine as far as I could tell. I'd have thought it came naturally to you. How on earth did you master the Celtic language?"

The red-haired woman answered. "My speaking accent is natural. I'm Irish. The Celtic lyrics I just learned from one of the troupe," said the harpist, casting a look and a nod across the room in Wendy's direction. "Her, there." She plucked from the harp a minor chord muttering, "Bernard's fancy." Casting a quick look up at Meg, she said, "By the way, thanks for sharing your cat with us. White cats bring good luck, you know," and without missing a beat moved into another haunting melody, of which the two women understood not a word.

They listened for a long time to the enchanted music, letting their thoughts be taken far away to a green land they had never seen, in the long distant past they had never known, feeling a visceral sorrow for they knew not what.

Wendy, finished with her kitchen chores, joined them then, to lead Cassie off for their girl talk. Cassie and Meg said their goodnights, each telling the other to call if she needed anything, sleep well, then Meg climbed the stairs to attend to her cat while Cassie and Wendy, by way of the back stairs, made their way to the secluded room where Cassie hoped to learn much from this strange young woman.

Thirteen

Cassie followed as Wendy led her up the stairs as if to the guest rooms, then down a hallway and down another half-flight of stairs to a sort of balcony floor that seemed to be somehow wedged in between the first and second floors. Wendy was right. The little room was quite hidden, and there was a chill in the air, but the room was clean and tidy. Cassie was drawn toward the large comfortable chairs placed just right for conversation. Wendy took a match from the brass canister on the mantle and lit the kindling under heavy oak logs as Cassie's gaze scanned the room. Against the far wall was a small cabinet housing a white enamel sink. On the counter beside it sat a hotplate, cups and a box of cocoa mix.

When the fire was crackling cozily, Wendy prepared two cups of cocoa, handed one to Cassie and sat down opposite her before the fire. "Tell me about how you came to Hartsville. Someone said you had only been here a couple of years."

"Closer to six by this time, I'd say," Cassie began. "Before I came back here, as you know, I was a nurse on the Hopi reservation in Arizona. We, my husband and I, had been there a couple of years, and had actually planned to stay, had not thought of leaving. He was a teacher, and really did love working with those little tykes. Then he died. I stayed on for a while with my parents but finally I had to leave the reservation. That's when I came back here, and moved back into their house."

"Coo-ee, that's awful. I mean, you're so young! What did he die of? Must have been an accident of some sort."

"No, he just became really sick, but no one ever found out for sure what it was. I tried, though. I had promised him at his grave that I wouldn't rest until I learned the truth. I started my own little investigation of sorts, but nobody wanted to talk to me about it much. I did a lot of research on the symptoms he had, and I actually felt like I was getting close. But they made me stop. It was getting to be too hard on my parents."

"So did you just leave?"

"Not at first." Cassie paused for several seconds, scrutinizing her hands as they lay on her lap. She had never given anyone the full account of what had happened to make her leave the reservation, not even to her parents, though they knew some of it. In fact, she had never talked much about it at all. But there was something about this stranger she sat with, this young woman who was alien to the town and to her, this person who, like Cassie, had the ability to keep herself to herself while socially interacting with others. There was something reassuring in the cozy fire, their isolation in this room from the rest of the hotel, and the hotel from the rest of the world because of the snow, that made her feel safe in talking about those terrible days that almost cost her life. Had no one ever asked what had happened? Would she have told them if they had? She couldn't remember, but now that she had begun telling Wendy the story, just the thought of letting go of that burden brought a sense of relief and release to her.

"I had learned that Matt's symptoms right before he died were just like those experienced by people who had ingested a certain kind of plant that grew in some high places in the Southwest. After thinking about it for a long time, I decided to look for one of those plants. Anyway, when I started looking for it close to home, I couldn't find a bit of it. I started riding up into the mountains and parking the car, then walking as far away from the car as I could and still keep the car in sight. I told myself I was looking for the plant, of course, but mostly I think I was just reliving memories, enjoying the mystery of the desert, imagining the times when the red men were free to roam the land in bands.

"One day, at about noon, I went up and parked the car close to the cliffs. There was no road, nothing that I could see that would interest people except more rocky desert. Back in the last century the Indians used to pitch their tepees at the foot of those cliffs for protection from the north winds in winter. They'd spend the winter there chipping arrow heads out of the flint rocks that had fallen from the face of the cliff since the winter before. They'd put big rocks around the edges of their tepees to hold them down when the wind started blowing. The teepee rock rings are still there." Cassie's eyes looked far into the past, the flickering firelight reflecting like campfires in their depths.

Wendy was watching, listening wide-eyed in awe, almost holding her breath as Cassie continued. "One day I went up there, it was about noon, and I thought I'd have a lot of time to look around and explore. I parked the car and walked along the cliff edge, just looking at the stark beauty of the place. Then I found a trail leading down toward a ledge, where it stopped. Without even thinking I just started down it to see what was at the bottom, behind that ledge. There was a cave down there, and I went a little way in. I didn't see anything except what looked like the remains of an old fire, and some dried plants hanging from outcropping rocks on the walls of the cave. I started back up toward the top, and just as I got there, something hit my shoulder and I lost my footing. I tumbled all the way to the bottom of the cliff."

She lapsed into silence, shivering as she remembered the fear and panic she felt as she fell, and the pain that dominated her for hours after she regained consciousness. Wendy leaned forward, eager to hear more, but waited until Cassie brought her focus back to the present and took a sip of cocoa.

Wendy got up and refilled the kettle, turning the little hot plate on again. "Is that how you hurt your leg? I've noticed you favoring it, sometimes."

"Yes. It was broken in several places just from the fall, but the ankle was pretty well crushed by a large boulder I dislodged as I fell. It rolled down with me, then rolled back and settled onto my foot. I was completely trapped by it, even if the leg hadn't been broken. The pain was just unbearable. I passed out again almost immediately. I didn't know till later how I got out of there."

"How did you get free? Someone must have come along and helped you."

"Someone did. There was an Indian couple that Matt had helped a lot while he was teaching their children. They lived out beyond the cliffs. He was on his way home that evening and recognized my car. It was getting late, so he started looking for me. It was almost dark when he found me. He had to go for help before he could get the boulder off my foot and get me to the hospital."

The kettle whistled and Wendy made fresh cups of cocoa.

"How long were you in hospital?"she asked, handing Cassie another serving of the steaming, delicious brew.

"About six weeks, then I stayed with my parents for a little while, maybe a month. Dad helped that poor man's destitute family get resettled in a better, safer place and helped him get a better job. He and Mom are missionaries out there, you see.

"As soon as I could, I started looking for answers again. Then one day soon after that, Dad told me that my questions and prying were having a bad effect on his mission work. It seems that every day or so one of the officials would approach him with another setback in his work, and always ended with a suggestion that he try to help me put Matt's death behind me for my own mental health. Dad stressed that it had already been attributed to natural causes, and said I should just leave it at that."

"And is that when you came here?"

"Yes. Dad and Mom offered me the use of their house here for as long as I want it. They bought it before I was born, and I was born here, but when they started going off to the missions they weren't here all that much. I came back and had a lot of repairs done on it so that it will be in good shape for them when they come back. When they retire, I'll find another place, but houses like to have somebody in them, I think. They tend to fall apart if they aren't lived in."

"Lucky for you to have it, then. What made you decide to stay here?"

"Matt and I came back for a visit several years ago. He fell in love with the way the houses are built right into the mountainside and the way the roads just amble along wherever they want to go. He liked the way that nothing in this town seems ordered and rigid. "Life just is, and it is good," is the way he described it. That was the way we felt then, and every time we got a chance, we came back for a week or two.

"So when I left Arizona, this is the one place I knew I could find solace. So here I came, and here I've stayed."

"And is it still as healing a place for you as you thought?"

"Oh, yes. It feels safe and strong and, oh, sort of eternal, if you know what I mean."

Wendy looked off into the flames and sipped her cocoa, quiet and thoughtful for a moment, then said, "It doesn't feel that way to me. No place has ever felt that way to me. Ever."

"Not even your childhood home?"

"I didn't really have a childhood home." She gazed down at her hands, picking and picking at a fingernail, Without looking up she continued, "I was just sort of passed around from one house to another, mostly."

"What about your parents?" Cassie asked after a little silence.

Wendy watched the flames send out sparks like shooting stars. She took a deep breath and held it in her lungs for a moment, then let it drift out like smoke on her voice as she spoke, giving an impression of the smoldering depths from which her words rose. "Parents. Parents are people who love you and look after you. They keep you and nurture you. There was a woman who gave birth to me, but she did not give me any sort of life. She gave me away when I was just a toddler. There was, I suppose, a male involved with her, but not with me. So, no, I had no parents."

"Are they still alive?"

Wendy gazed into the distance for a moment. "I really don't know," she said.

Cassie was surprised by the lack of emotion behind Wendy's words. From lessons learned while taking care of people with all types of illness, she assumed a passive attitude and, folding her hands in her lap, left an inviting silence for Wendy to fill if there was more she needed to say.

There was. "My first foster parents were an old couple she knew. They lived in Brandon, a town nearby. They always reminded me how much they loved my mum and said they gave me a home for her sake. They had a lot of children of their own, but they somehow managed to always keep me separate, making it plain that I wasn't one of them. I didn't get quite as much food as the others, and they gave me very few treats. They'd just run out by the time they got to me. They sent their kids away to school, but I went to the local one so they could keep me at home to help with the chores and housework."

She stood up and began to pace, refilling the kettle and putting it on to boil as she spoke. "I was quick in school, I have to say that. I dreamed of going on and getting a proper education, but it didn't work out that way. The wife died, and after that the old man didn't even try to pretend I was anything other than a servant. He kept his kids away at school or at relatives' almost all the time. Me, he kept at home, and by then it wasn't just for housework, if you know what I mean." Cassie cringed at the volumes of the insult and injury that reverberated in her voice from wounds that haunted her still.

"You don't have to tell me all this, Wendy, if you'd rather not talk about it."

Wendy seemed not to hear her. "The old man died some time later. I was maybe twelve by then, and I went from one home to another, always the same, never as a child, always as a servant. Finally, I got a proper job at this big house out in the country. The people were nicer there, and I did really well. That's where I was at last able to get away from the past a little bit."

She settled down now and looked into Cassie's eyes as she continued. "Being in those better surroundings made me realize I wasn't doomed to the kind of life I had started with. I set out to learn as much as I could about running things. First I stuck close to the housekeeper and learned how to run a house and manage cooks and maids. From the cook I learned how to plan menus and order groceries and supplies and prepare meals for large crowds."

She quickly brightened and said, almost as an aside, "Sometimes they'd have fox hunts and there'd be dozens of people to house and feed. Those were great times. I loved being a part of those crowds." The kettle sang like a hunting horn, and she rose to make more cocoa.

Handing Cassie a cup, Wendy sat down and continued. "When I got a little older, I made friends with the estate manager. He taught me how to do the books, pay the taxes, pay the help, all of it. He said he was surprised that I was still only a servant when he found out how sharp I was. That was like a healing for me, almost. It made me realize that I am worth a lot more than anyone else ever thought of me being, even my own mother. I guess if I got to choose a place to call home, that would be it."

"Of course you deserved a better life than you were given. Anyone would. What a sad situation to leave a child in. I wonder your mother didn't make some better arrangements for you, no matter what her circumstances."

"Yes." She offered no excuse for the woman. "I always wondered about that, and would cry myself to sleep at night. Then after a few years it quit hurting and I didn't feel anything or think any more about her."

"What about now? If you had the chance to meet her, for instance, if you learned that she needed you, what do you think you'd do?"

With a studied lack of expression, Wendy replied, "Why I'd just go right on with whatever I was doing."

"Do you really feel that way, Wendy?"

The girl did not answer, except for a slight shrug as she finished off her cocoa. Perhaps she, Cassie, had bitten off more than she wanted to chew, seeking to befriend and get to know this young woman, if she really wanted to remain uninvolved. She had discovered a woman who had suffered such deep emotional wounds that she, with all her training and experience, felt useless in the face of them. But Wendy did, after all was said and done, seem to have come to some sort of terms with the pains of the past and had made a better life for herself.

As if by agreement, they both stood, signaling that their girl talk was over for now. Wendy washed their cups and led Cassie back the way they had come. At the stairwell Wendy went on up to the next floor where her quarters were while Cassie turned down the hall toward her own room.

In light of Wendy's life, Cassie knew her own troubles of the past few years were not nearly as devastating as she had at times allowed them to be. She had known the love of devoted parents, the security of a good home, the happiness of loving and being loved by a good man. Wendy had suffered far more, yet she seemed to have found a lifestyle that suited her, and was not held back by the past as Cassie was allowing herself to be. She determined that she would begin now to let go of the pain of her own recent past and put her energies into making her future as fulfilling and productive as her parents and Matt would want it to be.

Tired from the day's activity, mentally and emotionally stirred by the conversation with Wendy, but physically warmed by the hot cocoa and restful atmosphere of the little lounge, Cassie dressed for bed and breathed a grateful sigh as she crept beneath the covers.

But sleep was not quick in coming. Her mind went almost immediately to Jesse, wondering what he had learned, when they would hear from him, why he decided to go away without so much as a toothbrush, where he was at this moment, and when would he return. When would she know what was going on? She reasoned that the absence of his quiet confidence in this cruel time left a gaping hole in the fabric of life. Her circle of friends was incomplete. She felt like things would go much more smoothly if he were here and she knew where the investigation stood.

Then, realizing that things were already moving along quite well and that Gillis could tell her all she needed to know, she wondered if it was really her unbridled curiosity or if, in fact, she really did miss Jesse and would be more at peace if he was here. Well, until her promise to Matt was fulfilled, she wouldn't allow herself to become too interested in the presence or absence of any man, least of all the one who had been her neighbor and friend these past few years. She knew she was now ready to let go of the past, but that must actually happen before she took hold of the uncertain future.

She put those thoughts aside and began to muse over the death of a young man so little known in this community of people who seemingly paid little attention to outsiders. As she sought sleep, her mind was still probing the unknown for news about what the coroner may have found and what they would eventually learn.

Fourteen

Night had spread a darkening mantle across the expanse of snow, and an icy wind made a crunchy frosting on its surface. The car strained and swerved as Jesse and the sheriff pulled into the street where Olivia's house stood. Lights were on in the house next door. As Jesse and Bob Maddox slammed the car doors shut, a curtain was pulled aside and the face of a scrawny harridan peered out. Jesse waved and the curtain quickly dropped shut as the two men clumped through the snow to the back door of Olivia's dark, somber house.

Jesse fitted the key into the door and as they entered the gloom, Bob produced a small but powerful flashlight and kept it available even though the house lights came on at the first touch of the switch.

"Which rooms did you go in, Mr. Lankford?" The sheriff asked, heading for the front room.

"All of them, at least the ones on the first two floors. From the outside it looks as if there might be an attic, but I don't remember..." his voice faded into his thoughts.

Together they moved through the downstairs rooms, turning on lights as they went. The air inside was even colder than the air outside, or so it seemed to Jesse. Everything was as it had been earlier when he was here. They climbed the creaking stairs, Jesse leading the way, and made another cursory tour of the bedrooms and bath on the second floor.

"If you were going to build an attic on this house, Bob, where would you put the stairs?" asked Jesse, failing miserably in relieving the tension that held them bound.

"Don't know. Just have to look, I guess."

Until now, Jesse hadn't noticed how many narrow doors interspersed the walls. He'd never before gone into any of the bedrooms other than his own and once to Olivia's when she was ill. In each bedroom there were at least two doors, the one they entered and the other to the closet.

In the hallway itself were six main doors. Jesse methodically inspected each one, only to find that two of them were closets, one of them, already open, was to a bathroom and three of them led to bedrooms. Coming out of the very front bedroom, one that was, in Jesse's memory, usually unoccupied, they found a nook behind the wall that backed the stairwell. Almost hidden from casual view by an array of coats and robes hanging from hooks along the top, they found another small door.

This was the last place left to look. There were no other areas or doors in the little house. Jesse didn't want to open this door. He started to turn away, and Bob, ever sensitive to the body language of others, said, "Here, let me. We both know what we are looking for and what we are apt to find."

Maddox shifted the garments aside, then lifted the bar latch and turned the knob, and carefully drew the door open.

Olivia Howe was not at her best for receiving visitors, but then she hadn't cared for a long time how disheveled or puffy she looked in life. She looked no better in death.

Fifteen

Bob Maddox gave silent thanks for the freezing air that spared them most of the effluvia that should have accompanied such a scene. He took a firm hold on Jesse's arm to steady him.

"Sorry, man. You don't need to stay here. I'll just look around a bit."

Maddox looked at the dried and crusted trickle of blood that had run from Olivia's ear downward toward the floor, and knew that she had died where she lay. He touched the dry, waxy skin of her hand and determined that death had occurred many hours, perhaps days before. The Medical Examiner would, of course, be able to fix the time more exactly. He closed the door without difficulty as the body, still in the position it had lain in since life had fled, had not moved.

When Jesse had performed his private functions in the bathroom, washed his face and brushed back his hair, Bob was waiting at the head of the stairs with his back to Jesse and his hands in his pockets. "Let's go downstairs. I'll just see if the phone's working."

Jesse could have told him it was not, but he let Maddox go through the motions of his office, however futile they proved to be. At least though, while the highways leading into Hartsville had been hard hit and made impassible by the storm, Cherry Lake, lying protected at the foot of the mountain, still had open roads to the outside world.

"Come on. We'll go to the cruiser. I'll radio the coroner and call for an ambulance from there."

When at last the sad remains of his aunt had been taken away, Jesse and Maddox made the return trip to the station in comparative silence, broken only by Jesse's occasional questions that all came out being, why?

He was filled with anger, remorse and confusion. Why had both Olivia and her only son, Jamey, died in such terrible circumstances at the same time? What had either of them done to deserve it? He knew of course that murder victims very often did not deserve to die, not even in a gentler way. He didn't know what sort of young man Jamey had turned out to be, but he did know that Olivia had done nothing more offensive than drink herself into a stupor several times a week. Unless, of course, you remembered that Jamey's father had a lawful wife and child in Hartsville. Jesse could not bring himself to even entertain that thought.

His mind darted here and there along random pathways. Olivia's neighbors would have to be told. He would need to plan a funeral or memorial of some sort for both Jamey and Olivia. May as well have both together. Olivia would have wanted it that way. Then he forced himself to face thoughts of the man he had seen leaving her house all those years ago, the man who was Jamey's father. At some point he would have to tell all this to Maddox, but before he did, he would accept Maddox's suggestion that they stop and have a cup of hot coffee at the first café.

With the coffee hot on his tongue and the cup warming his hands, he was able, after a few false starts, to find his voice. "What do you need to know first?"

Maddox looked at him, long and deep as if looking into his soul, then began on a soft note. "When did you last see your aunt alive?"

Sixteen

Wednesday, January 15, 1985

Morning came slowly to Cassie. Unable to fall asleep last night, she had got up again and stayed up late, working on her notes and thinking through the tidbits she had gleaned here at the hotel. She felt drained by the excitement of the past twenty four hours. She debated whether to go down for breakfast or stay under the covers and read until noon.

She heard Meg moving about in the next room, heard Raucous telling her exactly what she wanted for breakfast, and Meg's voice demanding respect from the cat before it got its meal.

Raucous must have complied, for soon Meg tapped on their adjoining door and called, "Get up, sleepyhead, you're going to miss breakfast."

Cassie suddenly felt a strong yearning for a cup of coffee laced with gobs of sugar and cream. Since room service was out of the question, going downstairs was the only way she was apt to get it, so she got her body out of bed and pushed it into submission.

Ike, Evelyn, Wendy and Ben were all on duty today. Cassie felt a pang of guilt, fostered, she knew, by her early years in nursing when people viewed professional nurses as servile nursemaids, and she, out of compassion, had let a lot of them get away with it. Yet she still felt the guests should be allowed to pitch in, if they wanted to. She would bring it up to Evelyn, she decided.

The faces around her wore a glazed look, as if everyone present was about to succumb to either fear or ennui. *They need a distraction*, she thought, suddenly aware of a way she could relieve both situations in one fell swoop. It occurred to her that Evelyn, as hostess, would not ask for assistance, but Cassie, as a guest and latent nursing supervisor, would. She raised her hand in a tiny beckoning motion to the innkeeper's wife.

Evelyn, having found a lull in the serving of guests, came to join Cassie. She brought a plate filled with eggs, bacon and toast and a cup of coffee with her and as soon as she was seated, scooped up a fork full, eating it with a generous appetite.

Cassie greeted her. "Hi. How are your guests maintaining?"

"They seem to be keeping busy," Evelyn said when her mouth was available for speech. "Some of the older ladies and men have offered to help out with the chores. Do you think we should let them?"

"Of course. In fact, I was just going to suggest it myself. All that food preparation has to be more than Ben can handle alone. Is he getting any help at all this morning?"

"Just Wendy, but a few of the guests really want to. I guess I'll let them. They keep saying they were raised in a time when people pitched in to help in times of need. I heard one say something about 'putting back into life as much as you take out', and I think I kinda like the idea. It has a good ring to it," she laughed her soft bubbly laugh and pushed hair back from her face, concentrating on another foray on the eggs.

"You look as if you could do with a little help yourself," Cassie observed.

"I could use a break, but Wendy is helping in the kitchen. If one of us doesn't help him organize the helpers, Ben will never get a minute to cook." She stood and stretched her back.

"Let me sit at the desk this morning so you can relax for a minute," Cassie offered, and Evelyn was quick to agree. They finished their meals and left the dining room before the others were through.

Taking Evelyn's place behind the desk, Cassie said, "Before you go, Evelyn, I've an idea for something that might help everybody. We used to do it at retreats and week-long workshops, just to break the intensity of the times. I've been thinking it might be fun if we got the actors to put on a little show for the crowd, if they will, and being naturally inclined to being on stage, I should think they'd jump at the chance. I could set it up. What do you think?"

Evelyn beamed at her. "I think it's a wonderful idea. I'm not even going to ask Ike. You just go right ahead."

Alone at the desk, Cassie began leafing through the registry book, looking at the names of all who had registered since a few days before the snow. Among the actors she found Regan's and Bethany's names and their locations. They were staying in the same room. She wrote down the number and looked for others. Most of them, she saw, were staying on the same floor. The numbers were low and all two digits, so Cassie assumed they were at least ground floor or maybe even basement rooms. She looked back through the register for the past few months, but nowhere was there a listing for Janet Wright.

Later, when Evelyn had resumed her responsibilities at the desk and Cassie was free to roam she started down the long hallway that led to the east wing, in the opposite direction from the dining room. These room numbers all had three digits, beginning with "1", so she turned back. Passing a door marked STAIRS she pushed through. It only went down. She did likewise, and found herself in yet another ground floor wing, only this wing was built on a different level of the mountainside, facing out toward the back of the hotel into a little declivity, somewhat lower than the hotel's front entrance.

The room numbers in this basement wing consisted of only two digits, beginning with 10. Finding the number she needed, she tapped on the door with one knuckle. After a few moments the red-haired Regan appeared in the doorway. Cassie explained what she wanted, and Regan turned for a brief exchange with her roommate, Bethany, who joined the other two at the door. Cassie wrote down a few names of others whom Regan thought might participate, and soon Cassie was on her way to the next room, smiling, followed by both the harpist and her singing partner. Soon they had knocked on every door, some of the occupants answering and others not.

Regan and Bethany had quickly taken over the task of organizing the show, and Cassie left them to it, making it clear that she'd like all of the actors to be asked to participate, as they added so much flair to this enclave of unwilling exiles, mentioning that they, the actors, were the focal point of the guests, an idea bought hook, line and sinker by the two performing artists. Back in the lobby she confirmed the plan with Evelyn.

Evelyn began immediately informing the other guests of the coming event. Wendy was appointed to make posters to place in the lounge and the dining room, and then to arrange some decoration for both rooms, if any decorative items could be found. Neither Evelyn nor Ike had yet explored the many hidden nooks and crannies of the old building. It turned out, though, that Wendy had come across several boxes of a wide variety of decorations for any festive occasion. "Where on earth did you find those?" Evelyn inquired, evidently impressed with Wendy's ingenuity.

"Oh, I'm not in any place very long without finding out just what is where and where is what," Wendy quipped. Seeing that Evelyn had taken her remark lightly, she began sorting through the gewgaws and doodads. As some of them dated back to a much earlier time, they decided to use those for a lamplit theme to enhance the Shakespearean mood.

Cassie and Regan who, as it turned out, was the director of the Shakespeare production as well as director of this revue, held many discussions about the program to make sure the material was suitable for the older people who may have no interest in some of the more modern types of entertainment.

By the time the lunch gong sounded, the program was set. Nate had shown up in time to offer a few suggestions of his own, and arrange for Cassie to cover the revue for the next edition of the newspaper. Gillis showed up soon after.

After a lunch of pungent, spicy chicken gumbo, rice and salad, they slipped away to the little room behind the stairs, where they discussed their findings in the investigation. Nate had found no one in the hotel who either answered to or knew anyone who answered to the name Janet Wright. The car must be a borrowed one, but nobody would claim it. It may even be stolen, he concluded.

"I've talked with a lot of people here, as I told you before, and haven't heard anything that made me suspicious. Nothing out of the ordinary, anyway." She thought about the conversation with Wendy, but found no connection between it and the dead boy. She didn't want to waste their precious time with idle gossip and decided it could wait.

"But there are a couple of people I just cannot question very much, because I cannot stand the thought of either of them being connected with this," she continued.

Gillis nodded. "I know. I don't want to even think about either Meg or Ben having anything to do with it, either. But they are the very ones who are closest to the situation. No matter, though, because if either of them is involved, they will cover for each other."

Cassie thought for a moment. "I need to check and see if anybody knows for sure that Ben was here, that will help, but Meg has already told us she was right there at her house, alone, when it happened. Maybe that means she's confident she doesn't even need an alibi."

"May be. One thing is for sure. She will be here when all's said and done, and we can't be sure about any of the others. Let's just concentrate on them first. Well, at least I will. You two just keep listening. Like I said before, don't get too obvious with your questions. Especially you, Cassie. Nate is a newspaper man, he's supposed to be nosey, but you ... you don't have quite that much latitude."

"Yeah, I know. I'll be careful." Gillis walked to the door and held it open as the other two passed through, and they went back to their own pursuits.

Cassie had plans of her own. Regan had told her that the actors were doing most of their rehearsing in the carriage house behind the hotel, using the alcove inside mostly for late auditions. In her own room again, Cassie dressed in two of everything, covered the lot with her full length leather coat, and wrapped a woolen scarf around her head and neck. All that was needed now were the fleece-lined leather gloves, which she pulled on over a pair of insulated glove liners. She had often needed these items in the Southwest, and now she was glad she had kept them. This blizzard had made their storage space worthwhile.

She decided to take a short cut through the kitchen as it was nearer the carriage house where rehearsals were now in progress. When she reached the dining room, she came to a full stop as the yeasty smell of homemade breads seemed to wrap itself around her and draw her in. Amy was there playing with paper dolls and talking with Wendy and Ben as they mixed the batter for bread.

"Oo-ooo-oo, that smells wonderful!" Cassie said as she came through the swinging doors.

"Nothing like it's going to taste," replied Ben. "Want to knead it a bit? Get your hands in the dough?" as if everyone shared his penchant for cooking.

"Well, not right now, thanks," Cassie replied, holding up her gloved hands and wiggling her fingers for Ben's inspection. "Maybe someday when I learn to make biscuits that aren't so hard you could play croquet with them, maybe then I'll try yeast breads. Until then, you just carry on."

"Where you going, Cassie?" asked the little girl.

"Out to the carriage house. I'm going to watch the actors rehearse. They're putting on a show for us soon, did you know that?"

"No. I don't like shows. But I like snow. Can I come with you?"

"Only if your Mom and Dad say so," Cassie said, winking at Ben and Wendy, certain that the child's parents would say no.

"You wait for me. I'll go tell them I'm going with you."

Cassie and Ben exchanged glances with raised eyebrows. Wendy said, "That's my girl!" as the child ran from the room, and slanted a wicked grin in Cassie's direction.

In less time than it took for Cassie to learn the menu for the evening meal, the girl was back, dressed in a down filled coat, nylon gloves, a long red scarf and ski cap, much to Cassie's chagrin, but not to her surprise. They both caught their breath as they stepped out into the cold air. Cassie considered her dilemma: how was she going to keep from exposing this innocent child to whatever the actors might be up to in the carriage house? Then on a sudden inspiration Cassie asked, "Did you ever build a snowman?"

"No, I've never had enough snow."

Cassie considered for a moment. This may be the only chance the little girl would ever get to experience that particular joy of childhood. Too, if she got her interested enough and tired enough, she wouldn't pester Cassie to go with her into the carriage house. If, in fact, Cassie herself was to be allowed in.

Starting with a hand packed nucleus of snow, Cassie began rolling it in figure eights, circles, squares, and in every direction, with every step followed by what appeared to be a four-footed snowball with a long tail. Raucous had somehow escaped her confines and followed them out, flicking the snow off a paw now and then, and swatting at the growing snowball as they rolled it along. It would be so easy to lose that cat out here, Cassie thought.

Soon the growing mass of snow was large enough for the little girl to take over. Amy laughed and chattered as she pushed it around and around, back and forth in long paths and zigzags until the body was formed.

Their breath came in sharp stinging gasps, and the air they exhaled was white as the snow but they took no notice. "Now we have to make his chest. You do it this time while I find something for his arms and face. Go on now, get started. I'll be right back."

The child began as she had seen Cassie do with the first ball of snow and soon was enrapt in developing her first snowman's torso.

Cassie turned toward a couple of outbuildings, one quite large with good, wide doors on it. That one must be the carriage house. She trudged across the snow until her path intersected with a well-trodden one between this building and an obscure access to the hotel. A fire door, Cassie thought. The clever mummers had probably deactivated the alarm so they could come and go as they wanted. Well, she thought, no harm done. They are, after all, known to be creative people who often felt that rules applied only to others and that it was their duty to prove it.

Opening one of the wide doors, she stepped inside. Conversation and action dwindled away as every actor and actress turned to look at her, waiting for her to speak. "Just came to see how things are going," she said. No one uttered a word.

"Do you need anything? Can I be of help?" A few of them shook their heads, some muttered no, thanks, and all of them turned their eyes away. The air inside the building was cold in spite of the fire in the wood-burning stove. Here and there a group sat together with downcast eyes, their faces bearing traces of sadness, and Cassie realized they were mourning Jamey, their fallen comrade in make-up, in their own way. She feared for a moment that she may have interrupted a sort of memorial service for him.

Then she noticed another aroma overriding the smell of burning wood, an aroma Cassie recognized from her years in the Southwest. At least some of these young people were smoking strange substances, she decided, and made a hasty exit after giving Regan and Bethany a wink. At least they were not smoking in the hotel itself.

She couldn't leave though, without knowing what else they were doing. As she watched through a crack in the door she had just closed behind her, a singer resumed his singing. Soon, one group began enacting a scene that Cassie recognized from one of the Wodehouse books, the youthful performers swaggering and swanning to beat the band. Meanwhile, a group obviously portraying Oberon and Titania and their fairy band consulted on the best way to emulate the concoction of a potion with which to enchant the local mortals.

She hadn't done what she set out to do. She had planned to blend in with the people in the carriage house, keeping alert for any mention of Jamey or Janet, but she realized now it would require more than just mingling. It would require conversations with each one of them individually, something she and Nate would have to do inside the hotel. They would have to win their confidence if they were to get any information from this group.

Satisfied that she was no more needed than she was welcome in the carriage house, she moved on to the smaller building. A hasp was slipped over a metal half loop from which hung a lock. The lock was not closed, so she lifted it out and opened the door.

The darkness inside was thick until, from her position on the ground outside the doorway, she spotted a flashlight on a low shelf just to the left of the door. She switched it on and moved the beam around the room. Along the back wall loomed the bulk of several large objects that looked like pieces of furniture covered with tarps.

She could only see bits of it at a time, where the light shone on it. The closest one, the only one she could see well without removing the tarp, was a table similar to the one that sat in the hall in the hotel. A pity, she thought, if these are all antiques left out here rather than being shown off inside. Perhaps they were here for repairs. Ike, having once been a furniture maker, would probably be able to restore the pieces that needed it.

Stepping up into the building she selected two pieces of an old broken dowel that lay several feet from a group of others and then pointed the light into the corners and against the other walls. She located a stack of flower pots, and found one of them half full of pebbles. She grabbed a handful before she stepped outside, then replaced the flashlight beside the door and shut it quickly, barely missing closing the door on Raucous' tail as the cat scampered out.

The little girl stood beside the two mounds of snow, bewildered. "I can't get his chest up on top of his big fat stomach," she protested. Cassie bet it wasn't often this child failed at anything and was not surprised that it didn't set at all well with her.

"Here, let's both do it." With four hands and arms and multiplied strength on their side, the two of them lifted the torso into place. "Now for the head, just a normal size one," Cassie directed as Amy began packing snow for the next rolled ball, her ice crusted gloves sounding hard against the snow pack as she molded it into shape.

They inserted the dowels where the arms should go and made him a face from the pebbles, and at last, the snowman was done. "I'm going to call him Commissioner. He looks like some of Daddy's friends that he calls Commissioner."

"Yes. I do see your point." Cassie agreed. "Now let's go get warm. What d'ya say?"

The little girl looked around, apparently making sure she'd done everything she came out to do. "Okay. For just a while, anyway."

Cassie didn't give voice to her thoughts that if the child intended Cassie as a permanent playmate she was in for an awakening. Taking the little girl's hand, Cassie led her toward the kitchen.

At the door they turned and looked back at their work. Amy waved goodbye to the snowman. "See you later, Mister Commissioner." Cassie gave the snowman one last glance, stomped the snow from her boots, brushed the snow from her gloves, and went inside to thaw out. Their wet boots were left at the door and their cold, damp socks laid over a chair back near the warm oven. For the first time Cassie and the little girl were aware of just how chilled they were.

Hot cocoa was served by Ben and greedily accepted by the two adventurers. "Thanks. Just the ticket to restore body heat," said Cassie. Their furry little helper only mewed her thanks for the bowl of warm milk that was put down for her.

"Good snowman," Ben said to the little girl.

"He needs a hat," was Amy's only response.

Cassie's taste buds began to dance at the aroma issuing from the oven. It was obvious that roast chicken was on the menu, complete with stuffing. When she had drunk her cocoa, she went to make sure Raucous was safely back with Meg.

At dinner that evening Nate came and sat beside her to update her on his findings, which were few. He still had no information on Janet Wright. He had learned from Regan that Bernard was at least infatuated with Wendy, but the attraction was not mutual. And he had learned that Jamey and Wendy seemed to have been good friends. It wasn't much, he said, but he would keep delving.

"At least they will talk to you. I went to the carriage house to see what they were working on this afternoon and you would have thought I had come in carrying a machine gun, yelling 'freeze.' Everyone just stopped and stared at me. Well, that's all right, because I nearly froze myself. Amy and I built a nice snowman. Her first one. Maybe her last, if she stays in this part of the country."

Nate's smile was fleeting. But by morning, as if in mystical response to the child's wish, Nate's hat graced the head of the Commissioner. How it got there, no one seemed to know.

Seventeen

Thursday, January 16, 1985

Gillis' arrival at the hotel that morning was a welcome change. Snow still flew past the tall windows with no sign of let up. The residents of the hotel, shut in together for two days, had begun to wear on each other's nerves and some of them snapped at their table mates. But Meg and Nell, both fresh from a good night's sleep, seemed determined to put a good face on the new day. Nell greeted Gillis with excessive enthusiasm, and Meg graced him with a conspiratorial smile before returning to her usual prickly self.

Cassie and the other residents hovered as near him as possible in hopes of hearing something new and comforting, if not encouraging, about the recent tragedy. They soon found that he had nothing new to offer and, disappointed, they all moved toward the dining room.

With their plates filled from the serving counter, they sat in the same seats they had occupied at previous meals, with one exception.

Gillis sat in the chair beside Cassie where Jesse first had dined. Nate still spent most of his time among the company of actors.

Cassie did not let the opportunity pass. "Have you heard anything from Jesse?"

"Heard from Bob Maddox over in Cherry Lake. Jesse will be awhile coming home. He's helping with the investigation over there."

Hearing this, Cassie laid her fork down and made a thin mouth at Gillis. "When the British say someone is helping with an investigation, they usually mean that person is under suspicion. Is Jesse actually helping with the investigation, or is he under investigation? And if that is the case, it is the most ridiculous thing I've ever heard! And besides, why is Cherry Lake interested in this investigation at all?"

"It seems the boy came from over there. Jesse used to live there, too, in case you didn't know it," Gillis said, using his napkin perhaps to hide the fact that he was measuring her reaction.

Cassie said, "No, I didn't know that, but then there is no reason why I should." She said nothing else but her eyes flashed a profusion of unasked questions as she turned back to the food on her plate.

It didn't work. "What else?" she asked, paying particular attention to the bit of bread she was buttering.

"Oh, yes. He sent you a message, too. Something about taking care of the family treasure, or something like that. Is that a personal reference? Was he referring to you, do you think?" He didn't even try to hide his teasing now, and she could no longer avoid his laughing eyes.

"No, of course not! Now stop being ridiculous and tell me the rest."

"Oh, all right. It seems they've found the boy's mother," Gillis said almost in a whisper.

"Poor woman. She must be crushed. I wonder if he had any brothers or sisters."

Their voices were low enough to allow for privacy but those nearest them were trying very hard to act as if they weren't trying to overhear.

"None that we know of, but at any rate that isn't the major issue right now. The thing is, the mother never knew her son was dead.

When Bob and Jesse found her, she was dead too. Had been dead for a while, in fact."

Cassie dropped her fork, barely catching it before it bounced off the table into her lap.

"What! I don't believe it!" she said, louder than she had intended. She looked around to find several people looking at her, but their gazes fell quickly when their eyes met hers.

"Eat," she said, "then meet me in that little room where I've been working. We have to talk in private." Whatever other shocking news he had to share with her would just have to wait. They turned their attention back to their breakfasts.

Ben's menu today was as generous as yesterday's and for a while they ate in companionable silence, hearing bits of conversation from the guests. When they saw Wendy wheeling the urn of steaming coffee through to the lobby, they followed like rats to the pied piper.

A crowd gathered around Gillis once again, this time to hear the latest news about the weather conditions and whether it was safe for them to go home again.

"There's no help in sight for the telephones. Most of the areas down here still have electricity, but you folks up the mountain have probably lost it by now. A lot of those snow-laden limbs have fallen and you know how the electric lines run up there. Some of the lines themselves got so heavy they've pulled loose from the poles. So if any of you want to go home we'll do all we can to get you there, but I don't advise it." He paused and changed his stance, as his next words revealed a change in his tactics.

"I'd be happy if you'll all just make yourselves comfortable here for the time being," he said. "Keeps me from having to run up and down the mountain telling all of you what's going on and asking whatever questions need answering." His tone of voice was light, but the atmosphere his words created was not. Every face grew solemn as the little group closed in tighter around him.

"What about that boy? Was it an accident, then? Was it a hit-and-run?" Nell asked.

"A hit-and-run isn't considered an accident. If a person dies as a result of a hit-and-run, it's considered manslaughter at least, but in this case there is something else. Jamey...," he looked around to see their faces when he gave out the name of the victim. The only meaningful change he saw was on the face of Meg Dothard and he knew that it only reminded her that her son might be involved.

He continued, "Jamey may have been hit by a passing car, but the autopsy showed a lethal dose of some substance in his blood, as well." A look of concern in Doc's eyes, total blankness on the faces of some others did not escape him. He registered as many reactions as he could before they all had time to put on new faces. For the most part, he saw only attentive concern in the faces around him.

"So where did the blood in the snow come from?" asked Doc.

Gillis looked at him a moment before answering. "I guess it won't hurt to tell you. He had a bruise on his face, like he had fallen on a rock or something. It nicked a blood vessel on his forehead, well, in his temple actually."

Doc returned Gillis' lingering look for a moment before they both turned away. Cassie looked at neither of them. She knew that if there was blood at the scene, the boy was still alive, at least to some degree, as he lay there.

"What was it in his blood? Alcohol? Drugs?" asked Meg. Her own son didn't drink alcohol, she knew that. This couldn't involve him at all, she told herself.

"Alcohol, yes, but something else, too. I can't call the name right off. Not one of your common recreational drugs, I know."

"Well, people never learn about mixing prescription drugs and alcohol. They just never learn," intoned a drooping Doctor Abbott. The weight of all mankind seemed to rest on his shoulders.

Cassie was not the only person in the room who wondered what medication Doc may have prescribed for Jamey, forgetting to warn him about the danger of using alcohol while he was taking it.

They were all quietly entertaining their own speculations, so they were able to hear the whoosh of a door swinging shut behind them. Gillis looked over their shoulders just in time to see the movement, but did not get a glimpse of the listener.

Ike had joined them late. Gillis asked, "Did anyone see who just left this room? Who all is missing from this group, Ike?"

After a quick glance around the crowd Ike said, "Evelyn, Wendy and Ben. And that little girl. Some of the guests could be missing, and some of the actors of course. Hard to keep track of all these people on short notice." His sacrifice went unheeded.

Gillis dismissed the information as being acceptable absences. Whoever had been at the door had probably only been going about their chores. Except the child, and she hadn't needed to hear any of it. But she was, after all, the mayor's responsibility, not his. The thought made him smile.

The door swung open again, and this time Wendy entered. Her face was drooping and she looked haggard. She leaned against the wall for a second, watching the people around her, then moved to the juice and coffee bar.

Ike saw her movements and took a cue from them. "Bar's open, everyone. Juice, coffee, and anything extra you want thrown in. It's early in the day, but what the heck? Have one on the house." Wendy served a few drinks until Ike got there with several bottles of wine. She poured glasses of red wine for Evelyn and herself. She looked at the liquid in her glass as if it were water in a desert before she sipped from the rim of the glass in quick small drafts. Cassie shivered. When Wendy poured the wine into their glasses, for a brief instant she imagined it looked like blood.

Gillis at last got free from the crowd and caught Cassie's eye. She nodded toward the foyer and he followed. They went along the short hallway to the back door of her little study. Making sure Ike was not in the office next door, she motioned him into one of the rickety chairs while she took the other. "Tell me now, what's going on up there?" she implored.

"I really don't know much about it. Bob Maddox just radioed me from Murphree last night and told me what I've already told you. Boy, you never know how much you depend on the telephone until they go out on you. Maybe they'll get some of the lines repaired today or tomorrow and I can find out more details. What have you learned here?"

"Not much, really. I've found out that one of the guests during that big tornado left a burned place on a couple of pieces of this old furniture, it was old even then, antique. I'll tell you all about that later, or you can read my book, and they made him pay, but never repaired the damage."

"That's wonderful, Cassie. Just great." The sarcasm dripped from his words, and Cassie didn't miss it. Neither did she cringe before it. Instead, she laughed deep and loud as Gillis continued, "Now if you can tear yourself away from your research for a minute, tell me what you've learned about people's whereabouts Monday afternoon and evening."

"I've talked to some of the local people, but they don't say anything, they just ask a lot of what-if questions and speculate about any newcomers. I'm sure they include me in that. I did find out from Evelyn that Wendy and Jamey left here together Monday afternoon. Then, according to Wendy, they went their separate ways early and he went on to meet somebody else. She came back here, and Evelyn confirmed that. She saw Wendy in the kitchen but not Jamey." She realized now that she didn't know what time Evelyn saw her, but she didn't tell Gillis about the oversight. He didn't need any further convincing of her spaciness.

"Evelyn herself was out to the beauty shop and boutique for a while but got home early. Ike says he didn't leave, but that he sent Jamey out on an errand and Jamey never came back. If Jamey left with Wendy to do an errand, then left her to go see someone else, it makes you wonder how reliable he was, not that it has anything to do with the problem at hand," Cassie said.

"You could wonder how reliable Jamey was, or how believable Ike is." As soon as he said it, Gillis' gaze dropped to his hands, which picked at each other like testy children. "I shouldn't have said that out loud."

"Said what? I wasn't paying attention."

"Thanks. But it may have more bearing on this situation than you think. If we can find out who he was going to meet, or to see, we may find out how he happened to end up in Meg's ditch. What was the errand, by the way?"

"Ike didn't say and since he's a suspicious old crab anyway, I didn't want to appear too nosy. And another thing, Evelyn said that Ike came in late Monday night, but Ike told me only a little while later that he hadn't been away from the hotel in a week."

Gillis gazed at her thoughtfully and nodded, and Cassie continued, "Jamey was part of the Shakespeare troupe. Maybe one of them knows something."

"And good luck questioning that bunch," said Gillis, rising from his chair. "Let's go get acquainted with them."

"Nate is exploring that area, especially about the Janet Wright thing. They seem to like him, probably because he's their only media connection right now. We need to talk to him, too," Cassie said, locking the door behind her. She led Gillis back to the little alcove where the actors moved about and read their lines, being cued by a mousy little woman sitting on a stack of cushions. They found a suitable spot out of the way where they could both see and hear, and watched for a while.

"Do you like Shakespeare, Gillis?"

"Never thought about it much since high school. He doesn't hang out on my turf a lot," he added, grinning. A large white gossamer-draped figure that Cassie took to be male, spoke and gestured gracefully to a small thin boy in pixie clothing, obviously Puck, who flitted and pranced while explaining something to the angry larger sprite. "See that big one? That's Bernard!" exclaimed Gillis, grinning from ear to ear.

"So it is," agreed Cassie after a closer look at the pair. "Bernard playing Oberon," Cassie explained to Gillis. "Puck's cast a spell on the wrong lover and upset everybody's plans."

Gillis looked at the pair of 'faeries', looked at the nearby group of young lovers and another group of ordinary men, especially at the one wearing the papier mache donkey's head. He looked from group to group and shook his head. "'Lord, what fools these mortals be!'" he said in as near a British accent as he could muster.

Cassie gave him a sharp poke in the ribs for his mischief. "Evidently, you have been hanging out with the bard somewhere. What were you, The Bobby of Avon or something?"

"I played the role of Bottom in high school, actually," he admitted. "That line I quoted back there was really Puck's line." He turned to face her. "But don't you dare tell anybody else, especially Thacker. He'd disgrace me forever."

"No wonder you looked at the donkey's head with such longing just now. You are perfect for the role of Bottom, seeing that he, too, is being an ass!"

"I work at it," Gillis said.

They paused near the harpist as she plucked a beguiling melody. The pretty dark-haired girl was not with her today, and the harpist hummed alone, watching from her cushion as the various contenders for roles played out their hearts before her, interrupting them now and then with some directive comment. Gillis listened for a moment then said, "I'm glad to see Bernard is playing Oberon. What role was Jamey hoping to play?"

Regan, without taking her eyes from the players or her fingers from the harp, said "Puck. He really got into the role. This one fits it better, though. Smaller boned, lighter on his feet." She never looked at them and soon seemed to have become oblivious to her new audience and the pair soon moved off to linger over other sets and scenes.

Gillis watched and listened to the music for a few minutes, then turned to Cassie and said, "I'd like to use your office for a while if you don't mind, to talk to some of these folks."

"By all means," Cassie agreed and handed him the key. "Just help yourself to pens and paper, whatever is there that you need. They're all on the table." As Gillis went to choose his first subjects, she returned to her room to collect her thoughts and plan her next moves.

Eighteen

When she had seen Gillis off again Cassie returned to her little room with its smattering of history, determined to get all the information it had to offer before the time came for them to leave the hotel and return to their homes.

Ike was in his office, head bowed over a stack of papers on his desk. He looked up when Cassie entered, his hands hovering over the page in front of him. When he saw her and realized that she wasn't stopping, he muttered a greeting and returned to his work. Glad that he didn't want to talk, Cassie went into her study and closed the door.

Silence came down like a heavy fog and enclosed her, but she was not aware of it. She was lost within the last century, almost seeing and hearing the people who had occupied this wonderful building when it was, indeed, the grandest hotel in the mountain country.

When she could read no more because of the burning of her eyes, she closed her books and gave her eyelids a good rub, never mind the dangers. She stood up and leaned forward from the hips, dangling herself about like a rag doll to relieve the cramping of her back and shoulders.

She replaced *Volume Two* on the shelf, and with a sense of finality took *Volume One* and carried it to the table. As she read the first page, she gave a little sigh of relief. This was it, the record of the birth of a landmark. She turned the page and continued to read. What she now held in her hands was not only a register used to record the very earliest visitors to the hotel, it was also a record of opening expenditures, and an inventory of the treasures with which the founder had furnished his new refuge. He had brought them in, thinking they might add a special cachet to the hotel.

After an hour or so Meg came in with a tray of sandwiches, soup and tea. Cassie kept on reading and making notes as they ate. Meg sat quietly, looking through some of the later records for any names she might recognize from recent years.

They spent the next half hour in silence, Cassie occasionally calling Meg's attention to something in the earliest pages.

Cassie spoke at last. "Look at this one, Meg. This one I just found. It's labeled as a register, not as a ledger. I guess that's why Ike missed it when he took the ledgers out. It tells about the very beginning of the hotel and how they got the things they would need. You know, like 'one sorrel horse, $25.00. One leather saddle, $250.00'. Things like that. It tells about the original land grants, the name of the builder, where the marble and stuff came from."

She closed the book and held it in her hands, looking at it as if it were alive. "This is exactly the sort of thing I wanted. It's full of real information, and there'll probably even be a lot more stuff in here that I want to use. Don't mention it to anybody, though or Ike will take this one away. I want to keep it until I get every morsel of interest out of it."

"I won't say a word." Meg had grown restless and began moving along the shelves where other books stood, ones not connected with the running of the hotel, picking out a book here and there. After leafing through each one, she returned it to its place and selected another. One of them caught her attention more than any of the others. It seemed to be a narrative, a diary, about the settling of Hartsville with its mineral springs, and the Corona, where the patrons stayed when they came to "take the waters."

"Look here, Cassie. Did you see this?"

Peering over Meg's shoulder Cassie saw, stuck in between the pages, a picture of the hotel. The page beside it was covered in faded and fancy handwriting. It spoke of the early days of Hartsville, and was dated only a few years after the hotel's grand opening. The following pages were devoted to the richness of the Corona's interior and decor. Every ornate piece of art, every piece of elegant furniture, was pictured, either by pen and ink drawing or by an old black and white photo, and written in the pages was the provenance of each item. She recognized some of the other pieces in the lobby that, according to the ledger, had been bought new for the opening. They too would be antiques by now.

Cassie sat down with the books and breathed a sigh of relief that Ike had not taken them. Then she realized that he may not even know they existed.

"May I go now, or do I need to stay and help you with something else?" Meg brought her back to the present with a start.

"No, I'm going, too. I've absorbed all I can handle for one day, I think." She began to look around for a place to hide the books from Ike's watchful eye. "On second thought," she said aloud, "I'm taking them to my room." She shoved one volume at Meg. "Put this under your sweater. I'll smuggle the other one out." She tucked it into the elasticized waistband of her slacks and pulled the bulky sweater down over it and helped Meg rearrange herself to conceal the contours of the contraband. Meg was flushed and smiling, having had her day made by participating in something she considered subversive.

"I'll take this one up now, and put it in your room after I've glanced through it. You stay down here until I get back. Keep old Ike distracted if you run into him. And if you're going to start pilfering hotel property, I really think you should pick up your key from the desk and keep your room locked, don't you?"

"Yes. And you can ask for yours too, if we're going to leave our adjoining doors open for Raucous."

"Good thinking," said Meg, and she was gone and Cassie returned to her work.

For the moment satiated with what she had learned, Cassie made sure the pilfered book was secure in her waistband then closed and locked the door that led to Ike's office and went out the other door into the hall that led to the foyer.

Pausing there, she rubbed her hand along the damaged table, feeling its texture. Strange, she thought, perhaps it was just her imagination but this piece felt like any other table would have. She would have expected it to glow, sort of, to emit some sort of special vibration, some richness from being steeped in history. But it just sat there. She moved the runner and the tray to look at the burned place again, to commiserate with the table. Her brow creased as she touched the spot where the tray had rested. There was no trace of a burn on this table. Her heart lifted. Maybe Ike, with his woodworking skills, had mended it. If so, he must have been a master at his trade, for the finish was now seamless and flawless.

Replacing the runner and the tray, she went into the lounge and found Meg already back. Cassie took her bit of contraband to her room then came and began to bring Meg up to date on the things she had discovered.

"In one of those books there is a mention of that piece in the foyer. Someone, a man named Benefield, laid a lighted cigar or cigarette on that one and burned it. Once when I was here with Nathan, I saw it. But now, well come on. I'll show you what I'm talking about." She dragged Meg into the foyer and moved the runner aside. "Look." She pointed to the place where the scar should have been. "It was burned right here. Look how well it has been repaired! Do you think it is possible to do that good a job at removing a burn, or do you suppose this might be just a copy of the original table?"

"You're getting a little too caught up in this mystery stuff, Cassie. Your imagination is on a rampage," Meg said, turning to go back to the lounge.

"You're probably right. The mystery is happening now, not back in the sixties."

"Well, I'm going to call it a day, I think. You coming up now?"

"Yes, I think I will."

All was quiet as they crossed the lobby. Cassie knew what she wanted to do, but her body and her mind screamed for rest, so she climbed the stairs for the last time that day and gratefully found her bed. The curiosity that now piqued her would have to be laid to rest for the night. Or so she thought.

Nineteen

In her warm comfortable bed Cassie closed her eyes to welcome sleep, but it eluded her like fog before sunshine. She found that although her eyes and body wanted rest her mind broke free from all control and prodded and poked at her until, as a last resort, she turned on her side and drew her knees up into fetal position and shut her eyes, willing herself to sleep.

The present began to fade and blurred images of desert lands began to form in her mind. Somewhere nearby she heard a sound like the keening of a newly widowed Indian woman, and in her semi-somnolence Cassie felt a chill creep along her spine.

Was she dreaming or was it real? *Do I need to think about it?* she asked herself. No, just try to sleep. She lay in the dark with her eyes closed and did a relaxation technique, starting with her toes and working upward. "Relax, darn you!" she insisted. But some basic instinct kept nudging her, pricking at her intellect, telling her to think, think, think. Of what? she demanded of it.

At last it came. What Gillis had said about Jesse's message to her. Why would he think to send her a casual greeting when there were so many more important things to consider? Well, perhaps it wasn't so trivial. What was it he had said about treasures? Was it family treasures? And why would he tell her to look after them? They were certainly not in the same family. No, wait. It was family heirlooms. The only thing he'd said about that though was about putting a couple of letters in with his socks, for heavens sake! He must have been referring to their conversation about Ike's offer to take care of their valuables. Well, she did have a tendency to be a very literal person at times.

But wait. The letters. He had left two letters in his room, referring to them as family heirlooms. And they were important enough for him to have gone back into his house to get them when they were leaving for the hotel. But surely he wasn't referring to them in his message through Gillis. Well, whatever he meant it would have to come to her on its own. She couldn't come up with an answer through sheer reason. Then she recalled the crash she had heard from his room, and hearing the sound of footsteps running down the hall afterward. If the letters were his only valuables, and if someone else thought it profitable to search his room, they must contain information of some importance. She slipped out from under the covers and found her robe and slippers.

At the door she paused in reflection of the words of the sheriff in Arizona, telling her to keep her nose out of the law's business. He had turned a deaf ear to her promise to Matt, to find the cause of his death. He had ordered her to cease and desist, and then made it impossible for her not to do so.

Was she now committing an even greater offense? Was she justified in prying into others' affairs just because Gillis had asked her to help him? Or because Jesse had sent her a cryptic message to protect some unnamed treasure? But then, if he had to be cryptic when sending his message through Gillis, he obviously didn't want Gillis or perhaps someone else to have access to whatever secret he was hiding, and what more apt place for secrets to be exposed than in letters?

Well, there would be no harm done, she decided, if she brought them into her room for safekeeping. She had no idea what was in them, but the more thought she gave it the more sure she was that Jesse's message had to be in reference to them. If he was offended later, if this was not what he had meant, then too bad. The idea of the possible presence of a killer in their midst was the deciding factor for her.

Stealthy as a cat she opened her door, crossed the hall and entered Jesse's room. She felt a little twinge of doubt, but quickly suppressed it. She proceeded with a small measure of confidence across to the chest, and opened the top drawer. That was where Matt had always kept his socks, and she assumed other men would do likewise, so she was surprised when they were not there.

It took her quite a while to locate them, in the drawer of the bedside table. Her face lit up in amusement as she gazed into that last drawer. There they were, six pairs of black socks, the tops of each pair tucked into each other just as Matt had done.

For an instant she had a vision of Jesse, waking from a good night's sleep, reaching for his glasses then pulling on his socks before stepping out onto the cold floor. It didn't take her a second to sweep the socks aside and find the white envelopes Jesse had held in his hand the day they arrived.

As quietly as she had come in, she left the room and returned to her own. Once inside she dug down into a stack of papers in the drawer where she kept her notebooks and research notes, thinking of something Matt had once said when they were secreting some valuable papers among a few pieces of junk mail while still on the reservation: "A good camouflage is better than the best hiding place." *Let's hope he was right*, she thought, as she pulled the cover up, hoping too that this time she would sleep.

It was not to be. The longer she lay there, the more she thought of what she had done. What if Jesse hadn't been referring to the letters at all? What if he were to come back tonight and find them missing? She would have to own up to taking them, and wouldn't she look foolish, not to mention guilty, when it came out that she had prowled through his drawers, then brazenly tampered with his private correspondence?

Cassie lay with eyes closed, alternately counting sheep and mentally commanding herself to "sleep...sleep...sleep...," summoning the needed respite that would not come.

What did come made her blood run cold.

Twenty

A bone-chilling scream shattered the silence as a screech owl swooped above the snow-covered mountain alert for any movement on the ground below. His quest led him to the dense shadows cast by the moonlight around the old hotel. He came to rest on a bare and frozen limb where vestiges of an eerie light crept out around a shuttered window high above the ground. His primeval cry pierced the icy night, portending death to any stirring creature. He watched the ground below for any cautious or defensive movement evoked by his menacing scream.

Hearing the screech owl's death knell, Cassie jerked upright in her bed. Swinging her feet from under the covers, she pulled on faded jeans and a sweater over her pajamas, then drew on a bulky sweater and thick socks, the clothing she had laid out for the next day.

She felt as if she had been stalking sleep for hours, but now she would have to face the fact that she wouldn't catch it tonight. The rest she so desperately craved had fled away in the echo of the screech owl's threat.

Fully clothed now, she looked at her watch. One o'clock. She was sure the rest of the hotel had been sleeping for hours. If she must be awake, she could at least do some more reading. There was that old book Meg had found. It would be more entertaining than the one she had brought up.

She looked in all the logical places where one might place a book but found nothing. Meg had said she would put it in her room after she'd looked through it, but she must not have finished with it. It was probably in Meg's own room. Oh well. As long as Ike hadn't confiscated it.

Cassie decided to go downstairs and look for something light to read, something that would put her to sleep. She eased her door open and crept out into the dim light of the hallway. As her foot touched the first stair a chill ran along her spine as the voice of the screech owl again pierced the night. She withdrew her foot and stood quite still for a long time. No more sounds came through the darkness, but now she wasn't in the same frame of mind about going downstairs, alone, not this late into the night. Not with the undeniable possibility of meeting a murderer down there.

Gazing along the hall, she could just make out the glow from a window at the end of this hallway, where the east wing passageway branched off from it. Moving quietly, she let herself be drawn toward that window. But once there, she looked northward along the hallway and saw defined in eerie light not a window but a French door, leading to a balcony. That was where she would go, she decided, outside on the balcony where she could get a good view of the night, maybe even a glimpse of the owl.

She went back to her room for her heavy coat and put on some shoes and gloves. It was far too cold to risk getting a chill in the night air. She had heard all her life about the miasma that permeated night air, causing all manners of illnesses, and she was a firm believer in the truth of that maxim.

Warmly dressed now she unfastened the latch on the French doors and pushed one open, making sure the lock was off before she stepped out into the frozen night onto a wide balcony. The snow was taking a rest, and the cold air seemed to cut right into her lungs as she stood in the semi-darkness, feeling as if she had found a wakeful moment in a world all her own, in which she could detach herself from the events of the last two days and from the horde of people now sleeping inside the hotel. Standing here alone, far above the ground, she began to feel as if she owned the very night and that she had been pulled by an unseen force out into this peaceful place above the world.

She stood now at the edge of the balcony, which served as a roof for the veranda below, and rested her arms on the high balustrade, looking out into the night. Across the valley, slivers of light glittered through the misty moon-made twilight.

In the distance across the valley, a fountain of light rose upward to illuminate the giant statue of a benevolent Jesus, his arms outstretched in a gesture of enfoldment, belying the uncertainty born of the events of the past few days. She watched in sorrow as a hazy fog enveloped the base of the figure and crept upward to enshroud the outstretched arms of the welcoming Christ.

To her it seemed symbolic of the grim activity, the threat, that had crept into and changed the lives of everyone she knew, all her friends, all the people she had just begun to know and some she had learned to trust, whom she now realized were comparative strangers to her. She wondered if they harbored those same feelings about her and about each other.

From far away the occasional crack of breaking snow-laden limbs echoed through the icy air. Below her the outbuildings at the rear of the hotel huddled in dark silence. As she watched, a short burst of light poured out from the building where she had found the dowels, the snowman's arms, as someone opened the door and stepped out, but then the light vanished and all was silent again.

She realized now that there were no windows in the building and wondered why. Perhaps Ike had thought it more expensive in the construction than practical. Also, if the building was to be used for storage, windows would only allow the contents to be more exposed to damage from the elements of light and temperature changes.

She was near to freezing now and her bare head hurt from the cold. The chill penetrated through to her bones. Though beautiful and eerie, the night now held a different but very real threat for her in continued exposure to this cold. She had suffered bouts of pneumonia in the past from less provocation than this. She knew she should get back inside soon, but the distant ice-sparkled lights and the dark misty air held her captive. Just a bit longer, then she would go in, she told herself.

As these thoughts passed through her consciousness, Cassie heard a sound at the door behind her. Meg must have heard her leave her room and followed her.

Without turning she said, "It's so peaceful out here! Look how the lights glow through the fog. Looks almost unreal." Silence absorbed her words. There was no sound of voice or footstep behind her. By the time the last word was uttered a shiver ran down her spine, not only from the coldness of the air, but from the chill of a sudden warning within.

She spun around, half expecting to be attacked, but there was no one there. Suddenly a whirring sound surrounded her and the cry of the screech owl just overhead penetrated the stillness like the scream of a tortured soul. She dashed to the door and turned the knob. It did not move. She was locked out.

She wasted not a thought on yelling for someone to open the door. Instead she pulled her hand up into the sleeve of her jacket and smashed it through a pane of glass, carefully reaching through to open the door from within. If anyone heard the breaking glass they were either too cautious or too callous to investigate. No lights came on, no doors opened so much as a crack as she sped along the corridor.

Inside her room she closed the door behind her and quickly retrieved her can of mace from her handbag while scanning the room for signs of anyone lurking in there.

Assured that she was alone, she peeked into Meg's room. Meg slept undisturbed. She made sure their doors were locked, then removed her chilled clothing and wrapped herself in a blanket from the bed while hot water ran steaming into the tub. As its warmth enveloped her, she at last tried to focus her mind, to think of anyone who would have done such a malicious thing. There was no thought in her mind of anyone actually trying to harm her, as breaking a glass to gain entry was such an obvious solution to the situation. Apparently, someone was only trying to annoy her, or more likely to frighten her. Was someone afraid she might discover some hidden fact or action? Had the person who opened the door to the little building seen her on the balcony and sent her a warning message?

That person would likely be none other than Ike, she decided. But why would he want to frighten her? With that thought came suspicion, based on things she had found in her research and more on certain details of the hotel furnishings.

Was he involved in something illegal? With his woodworking skill he could well be carrying on an antiques scam, substituting reproductions for the hotel's originals for his own personal gain.

If so, he would have to have help. Considering the size and heft of some of those pieces, it was most unlikely that he could even move them without assistance. If he had sought help, then the logical person to rely on would be a young man of good physique, such as Jamey, would it not? And if Jamey knew of such a scam, then he would have considerable power over Ike Farabaugh. And if he had been so foolish as to try to wield that power over a criminal mind then it was more than a mere possibility that the criminal minded would resort to criminal means to avoid trouble. Had Jamey been that naive? Or was Ike really that evil?

But she might be wrong. Ike might have a good man who came in to do the repairs privately so as not to disturb the guests. But she already knew that he was certainly capable of making the repairs himself. Logically, Jamey might indeed have been unfortunate enough to be hit by a passing motorist. After all, Ike had said he hadn't left the hotel that night. But Evelyn had said Ike came in late, and hinted that he had been drinking. Hadn't Gillis said there was also some alcohol found in Jamey's body?

Suddenly she found she couldn't think about it any more tonight. She was too tired, had had too great a shock, and was not sure she was thinking all that clearly. She would just let everything wait until she could look at it in the light of day.

Sinking low into the water, she allowed it to wash away her anxiety and lull her into tranquility. When the water cooled, she ran in more hot, until she felt relaxed and calm. When she stepped out of the tub and toweled herself off, she pulled a clean flannel gown over her head, crept back into her bed and was eventually wrapped in slumber.

She didn't hear the screech owl as he dove down deep into the shadows between the hotel and the stable. She didn't see him as he soared and flew away, a screaming rodent writhing in his claws.

Twenty-one

Friday, January 17, 1985

Morning buzzed with the sounds of activity outside her door as the guests made their descent to the dining room. Cassie wondered how many of them were hungry and how many were, like herself, just craving a steaming cup of fresh brisk coffee.

She lay under the covers, arguing with herself about getting up. She desperately wanted a hot drink and yet she hesitated, as usual, about leaving her warm bed.

The events of the night were as raw in her mind as if they had just happened. She was sorely ashamed to face Ike and tell him she had been locked outside as she stood on a balcony at one o'clock in the morning in the ice and snow and had broken a glass to get back inside. Well, dread or no dread, there was only one right thing for her to do about it.

Dutifully, she left the warm covers and went through her morning toilette. After showering, putting on makeup and brushing her hair, she pulled on the same clothes she had worn the night before, then shoved a foot into one of the socks she had dropped at the bedside.

Something sharp pricked at the top of her right foot. Examining the sock, she found a small shard of glass caught in the white fabric. Was it not enough to be pricked by her conscience? Did she have to be stabbed in the foot for her sins as well? Apparently so.

With that acceptance she tied a blue, gold and white scarf around her neck and began to search through her luggage until she found just the right herbal mix she wanted. Her leg throbbed from the effects of cold on the old injury, and her throat was scratchy. She felt the need of the soothing tea to help fend off a cold, and a couple of pain pills. With the help of an electric heating coil in her cup of hot water, she managed to brew up a fair potion. Having drunk it and taken the pills, she was now ready to face the day.

She knocked on the door between her room and Meg's.

"Come in," Meg called.

"Ready to go down for breakfast?" Cassie said, pushing the door wide for Raucous, who was already sniffing at the threshold.

"In a minute. I was just reading that book I found yesterday. Wanted to get through with it before I turned it over to you. I've just about finished. Or do you want it now?"

"Of course not. Keep it until you're through with it," Cassie said. Too bad Meg had kept it last night, though. If she had found it last night, would she have delved into it, instead of going prowling? Probably not.

"I'm glad you've got it, because when I couldn't find it last night I was afraid it might have fallen into Ike's hands and we'd never see it again. As long as we know it's safe. Does it have anything of interest in it?"

"It has a lot that interests me," Meg said, qualifying her response. "I remember hearing about some of these people, and I bet some of these families still live around here somewhere."

"Just the sort of human interest that makes history tolerable." Cassie opened the door and held it wide. "Coming?"

"You go on down. I'll be there in a few minutes."

In the hall, Cassie felt a draft of cold air, and wondered if it was creeping down the hall from the direction of the French door she had damaged. She intended to tell Ike about it right away, but what logical explanation could she give for being outside on the balcony in the middle of the frozen night? How could she explain the events that led to it being broken? How would Ike respond? Well, she would know soon enough. His response would perhaps tell her a lot more about him than just his overt reaction to the incident. How would he react to any infraction, a loose tongue for instance? Just how secretive and controlling was he?

She found him at the reception desk. When he saw Cassie his face seemed to close down, but he said nothing. She stopped at the desk and after only a brief hesitation dove right into the matter at hand. "I broke a window in the upstairs door to the balcony last night. I will gladly pay for the repairs. In fact, if you have a pane of glass that size and some putty, I'll put it in myself. I'm a pretty good glazier."

His scowl gave her no reassurance. "How did you happen to break a window there, of all places? Are you not satisfied with your room?"

"I couldn't sleep so I went out just to see the moonlight on the snow. I'd heard a screech owl out hunting around the hotel and I thought maybe I could see him, too. The door blew shut and locked while I was out." She knew she had unlocked it, but why bother with saying it? If he was the one who locked her out, he would deny it, and if not, he would probably just say she was mistaken. "Everyone else must have been asleep. I had to break a pane to get back in."

"It must have been pretty late at night, then." He turned back a few pages in his register as if looking for something, then back to where it had been open when she came down. Cassie waited, knowing he was playing for time until he could decide what he would say.

"Okay. I've got some glass. I'll cut it and put it in myself. Why don't you just try to stay inside while the weather is so bad?" His piercing look spoke volumes to her eyes. "Looks like you have enough to keep you busy, what with that research you're doing in my books. Snowmen, screech owls...." He shook his head slowly as he returned his attention to the register page.

She got the idea that, more than expressing concern for her welfare, he was telling her to control her curiosity. It was hard to be sure, as he was such a cantankerous old cuss anyway. Either way, she knew she would have to be more careful in the future. It brought back vivid memories of that other time, in Arizona, when she had been warned off. She tendered another almost sincere apology for the damage, and moved on to the dining room.

With the herbal tea and pain pills already working their wonders within her, and a breakfast of pancakes and bacon before her, Cassie turned her attention to the others at the table. "Did any of you hear that screech owl last night?"

Nathan had chosen to sit with her and Meg this morning, as none of the actors were in the room yet. He swallowed a generous mouthful of syrupy pancake and said, "I didn't hear anything after I went to sleep. Of course, I keep a little fan with me when I travel to create white noise at night. You know, so outside noises won't disturb me."

"I heard him, just faintly," said Meg. "I've always heard that if a screech owl lands on your house and screams, someone inside is going to die. I hope it's an old wives' tale, but I wouldn't swear to it. My Grandma died unexpectedly one night, and my mother swore they had heard a screech owl on their roof that same night. Is anybody missing out of this crowd, that you can tell?"

Cassie and Nathan looked around, knowing they wouldn't be able to identify anyone who was missing, but Cassie was also remembering how soundly Meg was sleeping when she looked in on her. That must be the sign of a very clear conscience, she decided, to be awakened by a screech owl's cry and go back to sleep almost immediately.

All the guests seemed to be present. Ike and Evelyn had joined them for breakfast this morning. Wendy was in and out of the kitchen helping to keep the serving dishes full, and Ben was, without a doubt, in the kitchen preparing more of this delicious spread for the few late arrivals.

"Does this mean that something could still happen to someone?" Cassie asked.

"Only if that old saying had a chance in hell of being true," Nathan said, debunking Meg's statement.

"You just watch your back, Mr. Know-it-all," Meg laughed. "You might make what started as a superstition turn into one of those self-fulfilling prophesies."

Nathan shivered, grinning. "Oooh, I'm scared."

"You better be. I don't like being wrong about anything." Meg's threat would have carried more punch if it hadn't been made around the strip of bacon she was nibbling.

"Well," Cassie lowered her voice, "I not only heard him, I saw him. He woke me up just as I was about to go to sleep, so I went out onto the balcony to look around. I got locked out somehow, and had to break one of the panes of the French doors to get back in."

Meg looked at her with wide accusing eyes. "If you don't have any better sense than that, then I guess the screech owl is justified in his predictions. You were begging to either catch pneumonia or be mistaken for a prowler and get shot in your tracks."

Nathan glared at her. "Yes, and worse than that, there is still the possibility of there being a murderer among us. Why don't you just keep a low profile and quit snooping before something serious happens to you?"

Cassie stared at him in surprise. Nate had echoed verbatim the words spoken by that sheriff in Arizona. But this was Nathan, her friend. His concern for her welfare was not unappreciated. It just wasn't like him to think such practical thoughts.

"Ike said almost the same thing this morning, only he wasn't concerned for me so much as he was for the protection of his own property."

"Then pay attention to him, why don't you?" said Nathan, looking intently into her eyes.

"How will anybody ever know what is happening around here if nobody tries to find out? Gillis can't be all over the town, in his office and up here all at the same time. It's not as if he has a full staff to back him up, with the whole northern part of the state being snowbound."

Nathan looked some unspoken thought at her, then turned back to his breakfast. Only then did Cassie realize that he could have meant something else in his earlier statement. *Did he mean I should pay attention to Ike's warning of potential danger, or that I should pay attention to his reactions, to see if they harbored some guilt?*

Meg was now involved in conversation with the person to her right. Cassie finished her breakfast in silence between her two good friends, remembering something Matt had once said: "People react in direct proportion to their emotional investment in any given situation." If that is true, then both Nathan and Meg must have a good little bit of emotion invested in me, she thought, as their responses to her adventure had been a little too extreme to be ignored.

About midmorning, forgetting the vow she had made to herself to stay out of trouble, she stopped worrying about upsetting Meg and Nathan. They had both evidently forgotten the moment by the time they left the dining room, so perhaps they wouldn't notice if she did just a little looking around outside.

Slipping away from the crowd in the lobby, she went up and added some more warm clothing to what she already wore, then took the same route she and Wendy had followed until she came to the little sitting room they had shared. Past there, she went down a flight of steps to a door that led outside, at the end of the west wing.

She eased it open, praying that no alarm would sound, and breathed in relief when none did. She was free now, outside without the little girl, without Meg, without Nathan, and without Ike, she hoped, for she was heading for the building where she had found the snowman's arms, where the light had shone last night.

She reached the door of the shed without being interrupted, and removed the lock from its hasp, putting it into her pocket. She may get caught and told off, but she wasn't taking any chances on getting locked in. Getting out of here would be a little more difficult than getting in through the balcony door had been.

As on her previous visit, darkness inside the shop was almost absolute. There were no windows at all in this building, but the flashlight that had rested just inside the door was now in her hand and she wasted no caution in shining it around, this time from well inside the room.

When she cast the light upward, she was surprised to see an elaborate track lighting system there. Nearby a bare light bulb with a pull chain still hung from its socket, but the chain was too short for her to reach, and besides, there was the other lighting available, if she could only find the switch.

A bank of switches had been installed in the middle of one wall but she had a gnawing suspicion that the light switch was not among them. To begin with, they were too near a table full of huge implements which she assumed were woodworkers' tools. All seemed to have motors, she thought, as they all smelled of oil and wiring. They probably all made loud noises when they were turned on, too.

She shined the light all around the walls again, soon spotting a small button set inside the vertical edge of a two-by-four upright, just stuck there with its wire running up the corner. She toggled it, and the room was full of light.

This part of the electrical system seemed to have been installed after the construction of the building was completed. It would be easy to remove the entire lighting package without damaging the walls or ceiling, she realized. It struck her that these lights could have been installed as a temporary measure, as if Ike might have brought it with him from a previous shop and put it in here to light his work, knowing that he could just as easily take it down again if he wanted to.

Having turned on enough light to last a week, she took a quick look around the room. On a work table lay what appeared to be the legs of some piece of furniture yet to be born. Against the wall sat a table like the gaming tables near the reception desk, except that those looked somewhat younger than this one. This one appeared to be worn, to have been abused, but she knew, from reading articles and advertisements about distressed furniture that if it was finished just right, it would look much older than it was.

It hit her like a fist. She knew now that the table in the foyer was an incredibly good copy, a fake of a genuine antique. Ike had made this swap, and she had no more doubt about his purpose in doing so. It wasn't for the protection and preservation of the antique itself. It was for the theft and possibly the eventual sale of that piece. That one, along with many others, no doubt. No wonder Ike liked auctions. He was replacing the hotel's original antiques with his own copies and making a fortune selling the originals.

She began to understand some of Ike's skulking behaviors. He had moved the ledgers to prevent her finding traces of the original pieces that had graced the hotel. He had meant to remove anything that drew attention to the furniture, either new or old.

She also began to realize the need to get out of this building. If no one had seen her come in and if she could get out without being seen, then no harm would be done. If Ike had seen her though, he may be angry enough to take away her research privileges, or worse.

Turning off the lights, she opened the door a crack and peeked out. All she saw was the snowman, but before she could take a better look, Amy appeared in the scene, adding handfuls of snow to the snowman here and there where he had shed an inch or two, and not, Cassie observed, from melting in the warmth of any sunshine, but from the cold wind tearing around his torso.

Cassie silently pushed the door closed and waited. After an interval that seemed an hour long, but that her watch said was only twenty minutes, she peeked out again, this time opening the door wider and wider until she was sure she could leave without being seen. With the flashlight back in its place by the door, she replaced the lock in the hasp as she had found it, and moved a little away from the building.

But glancing back to make sure the lock was intact, she was horrified to see her tracks in the snow, a dead giveaway. The first time she had looked in here, she hadn't worried about being found out, but the scenario was different now that she knew there was a reason for secrecy, a reason that Ike might object to her going into his workshop.

Moving with manic speed, she began at that point to fashion a wife for the snowman, starting her first snow rolling just where she had trod. In a very short time, the telltale tracks were gone, and the Commissioner had a little woman at his side. She had no arms, but she stood so near him his own arm could have embraced her, if only it could have bent a little.

Safely back in the hotel she found Amy and told her to go and see the Commisioner's bride. If she knew that little lass, she wouldn't leave an inch of snow in the area if that's what it would take to fashion a child for the happy couple. That little girl, Cassie was sure, would be outdone by no one.

She had spent a lot more time away than she had intended. She still had a lot to do in preparation for the thespians' revue. First she must make sure the camera she had borrowed from Nate was ready and loaded with film and placed on the shelf under the high receptionist's desk. That done, she arranged the chairs in semicircular rows and set up a stage of sorts.

Regan had assured her that the stage hands from the troupe would arrange whatever scenery they needed. The skits were all set in outdoor scenes, so artificial greenery from the lobby and throughout the hotel had been pressed into service and made a pretty good substitute for the great outdoors.

As a last minute thought, she found Nate and in no time got his take on a write-up of the performance to go with the pictures for the newspaper. Nate, still a little worried following the adventures of the night before, was nevertheless up to his ears in coverage of the storm for the next issue of the paper, and was only too glad to have her assistance. He hadn't had a story with this many angles in quite a while.

Twenty-two

By the simple artifice of removing lamps and light bulbs from the various fixtures of the lounge, leaving only the one above the receptionist's desk, Cassie had the seating areas in dim and shadowy light. Above the alcove already adopted by the actors as their theater hung a strategic arrangement of lights. The lighting director of the troupe had scavenged every extension cord in the hotel and borrowed the lamps and extra bulbs to create a fair representation of an outdoor scene in the daytime. It didn't take a very big leap of imagination to know that by the simple expedient of unplugging certain of the cords, a nighttime outdoor scene could be created quite easily.

The guests of the Hotel Corona, though probably none of them at all inclined to attend such mundane entertainment in the normal course of their lives, seemed to anticipate this evening's presentation with a certain degree of pleasure. This goodwill was probably directly related to the degree of their boredom with the daily routine they had endured during their enforced confinement.

Gillis had shown up in time for the performance, and he and Cassie were among the first to leave the dining room after an early supper. Meg went to the kitchen to help Ben and Wendy clean up so they could join the others in the lounge.

In low tones Cassie told Gillis about her trip out to the carriage house to observe the actors, and their reluctance to perform with her there, so she had nothing concrete to report about them. She also told him about her visit to Ike's workshop and the discoveries she had made there. "Do you think it's possible that he's counterfeiting the antiques in this hotel? Of course he could be just making duplicates to sell for his own purposes," she added as an afterthought.

Gillis gazed at her for a time, and said only, "I don't really know what he's doing. We'll just have to wait and see, after I talk to Jesse again. He may be able to give me more insight when he gets back from Murphree. I think there might be some other connection. But still no word on the Wright girl, huh?"

"No, not yet," she told him, and they moved into the alcove to watch the rehearsals for the revue. There the actors, hidden from view, sat on the floor or stood in groups rehearsing their lines, awaiting the opening of the show.

In one area an excited Puck was explaining to an outraged Oberon how he had managed to cast a spell on Lysander rather than Demetrius, causing an upset in the romances of several young lads and lasses. Oberon, powerfully portrayed by Bernard, upbraided him mightily.

Puck fled in hopes of finding a heartsick Helena to bring her back to the wood, while Oberon enchanted another potion to reverse the damage Puck had wrought with the first batch by dropping it into the eyes of the wrong young man.

Puck returned with both Helena and Lysander. He spoke to Oberon, with some help from the mousy prompter, who kept losing her place. Puck, in a fit of temperament, scolded her. "Can't you keep up with the place? It's not as if we're up here ad-libbing, surely!" His fine British accent blistered her face to a fiery red. She sank lower into the mounds of pillows on which she sat and a single teardrop landed on the pages of dialogue on her lap. Puck preened his spritely clothes and ushered his two charges into the clearing.

As he began his lines, Gillis and Cassie watched the prompter as she began to weep in earnest. Puck had forgotten his lines again and the prompter was unable to find the place fast enough to suit him. His look at the poor girl would have melted lead.

She turned the page, running her finger along the lines. "Just a minute, it's right here. I got something in my eye," she babbled.

When Puck, hands on hips, took a step in her direction, Gillis evidently felt it was enough. "That's my cue, I think," he said, taking long menacing steps in to intercept Puck.

He almost snarled as he pulled himself up into his authoritative stance. "If you can't remember your lines, I suppose it is only natural you would get your victims mixed up. Take that script from her and study your lines. And stop trying to be a prima donna. You don't have the presence for it."

Bernard stepped forward, placing himself between Gillis and the flustered Puck. "I will help him, he will do it right," he promised with a winsome smile.

Cassie squeezed his arm as they moved on. "Good for you, Gillis! He needed his wings clipped." She looked back over her shoulder to see the bewinged Bernard walking away with his arm around the shoulder of the undone Puck.

"Yes," Gillis said through a mischievous grin. "I've been wanting to do that to some of these young sprigs for years. That's exactly what our drama coach did to me in high school. I was furious and humiliated, but I learned my part. Maybe a little too well," he said as an afterthought.

Cassie gave him a very soft rendition of a whinny. She retrieved the camera from the receptionist's desk and they moved on through the audience.

Gathered in the lounge, the guests had seated themselves so as to get the best views of the alcove. Stage hands shifted the folding screens to and fro, making sure their movements emulated a curtain well enough to accommodate the players. Satisfied that this would work, they closed the screens and waited for curtain time. Behind the makeshift curtains much whispering and scurrying took place.

When the entertainment began, Regan played the harp as she and Bethany sang a lively Gaelic pub song as the opening act. When the toe tapping and rhythmic clapping grew into applause as they finished the number, Regan assumed the role of Mistress of Ceremonies. Speaking in her best polished accent, she introduced two men and two women who performed a skit they had adapted from a Wodehouse farce. Their rendition served as a warm-up for the heart of the revue, an adaptation of the livelier scenes from A Midsummer Night's Dream.

But the selected scenes lacked something in the way of lightness. Puck was not very convincing as a carefree fairy so soon after his encounter with Gillis. The scene was saved only by the appearance of a small white furry creature slinking through the scenery, whiskers twitching. Finding a warm pool of light shed by a 100-watt moon, it curled itself up into a ball and went to sleep. The actors, engrossed in their roles, never knew just what instigated the untimely burst of applause.

At the end of the show Wendy led in the Morris Dancers, with Regan explaining the origins of the lively folk dance, how the ancient ritual had probably come from the Morey's, or the Moorish, or perhaps from the moors of England, maybe even from some ancient European civilization. The dancers were dressed in costumes and wigs from the Shakespeareans' wardrobes. Wendy and her troupe performed the traditional rowdy, handkerchief-waving sets almost magically.

Cassie, standing in back of the room, had used a zoom lens and snapped photos of each scene as the different skits were performed. From among these she would surely find some excellent shots for the paper.

Gillis and Nate sat together off to one side, watching the crowd as much as the actors.

After the show was over, Nate and Cassie, bundled into the warmest clothing they could find, got Bernard to drive them down to the Newspaper office where Nate developed the film in spite of the cold. When he had finished, he handed the pictures to Cassie, saying, "Pick out the ones that are most colorful, not just the ones that depict your favorite acts. I'd like to feature this in the first edition after we're back up and running. I'd say, about twenty-five hundred words or so."

"Okay. I'll try to have it ready by tomorrow, just in case."

Back at the hotel they found that the stage had been struck, the lighting restored and the audience dispersed. Many of the guests had returned from the dining room with hot coffee or chocolate and were mingling and laughing instead of moving into their own little groups in which they usually sought comfort or escape.

Meg had taken her chair in the usual place near the windows from which she and Cassie could view the whole room. The fact that the bar was nearby meant nothing to her, except that tonight Wendy lingered near it, replenishing her glass twice before Doc joined her in conversation and they spoke softly and seriously for some time.

Meg had moved to the bar where she lingered over filling a glass with white wine, standing by the table just out of earshot as Doc and Wendy spoke in low, muffled voices. Passing near them on her way back to her seat, she saw Wendy's face become stony, staring intently at Doc before she put the glass down and swept out of the room, her face set in a peculiar grimace.

Returning to her place beside Cassie, Meg murmured, "Wonder what's going on there?"

"She's probably just one of his patients and he's concerned. She does look awfully pale, though," Cassie replied.

"I heard him say 'mayo'. Something about either mayonnaise or Mayo Clinic, I guess. Maybe they were talking about something else," she conceded. "Doc's such a silly old fossil, anyway. No wonder she gave him such a look."

The Shakespeareans, divided up into pairs now, had spread out to take advantage of the mood of the residents. Some of them were reading lines to one another. Bethany sat with an older man with drab brownish hair to his shoulders, and a beard carefully trimmed into the same fashion portrayed in all the pictures of Shakespeare that Cassie had ever seen. His eyes were a piercing blue, and he could well have been a descendant of the bard himself. Even his accent had the ring of truth in it. There was something, she couldn't say just what, that made her know his was a genuine accent.

When the girl spoke, her voice had the same quality. Cassie hadn't paid much attention to the changes in her enunciation or inflection when they had spoken earlier. All performers change accents from time to time. But listening to her now Cassie was fascinated. When the girl looked up and spoke to Cassie this time she stayed 'in character'.

"Would you mind doing me a favor?" Cassie asked. She had to know.

"And what might that be?" replied the girl, seeming to welcome a chance to speak with a mere colonial.

"Read one of those lines in your native accent for me, please." Again, the girl read the line, this time in what sounded to Cassie very much like a Cockney voice.

"No, no, I mean your American voice," she said.

"Aoh, w'y di'n't yer saiy sao, then?" came the response, and Cassie was now thoroughly confused. Again the girl read the line, and this time her accent was pure upper Midwest, USA. Or was it? There was that one little hint of a twist in some of the vowels, a little glitch in a diphthong or two. Cassie shook her head, thanked the girl and half turned away, then came back. "Amazing," she said to the actress. "How do you do it?"

"Aoh, it's dead easy, i'n't it?" came the reply.

"Well, thank you for indulging me. I wouldn't miss this season's production for anything in the world." This time, none the wiser, she did leave them.

In the alcove, the red-haired Regan plucked a chime-like sound from the harp. As if on signal, several of the others left their chosen niches and came to sit at her feet. The ballads they sang evoked again in Cassie's mind thoughts of dark misted moors, sweet heathered hills and peaceful green glens. *"Oh, to be in England now that April's there,"* came the plaintive phrase to Cassie's wistful mind.

Was England like that, she wondered, when Jesse lived there? And what was he doing right now? What was happening to him? *I'll have to ask Gillis,* she thought.

Twenty-three

Saturday, January 18, 1985

Gillis occupied the chair beside Cassie, as he usually did when having a meal at the hotel. Breakfast was one of Ben's finest achievements. The aroma of fresh coffee, sizzling bacon and warm, glossy eggs and fresh baked bran muffins made the mouth water as they took their seats at the table. Cassie passed Gillis the salt, accustomed now to his breakfast habits.

"How is the investigation coming along?" She ate a bite of muffin, savoring its buttery goodness.

"Slowly. Up until yesterday, at least, then things began to come together." He dipped a bit of muffin into the soft center of his egg and ate it. "The snowplow will be here this morning. They should have the roads in town open by noon. Probably not up to your place until tomorrow, though. You'll all still need to stay here a while longer."

"So, even though things are coming together as you say, you still want everyone to stay here until you catch the killer?"

His only reply was a thin smile.

She raised an eyebrow at him, but did not ask for an explanation to his cryptic gesture. He probably wouldn't have supplied one anyway.

"Oh, well, at least I'm getting a lot of research done. You'd be surprised how much information was written in some of those old logs. Almost like someone was using them as a kind of journal. But the information in the original records is nothing compared to the information in one of the other books Ike let me see." She didn't mention that he didn't know she had it. "It looks like things have changed a lot over the years. I'm really suspicious of Ike, actually. He just reeks of sneakiness. I wonder if maybe he is diddling the files?"

"Does Ike know you are suspicious? Does he suspect that you're onto something?"

"I don't think so. He acts just the same as always, too busy to care. He's in his office working in his books a lot of the time. I wonder what he records in those little books of his to require so much attention."

"Keeping one set of books is time consuming. Can you imagine how much time a second set must take? Especially when it might pertain to things as tangible and valuable as antique furniture."

"That's true, of course. He would have to be very careful, there."

Gillis mopped up the remainder of his egg yolk with the last bit of bread and placed it in his mouth like a sacramental host. "Well, you just keep a low profile around him. Now," he began, pushing his chair back. Resting one elbow on the table and cupping his chin in that hand, he placed the other arm around the back of Cassie's chair before he said, so softly that only Cassie, and maybe Meg, might hear, "I'm going to arrange for Bernard to bring you, Meg and Ben down to the station in a couple of hours."

"Whatever for?"

"You'll see. It's mostly Meg I want down there, but you need to come with her for moral support. In the meantime, help me fill a couple of carry-out boxes for my guests down at the jailhouse."

"You mean you've found somebody to arrest out in this weather?" Her face clouded. "You don't mean looters, do you? Are we going down there to identify our possessions?"

Gillis lifted his hand from the back of the chair to pat her shoulder, laughing. "No, no, nothing like that. Now come on, let's fix those breakfasts. I'll get some boxes." He went through the swinging door marked "Hotel Staff Only" and came out a few minutes later with Styrofoam containers. Handing one to Cassie, he heaped food into first one then the other. "Ben will meet you and Meg in the lobby when he's finished. You three can come down then. Bernard already knows to be on standby."

He pulled his dark blue overcoat up around his neck, pulled gloves out of the pocket and gathered up the bag of food. "Thanks," he said, looking deep into Cassie's eyes. "See you after awhile." He stopped and whispered something into Meg's ear on his way out. She turned quickly and looked at Cassie through bewildered eyes.

Cassie told her that Gillis had arranged for Bernard to take the three of them to the Sheriff's office when Ben was finished in the kitchen.

"What is this all about? I heard you and Gillis whispering, but I couldn't tell what you were talking about. What in the world is going on?" she asked

Handing Meg a fresh cup of coffee, she picked up her napkin and wiped at her mouth. "I don't know," she said into the paper folds. "It must have something to do with the death, but I'm sure Ben isn't involved. Maybe it's... oh, I don't know. We'll just have to be patient and wait, I guess."

They waited, but not patiently. It seemed like two hours instead of one before Ben came through the lobby door dressed in a parka and fleece lined gloves. Bernard appeared at their side as if by magic.

The Shakespeareans in their alcove stared in silent envy as Cassie's group turned to leave. The off-stage Bottom and Titania and company were clearly ready to return to their natural habitat at the trailer park. A faint dismal chord from the harp followed Cassie and her little group out into the snow.

Twenty-four

The cold outside was nothing compared to the chill in Cassie's blood when she stepped into the Hartsville Sheriff's Office. In a different setting she might not have given a moment's thought to the face now before her, yet the presence of the person behind that face demanded a long second look. Deep lines of fatigue drew down the corners of his usually crisp mouth and heavy bags under his eyes concealed their sharpness. Jesse Lankford was obviously in a state of exhaustion.

No words came to Cassie's tongue, at least none that she would say aloud, but questions raced through her mind. Was he under arrest? And if so, was he guilty as charged? Had he been under interrogation in Murphree for these past three days and nights?

Her next thoughts took the opposite stance. Had he been stranded in the snow somewhere, unable to get home? Had he, had he, had he. "Jesse, you look awful! Are you sick? I'm glad you're back. What's happened?"

Gillis, having made Bernard comfortable in Sheriff Thacker's office with the door closed between them, came to her rescue. "Jesse has been handling some problems in Murphree and Cherry Lake. He can tell you all about it later, but right now let's get comfortable and relax a little bit. Then we can talk."

Relax? Sure thing, thought Cassie. Meg looked as if she might explode. Only Ben remained impassive, looking from his mother to Jesse and back again. He sat down first, shoving his hands into his pockets and, sliding down in his chair, stared at the ceiling.

Meg sat on a straight chair, refusing to take Gillis' upholstered one behind his desk. Cassie pulled another straight chair beside Meg and sat there. Through all this Jesse sat impassively, his face expressionless, his eyes pained.

Gillis started the coffee maker to dripping and made sure cups and condiments were ready. "Help yourselves," he said, sitting down in his own chair. "Sorry to drag you out in this weather, and I do appreciate you coming. This isn't the scene where the detective calls the suspects together and tells them the solution of the crime, trapping the perpetrator in the process," Gillis began. "But Jesse has a story to tell us, and Meg, I think maybe you can help fill in some blanks too. I thought it best to do it here, where we have some privacy just in case anyone gets emotional. After everyone has his or her say and things settle down, we can all go back to the hotel and carry on as normally as possible. So, you go ahead, Jesse."

Cassie began to relax at last, only now aware of how tense she had been. Jesse spooned sugar into his coffee, took a deep sip and cleared his throat. "I've lived in Hartsville for quite a few years now, but I don't think anyone here knows about my life in England before I came to America, and I have to tell a little of that in order for the rest of my story to make sense.

"Cassie, I told you just a bit of it the morning all this started, and you, Meg, know another part of it. Outside of that I've kept a lot to myself in hopes that the truth would never have to be made public, that I could just let things lie where they fell and all would come right, just as it's always done."

Meg, still as tense as when she came in, interjected, "Some of us can appreciate that more than others, Jesse. We've all got secrets we don't want to come out."

Jesse's smile was weak and somewhat apologetic. "Well, as the saying goes, the cat's out of the bag now, no matter how much trouble it causes." His eyes locked in with Meg's. "Let's just hope we can protect those who are victims of circumstance from too much more grief."

Ben straightened up in his chair as if to speak, but then seemed to change his mind. He leaned forward, elbows on knees, and looked at the floor for awhile.

"Tell the story the way you see best, Jesse. Then the rest of us can have our say," prompted Gillis.

"I'll start, then, back when I was seventeen years old. Both my parents were killed in an automobile accident. They were archeologists, as I told you Cassie, and they were on their way home from a dig. I was still away at school, and it was decided that I should stay there until my early education was finished.

"The solicitors and our estate managers were to take care of all the business matters of running the place until I came home from school to take over the estate in East Anglia." He stood up and shoved his hands in his pockets, then took them out and offered refills of coffee all around. Only Gillis accepted a refill.

"After I'd finished my studies, I was at a loss regarding the rest of my life. Should I take over the estate, a chore I didn't relish, or was there some other route I could take? My parents had set up a trust fund providing adequate income for a living, and the estate certainly had no money problems.

"I could have, and now I wonder if I should have, stayed there until I died." He grinned, adding his true opinion of that option, "I don't think that would have been a long time, as I still recall the boredom I experienced with my parents' archeologist friends and their poses and stilted conversations.

"My parents had stipulated in their wills that the grounds would always be open for use in archeological studies." He stood again and walked to the window, looking out at the white world but seeing in his mind the green fields of England. "I'll never forget their excitement when they found the remains of a long fallen knight on the grounds. A group of archeologists found him while they were looking for artifacts. His armor was intact, and there were several ancient Anglo-Saxon coins scattered about. I was beside myself with excitement, but that soon faded when I was not allowed to touch or even go near the find, other than to look at it from about three feet away." He stood quite still gazing into the distant past.

"I still feel the yearning to touch that ancient armor, to hold those old coins in my hands and sense the history behind them...." He cupped his hands as if they rested in his palm, reaching toward a memory, "… to sense some of the adventure that must have caused this noble fellow to fall here on this spot." The bitterness of his boyish disappointment was still evident in the man, and had now grown into full-fledged resentment, especially for the science of archeology and its restraints. Suddenly, remembering why he was telling this story, he turned back to his audience.

"Well. That has nothing to do with why we are here. I'll get back to what matters." He prowled the room as he continued.

"There were endowments and investments sufficient to pay for the upkeep of the estate, but I was a sheltered twenty one year old, and was not ready to accept the responsibility of watching over it all. So, leaving all that in the hands of our trusted and very capable managers, I decided to come to America to visit my Aunt Olivia, and try to get a new perspective. She was my mother's sister. We met for the first time when she came back to England for my parents' funeral."

Jesse paused behind Cassie's chair, whether to avoid her eyes she couldn't say, but she turned in her chair to find him looking down at her. He quickly moved on. "I liked what I found in America and after a few weeks I decided to stay on. I felt that the only way I would ever overcome the grief of my childhood and of my parents' deaths was to write it out. I decided to write about the archaeological finds my parents had participated in. I arranged for the managers and solicitors to continue as they were doing with the estate until I got back. But I've never gone back."

He sat down and rubbed his eyes and Cassie saw the scraped, bruised knuckles on his left hand. Meg and Cassie had watched him closely as his story unfolded. Ben was less engrossed in Jesse's words and kept fidgeting and shifting positions. Gillis sat in his chair, his hands behind his head and his feet crossed on his desk, watching them all.

"Now this next part is where it gets a bit sticky. I'm just going to tell it as simply as I can, sticking to the part that applies only to me." He looked at Meg, then Ben, his eyes going from one to the other.

What did he mean by that? Cassie wondered, and looked at Meg for an answer. She received none. Meg's face was mask-like, and she now looked straight ahead. Ben stood up, walked to the window and looked out, then deciding to stay there, turned to look at Jesse. His expression tightened as Jesse got deeper and deeper into the story.

Upon his first arrival in Cherry Lake, Jesse had been surprised to find that his Aunt Olivia had a baby boy about two years of age. Jesse had never heard anyone mention Olivia's husband, though he had heard from his mother that she had gone abroad to marry her one true love, an American serviceman, a Yank as she had called him. She had met the American during his military assignment in England.

But there was no husband in the house in Cherry Lake. Olivia explained only that the baby's father was away a lot. Jesse assumed that there was trouble and that they were separated, and, not wanting to open any emotional wounds, never mentioned it again.

Olivia had encouraged Jesse to stay on in the house with them until he was settled, until he finished writing his book, until he knew what he really wanted to do and where he really wanted to be. She said that was the least she could do for her dead sister.

Jesse's voice cracked when he began to relate the events of the day when he finally met the child's father and learned why he so seldom visited; that he was in fact the man Olivia had come to America to marry. Jesse moved about the room, his face changing from grief to anger, to disgust, to sorrow as he went on.

The baby was by that time four years old. Jesse had come home from the library one day and found Olivia entertaining a guest. The child was playing in the yard and announced proudly, "My dad's here. He brought me these pistols! See? See?" he piped, drawing a small plastic six-shooter from the little leather holster attached to his belt. "Bang-bang!" He shot Jesse point blank, and Jesse obligingly fell to his knees.

The door to the house opened and a tall thin man emerged, holding out a dingy paw for Jesse to shake. "Glad to meet you. You must be Jesse. I'm glad you're here to look after Olivia and the boy. Sorry I can't stay," and he was gone before Jesse could respond.

Olivia was restless and nervous when Jesse entered the house. She poured a half glass of bourbon and drank it down before she turned to face him, waiting for him to speak first.

"Who was that man? He must be a very good friend, concerned as he was about you. He said he was glad I'm here to look after you. Your brave little tyke out there even called him his dad." Olivia said nothing, and Jesse busied himself moving a magazine from a chair, picking it up again, seating himself, crossing and uncrossing his legs while Olivia settled into a chair opposite. He thought about the lonely little boy outside. "Probably misses his real dad. He shot me with his new toy pistol. Good of the fellow to think about a little boy that way."

Olivia, unable to look at Jesse, examined her hands. "He is Jamey's real dad," she said softly.

"That was your husband?" Jesse found himself standing again, struggling to keep his voice under control. "Then why did he leave in such a hurry? Why doesn't he stay and look after you himself, if he is that concerned for your welfare? Couldn't he at least have stayed with his son a little longer?"

"He never can stay very long when he comes. I guess I should tell you, he's not my husband. He's married, was married when we met, actually, but I didn't know it till much later. He has another family." She poured another drink and again gulped it down. She said no more about the visitor and neither did Jesse. He stood gazing at her for some time, wondering how much else there was about her that he didn't know, and probably didn't need or want to know. She was, after all, only his aunt, a woman who had willfully left the family fold years before Jesse was of an age to pay much attention to his relatives and their affairs.

After that day he didn't feel quite the same about living in the house with her, not because he judged her but because he wondered if he was getting in the way of her private life. Before long he had sought and found his house on the mountain in the town of Hartsville where he could be alone and write, and where he could also be near enough to his only remaining relatives in case they ever needed him. He missed his newfound young cousin but was soon able to accept the arrangement as the best solution for all of them.

For some months he visited Olivia and the boy every other weekend. They seemed glad to see him but the child would soon become bored and go on with his playing, in his own little world. From time to time he would encounter the man there, and make his visit very short. The visits grew less and less frequent as the child grew older and became more involved in his own interests and as Olivia became more and more ill at ease, drinking throughout each visit.

Inevitably the time came when the boy was almost always out on his own pursuits when Jesse came, and Olivia was always drunk or entertaining the boy's father, and left him feeling a little unwelcome. It was then, about eight years ago, that the visits ceased altogether.

"I didn't want to desert them, but there seemed to be nothing I could offer. Aunt Olivia seemed to resent the fact that I wouldn't join her in her defeat, and the only way I could help the lad would be to take him from her. Knowing he had a father who also knew me, not to mention the fact that I had become friends with that man's lawful family, I could not do that. These were circumstances that I could not change, so I felt it best to stay away from the situation as much as possible while being near enough to help if I could.

"Once again, I faced my responsibilities like a spoiled child. That other child, though, haunted me. Still haunts me, and probably always will. That child," he paused again and now, standing in front of Meg, looking directly at her, "that little boy who had grown up and left home, is the boy who was found dead. That was Jamey."

Ben stood very still for a beat or two, then spun to face Jesse, taking a few steps toward him with his fists clenched. "You prick!" He shouted. Meg and Gillis both stood to intercept him but Jesse simply faced the boy with his hands at his sides, waiting to accept whatever Ben felt like delivering.

"Ben, calm down now," said Meg. Gillis, now at the boy's side, laid his hand on Ben's arm and said nothing.

"I'm sorry Ben, and I truly mean that. I wish I could have spared Jamey some of his hard times, but I didn't. I didn't know how, but worse than that I didn't really try to find a way. And I'm sorry you had to identify him the other day. If I could have been sure at the time, I would have spared you that."

"How could you not be sure?" Ben blurted. "He was your cousin, for chrissake! And for your information, I considered it an honor to tell the world I knew him. He was my...." Again Meg soothed her son as he stopped abruptly, regaining control of his voice. Very quietly he concluded, "He was my friend."

After a moment Jesse continued. "I hadn't seen Jamey in about eight years. During that time he had grown from a child to a man. I wasn't really sure it was him until I saw his birthmark when we got him to the... to Dr. MeHarg's.... " He couldn't bring himself to finish.

Meg uttered under her breath, "So that's why he looked so familiar." She caught herself and stopped, lest she say more than she wanted Ben to hear.

Cassie, looking at Jesse, now realized that the similarity she had seen in the picture Gillis had shown them was possibly from that kinship between the boy and Jesse. Perhaps, thought Cassie, perhaps after the shock of all this wore off, she would be able to sort out how she felt about it all. Perhaps her heart would not be crying out for Jamey, for Ben, even for Meg. Perhaps Meg's stoicism in the face of Ben's grief would not tear at her soul. Maybe she would find a basis of understanding for Jesse's behavior somewhere in her esteem for her fellow man.

But this moment, as painful as it was, could have taken place at the hotel. Why had Gillis brought them here? Right now she could only stay here and wait for what would come next.

What did come next was even more of a shock. Gillis sat at his desk, again in control of the situation. "I know you're all on edge and short on tolerance right now, I am too, but we still have one more camel to swallow before we can go back to the hotel." He leaned back in his chair and studied the little group before him, perhaps judging their explosive potential or their ability to weather another shock. Then having decided how he would proceed, he did so.

"Meg, I hope you'll forgive me for this, but I don't know any other way to do it. I want you to tell me what you know about your husband, what has happened with him over the last few years, if you don't mind. Now you don't have to say a word, mind you, and if you don't that's fine. But it would help if you'll talk to us."

"Why shouldn't I talk to you about it? Everybody else in this town probably already knows. Jack Dothard walked out on me more years ago than I care to count. Just like a lot of other men who have to be away from their wives for a long time, he found another interest. It doesn't matter how it happened though, because he never really was with us, you know, not really like a husband and father ought to be. After he came home from the service he was always gone off on the road selling stuff, or taking jobs here and there, and we saw him every now and then." Ben had walked up beside her and placed his arm around her shoulder.

Meg reached up and patted his hand before she went on. "He learned real quick that I didn't want any part time husband, but blast his soul, he was the only daddy Ben ever had or ever would have. Every two or three weeks when he came back this way I made sure he and Ben got to spend some time together somehow. I still do to this day. Oh, he knows to keep out of sight of the neighbors. I don't want to let on to the people in this town how often that man shows up after dark on my door step, and I let him come in and spend the night on my sofa, several nights in a row if he wants to, just so Ben can be with his daddy. A sorry daddy is better than no daddy at all, as Papa used to say. That's all I have to say about Jack Dothard."

"Ben, what about you? How do you feel about him?" Gillis asked.

"He's my dad. He may not be the best man in the world, but I can't change that. Whatever he's done over the years, he'll just have to live with it. All I have to do is remember who he is to me and what he once was to my mom. I don't have to judge him."

Four pairs of eyes rested on the boy's face, seeing again the man he was rapidly becoming.

"Well, Jack is back there in a cell—no, he's not under arrest, just that there's a place to sit back there while he waited for us to get through all this other. Now I'm going to bring him out here, and he's going to tell you some things you may not know, and in fact you may not want to know, but they are going to come out anyway so it's best if you know them up front. Then we'll leave you three alone for awhile if you want us to, Meg, or we'll stay, however you want it. But if I do leave you alone with him, you can't kill him. You have to promise me that." This drew a little ripple of laughter from the group, and they all relaxed just a bit as Gillis went back to fetch Jack Dothard.

Jack came into the room with his head down, and when he raised it to face them, Cassie hid her smile behind a gloved hand. Her eyes found Jesse's and she mouthed, "Good job!" For the shiner Jack sported around his left eye and the purplish bruise on his chin were clearly the calling card of a man in search of a reckoning. Jesse rubbed his bruised knuckles.

"Go ahead, Jack. Tell it like you want to. If you want to talk to Meg and Ben alone first, you can."

"No, it will probably be easier telling everybody. I'll have to face it sooner or later anyway," he began. "Meg, I never wanted to hurt you.

181

I always loved you, but you always seemed too strong and too high minded for me, especially after I came home from the service. Please try to understand what I'm going to say, now. While I was over in England...."

"Don't tell that in front of Ben. I've known about all that from before you ever came home. Your vicious sister over in Cherry Lake couldn't wait to tell me. She has told me all about everything that went on over there ever since. Didn't you know, you fool, that those two women were best friends, and she just delighted in rubbing it in every chance she got?"

Jack looked pained, even more so than the bruises would account for. "No, I didn't know about that. And you never told?"

"No, I never told. And you won't, either." She reached for Ben's hand.

Ben, making that last giant step out of his youth, stepped in and took over the conversation. "Okay, guys, let's be honest here. Mom, remember the day Jamey came to the house with me, waited in the living room for me to get my stuff?" Meg nodded, looking at Gillis, expecting him to ask why she had withheld this little tidbit. But Gillis wasn't paying her any attention. He looked at Ben and waited for him to go on.

"Well. He looked at the pictures you keep sitting around in there. After we left he asked who the man was with you and me in those pictures and I told him it was my dad. He got really quiet for a long time, and when I asked him why he had asked about my dad he said, 'Because unless I'm badly mistaken, he's my dad too.' We talked a lot about him over the next few days, compared notes on when we saw him and so on, and Jamey showed me a more recent picture of him." He looked now at Jack. "Finally, I followed you one day when you left our house and sure enough, you went straight to the address in Cherry Lake where Jamey's mom lives. So I know all about that part." He let his eyes rest on Jack's face for a moment, as if to let him know that he was exposed, that Ben had seen him true and whole, and was making no excuses for him. "Now is there anything else you want to tell us, Dad?"

"Only that I'm sorry, Ben. Meg, I'm sorry."

"Yes, Jack, you always have been sorry, only I didn't see it in time. Don't ask me to forgive you. Forgiveness implies caring, and I haven't cared a whit for you in years." She gathered up her gloves as if to go, knowing full well she couldn't leave until Gillis gave permission, but still the gesture made her point. It would do until she could do better.

Gillis stood up and walked around the little office, sometimes looking out the window, sometimes at his guests, while he talked. "Well, we've uncovered a little more of the story here, but there's a lot more to it yet that we don't have. Like, where is the car that hit Jamey, if he was hit? If he wasn't hit, what was he doing along that road at that hour?" He shoved his hands in his pockets and paced.

"We're a long way ahead but not home yet. We still have to find out who was the last person to see Jamey alive. I've asked a few people but nobody I've had a chance to question saw him after one or two in the afternoon. Ben, how about you? I haven't talked to you yet, but now I need to. Why don't all the rest of you just make yourselves comfortable, and Ben and I'll go back into one of the cells and talk." So saying he guided Ben through the door to the cellblock.

Ben never looked back, but Meg couldn't hold back a gasp, a sob. Cassie handed her a tissue, which she took and used to dab at her eyes.

Jesse intervened. "Meg, there's something else. Gillis and I have already talked about this and Ben doesn't need to know it right now. It needs to be kept really quiet, but you two need to know it because you might be able to help resolve the issue of Janet Wright.

"Last week I got a letter from Albert Goggans, the estate manager back home, telling me I need to come back and look after some things, but he also told me about a young lady who had been working there for a few years, a girl named Janet Wright. He said she looks just like Olivia did when she was that age. Then he told me that Aunt Olivia had been pregnant when Jack left England. She went away somewhere for a couple of years, then came back without the child and pretty soon started making arrangements to follow Jack back here. Goggans felt like Olivia had put the child up for adoption. He told me about it so that I would be prepared in case there was some later dispute over the inheritance or something. That's one of the reasons I have to go back."

Cassie, doing quick calculations, said, "If Janet Wright is Olivia's and Jack Dothard's daughter, then Ben has a sister, too."

Meg said, "He doesn't want to know that and neither do I. Just keep it to yourself, Jesse, if you find out it's true." She glanced at the door Gillis and Ben had gone through, and as if on cue they opened it and came back into the room.

"Okay, that's done. Everything's all right, Meg. Ben says he saw Jamey with the theater people, trying on the donkey's head. A little later, he thinks it was about two thirty, Jamey left the hotel. He saw Jamey and that new girl, Wendy, get into her car. That's all we know, until I can talk to Wendy."

"I talked with her a little bit that first afternoon," Cassie began, looking at Ben. He barely nodded, and she went on. "Wendy and Ben had been talking in the kitchen when I came in to see if I could help with the food. It must be pretty difficult, getting all those people fed without a lot of help."

"Not really. A lot of what I fix for lunch and supper is out of the freezer," he said.

"I'm glad to hear that, then," said Cassie, not believing him for a minute. She had seen him at work in his kitchen and very few other places during their stay at the hotel. She was silent for a moment, thinking that her own refrigerator, without the benefit of a backup generator such as the hotel had, might be in pretty bad shape before they were able to go home again.

Bringing her thoughts back to the present, she turned to Gillis and finished her observation. "Wendy got very upset at something that passed between her and Ben, or maybe she had just reached the point where she couldn't handle anymore, and ran crying to her room. I followed her and we talked a little while." She told them what Wendy had told her about the last afternoon of Jamey's life. "She said they left the hotel together but then they went their separate ways early in the day. She had things to do and he was on his way to visit somebody, but if she knew who it was, she didn't say."

After a little pause Gillis said, "Well, let's hope we can find out who that someone was." He turned to Cassie again. "Do you want to tell them about that other business at the hotel? No, on second thought, I think that can wait until after I talk to Ike and Evelyn personally."

"I think that would be best," Cassie said. "So far the atmosphere up there is calm. Everybody's just waiting. It's as if life is suspended until the snow melts and communications are restored." To Jesse she said, "We even had the actors put on a show for the residents last night. I took a lot of pictures, and I think I got at least one shot of everybody, in case anyone wants copies to remind them of this delightful little interlude."

Gillis looked long at her, then asked, "Where are those films?"

"Nate and I developed them down at his office last night. The pictures are up at the hotel."

Gillis looked thoughtful for a few seconds then turned to Jesse. "Didn't you tell me you talked to a woman in a diner at Cherry Lake who mentioned a girl who visited Olivia?"

Jesse grinned at Meg. "She's the woman Meg mentioned awhile ago. Jack's vicious sister."

Meg uttered "Hmmmf!" and busied herself smoothing the wrinkles from her dungarees.

Gillis stood up and said to Meg, "I want to bring her over here if I can get her to come. I'd like for her to see those pictures and then maybe go up to the hotel to see if she can identify anybody there as that girl without being recognized too soon."

"Oh, I can make her unrecognizable, if that's what you want," said Meg.

"No, Meg, not that way," Gillis chuckled along with the others. "What I was thinking was, Cassie, you try to get those actors to do another skit or two tonight. We can arrange the lighting so that it will be sort of dark in some part of the lounge. So if you don't want to see her, Meg, you can stay in your room. I just want her to see if that girl happens to be one of the girls up at the hotel, without tipping her off that we're onto her yet. We may be looking in the wrong town."

"I'm not going to let that nosey busybody cheat me out of another thing in this life." Meg cast a look at Jack that he must have felt as solidly as a blow. "It's through her you got your English...." She looked at Jesse, changed her course, and concluded, "English girlfriend over here."

"Well, yes," muttered Jack, "But I didn't have anything to do with that. Amelia went through some odds and ends I had left there and found Olivia's address in a letter she had written to me after I told her I was coming back home. They wrote back and forth some. I think she did encourage Olivia to come," he kept his eyes downcast as he spoke, never looking at Meg, caught in yet another deception.

"Oh, well, that makes it all right, doesn't it?" She arranged herself so that she seemed to be looking down her nose at Jack in spite of the fact that she was seated and he was not. "At least you didn't bring your odds and ends to my house."

"Okay, okay!" Gillis moved between them. "Meg, if you're going to be present tonight you have to promise to behave."

She looked up at him with a mischievous twinkle and raised her right palm. "Scout's honor," she swore.

Cassie glanced at Meg and thought, *Oh, my God! He can't do this to her!* Quickly she suggested, "Gillis, have you thought about just taking the pictures to the woman first? I mean, if you really want to spare her life. I don't like the look in Meg's eye."

"I did think of it. But do you think she'll be willing to talk to us honestly on her own turf? If we bring her here, she may take us more seriously. Because, if she's as scheming as you say...."

Jack moved from the wall he was leaning on to say, "If I go, she'll cooperate with you. If you act like you suspect me, she'd tell you just about anything to change your mind."

"Well, we certainly don't want that," Jesse declared. "We want her to be straightforward and honest, not defensive or scared."

"Scared she won't be, unless you bring her over here," said Meg. "What you can do is, take the pictures over there, and before she looks at them, just mention that if none of the people in those pictures look familiar to her, then you will have to ask her to come over here in a helicopter and see if that girl is at the hotel. She never did like flying, except maybe on a broom. If you mention bringing her over in a helicopter it would scare her spitless."

"Okay, we can do it that way. Jesse, you will go with me. Cassie, we'll take you and Meg back to the hotel. And we'll take Ben back, too. Jack, you can stay here or at the hotel, and we'll still let her know you're a suspect. I'm not locking you up right now because I don't think you'd get very far in this snow. But," he pointed a forefinger at Jack's nose, "You'd better be here when I get back. Understand?" The indicated nose rose and fell in an affirmative nod.

"Good. Now let's get up to the hotel and pick out some of those photos," Gillis said, looking at Jesse. He opened the door to the sheriff's office where Bernard had waited while they talked, and asked the driver to join them. "Let's take the ladies and Ben back to the hotel, and then after lunch, do you think you can drive us over to Cherry Lake, or should I radio for the chopper?" Gillis was becoming accustomed to being in charge and having Bernard and his powerful vehicle always there to drive them wherever they needed to go, but he need not forget that Bernard didn't even work for him.

"I will be happy to do that, and I think the van can get us there and back. I will hurry. I like working with the sheriff to enforce the law."

Twenty-five

Cassie worried all the way back to the hotel. What would she say to Jesse about his letters and the uninvited visitor to his room? She had to tell him, before he missed them, that she had brought the letters into her room and was keeping them for him. *What if he didn't mean what I thought he meant about the family treasure? He'll think I'm a fool,* she thought, and felt as if he may be right in that thinking.

The passengers in the van were quiet, most of them gazing out at the sun now glistening on the snow. All the clouds had gone at last and the sky was that deep intense blue that is usually seen only in October or sometimes on an especially fine day in February. How, wondered Cassie, could a day so beautiful have harbored so much pain?

Arriving at the hotel, Cassie hung back until she could speak only to Jesse. In a few softly spoken words she told him she needed to talk with him in private as soon as possible. She wasn't sure he heard her, so weary were his eyes.

Gillis raised his brows over devilish blue eyes as she passed him. "Anything I should know?" he asked.

"I don't know, that's up to Jesse," she muttered, following Ben into the hotel.

They were greeted by the other guests with every kind of response, from curious glances to bold questions.

"What's going on?" asked one.

"Where have you been?" asked another.

"What have you found out?" asked yet another, all of them in unison.

When they began to realize that Jack Dothard was among the new arrivals, those who knew him surrounded him with reserved handshakes and stilted greeting, a few of them enquiring about his travels and his general well being, but none asking about his black eye and bruises.

Slipping his hand under Cassie's elbow, Jesse led her through the crowd and toward the stairs. "You sounded urgent back there. Do we need to talk right now or can it wait until I get cleaned up?"

"There is one thing I need to say right now, but the rest can wait. It won't take long."

"Then let's go to my room, or yours if you prefer. If you can tolerate being around such a scruff as I must look right now."

"My room," she decided quickly, as she had the letters in there and was eager to return them to him.

As soon as they were inside and the door closed she motioned him to a chair. "Sit here. This chair is comfortable but it looks like it needs some attention to its upholstery. I'm surprised Ike hasn't done something about that," she said, taking the desk chair for herself.

"He will eventually, I'm sure," was Jesse's only response. "You had something you wanted to say to me?"

Now she was at a loss. Not knowing where to begin, she plunged right into the middle. "Gillis gave me a message he said you sent to me. I wasn't sure what it meant, but it did bring to mind something you said the day we arrived. Exactly what was it you said to him?"

He was quiet for a moment as if trying to remember, then said, "Yes, I did ask him to tell you something. Remember when we were talking about locking up our valuables, and I told you the only things I had of any value were a couple of letters?" Cassie nodded and he continued. "That is what I was referring to. I brought them to read over again while we were confined here, as the contents of both were sort of disturbing. Now it seems they may provide information that might or might not play a major role in Jamey's death, and probably Aunt Olivia's as well. If they did have a bearing on these deaths, then someone here at the hotel might have reason to look for anything that could be used as evidence. Since both are my relatives, my room would be the logical place to search. I just need to see again, in this new light, what information is really in them. It wouldn't need to fall into the wrong hands."

She nodded in relief. "That's what I thought you meant." Now that she was on a little surer footing, she relaxed. "At first I didn't want to bother anything in your room without being sure, but someone had already been in there. They knocked a vase over and the noise made me go to investigate. I heard someone running down the hall but have no idea who it was. Then I went into your room and saw the vase knocked over. Later on when Gillis told me what you said, I remembered the letters and went back in to get them. They're here," she said, searching through the stack of papers on the desk. She handed him the envelopes and stood up.

"Would you like a cup of herbal tea? I always keep a heating coil and some bags close at hand, especially when I travel." As she spoke, she was already preparing the cups.

"Yes, thanks. Then, if you don't mind, I think I'll get cleaned up, maybe rest a bit before I go downstairs again. While I'm doing that, why don't you read these and then later we'll talk more about it. I couldn't concentrate on them right now, and anyway, I'd like to get your thoughts about them," he said, and handed the letters back to her. "I'll get them back after you've done with them."

"All right, then," she said, relieved that he was not upset.

When Jesse had finished his tea and left her, Cassie, in the quiet and privacy of her room, sat down in the chair he had vacated and withdrew the pages from the first envelope, the one from England.

It started with a formal greeting to Jesse, then went on; "As you know, the present managers are getting on in years, and I may not have many more years left of my own, though I do seem to be more tenacious in my hold on mortality than most. Some of your finest staff are even now looking at retirement.

"I feel it my duty to your worthy father to share with you a little of your own family's history, which I will do in the form of several diaries that are now in my hands for safekeeping. There are many things that need your attention here, and my purpose in writing now is to attempt to influence you to make a trip to the family holdings in the near future.

"There is a separate matter that you should be made privy to, and as there is not a family member left who holds the same knowledge, I humbly ask your forgiveness for mentioning it. The information to which I refer is contained in the diaries mentioned above."

The letter continued on at some length, relating those things Jesse had already told them, and Cassie read with growing interest to the last page. "When you have completed your travel arrangements and have established a time of arrival at Heathrow, it would be an honor for me to arrange transportation and lodging for you in London and onward to the estate."

It was signed, simply, Albert Goggans.

Cassie sat in deep thought for some time before replacing the pages in their envelope. Then, opening the other letter, she quickly realized it had come from Olivia, and bore traces of smearing from droplets of some liquid, whether tears or drink Cassie could not determine. As she scanned the single page, she read only that a young woman had been staying with her, and had become a nuisance at times. She had asked the girl to leave and although she hadn't seen her for several days, she was fearful that she might return. She wanted Jesse to find out what steps she could take to insure that the young woman would not be allowed to bother her in the future.

Cassie didn't know how long she sat there with thoughts and realizations galloping into her consciousness. It all pointed in one direction, yet how would she obtain proof? And though there was nothing to connect any one person with Jamey's death, she knew there must be a connection there.

She was casting about for some idea of what she should do when Jesse came back, with Gillis in tow. Jesse looked somewhat fresher if not completely refreshed. "Gillis accosted me as I was leaving my room. I hope you don't mind me bringing him?" Jesse said as he settled himself into the lumpy depths of batting and crossed his legs. "Bring me up to date with what's been going on here while I was away, Cassie."

As Gillis listened, Cassie told Jesse of her research and discoveries of the last few days, ending with "If Ike is running an antique's scam, and it really looks as if he is, was Jamey helping him? And did he maybe threaten to spill the beans so that Ike had to silence him?"

"That could be the case," Gillis said. "What else have you got?"

Cassie considered for a moment. She was in no way ready to discuss the things that were on her mind as a result of those letters. She didn't like not sharing them with Gillis, but to tell him would, in some way it seemed, betray a confidence Jesse had shared with her. She shifted in her chair and said, "Let's just take each one of the staff, excluding Ben. Evelyn seemed to me at one time to have a certain interest in Jamey, young as he is, or was, and she was away from the hotel that afternoon. Do you think she may have met up with him after he left Wendy, maybe got into an argument and somehow managed to kill him? She may have been lying about the time she came home."

"Possible, but I don't see that her having a thing for him would make her kill him. Unless, of course, it could have been an accident."

"Given," said Cassie. "Let's see then. There's Bernard and Wendy. According to one of the girls in the troupe, Bernard 'fancied' Wendy." She sketched the quotes in the air with her fingers. "I have noticed him staying close to her when he is here, but she just walks away looking pretty fed up. Could he have been jealous of her leaving with Jamey?"

"Maybe," said Gillis, "but do you think he'd kill a boy over something that simple?"

"I don't know," Jesse answered. "I hardly know the man. What do you know about him, anyway? For instance, where does he live? Where does he work?"

"Evelyn says he had quit his job here at the hotel, planning to go back out to the Rockies for the skiing season there, but for some reason he didn't go. She thinks it was because of Wendy. He came back and wanted his job back, she said, but then Ike had already hired Jamey and wouldn't let him go just to please Bernard. And we already know that Jamey and Wendy were friendly, so maybe Bernard felt like Jamey was just too much in his way."

Gillis looked at her for a moment, then said, "Maybe so. But he just doesn't act like a guilty person. Let's leave that for a minute."

"Okay," said Cassie. "Did you find out anything about the automobile registrations?"

"They're going to get back with me when they can. There are just too few lines available right now. That information may be waiting for me at the station." He stood, preparing to leave. "I'll meet you downstairs in a few minutes, Jesse, unless you need a nap first?"

Jesse shook his head and made a dismissive gesture. "I got about twenty winks of sleep just now. That should carry me for a few more hours." Gillis turned, smiled and winked at Cassie, and left.

Jesse uncrossed his ankles and leaned forward, lacing his fingers together. "There's something I should tell you so you don't put yourself into danger. Ike's furniture transactions have been a matter of interest to me for some time. It wasn't Jamey helping him, though. It was Jack Dothard. I've been attending the auctions for several months and getting photos of the pieces they bought and sold. I've not yet had a chance to find their headquarters, so to speak, but I'll get around to that later."

"You? What are you doing investigating crimes? Are you a private detective, or insurance investigator or something?" Cassie asked, disbelieving.

"If Ike has bought the hotel intact, then the furniture is his anyway and there's no crime in selling what is yours. It is possible, though, that the hotel is owned by someone else, someone who hired Ike. In that case, we may have a crime. But I'm interested only as an amateur. The first time I saw them doing a deal, I couldn't believe it. From then on, they became a project of mine. That's how I knew how to find Jack Dothard, actually. Followed him home from an auction one night." He gave her an evil grin. "You, my dear girl, aren't Hartsville's only curious writer, to use a tactful term for what we Brits call a nosey parker, you know. I've even thought of writing a detective novel based on just this situation one day."

"Does Gillis know about Ike and Jack Dothard's activities?"

Standing, Jesse replied, "Not yet, at least not all of it. I'll probably tell him the whole story soon, though. But that's enough for now. Let's get downstairs and select those snapshots. We need to go find some lunch, too." He took her hands in his as she rose, and held them while he looked into her eyes. "But before we join the others, there is something I need to say. I want you to know how happy I am that you came back to Hartsville, Cass. I've always liked the town, but until you came I could be here or anywhere else, and never miss the place. But while I was off struggling through the ice and snow, I always felt warm and smelled cinnamon whenever I thought of you."

She looked at his serious face and his eyes that were the color of brown velvet, and saw in their depths a trace of Matt. *But Matt's eyes were sky blue*, she thought. There was much she wanted to say and some she wanted to do, but when she felt a blush creeping across her cheeks she reclaimed her hands and removed their empty cups. "Thank you. You flatter me," she said, allowing him a smile as she walked to the door, adding, "let's get back downstairs, then." From behind her she heard Jesse mutter something about safety in numbers, as they started back down to the lobby and the crowd.

They were the last ones down for lunch. Meg had finished her meal and gone. Gillis and Bernard were lingering over coffee, but joined Cassie and Jesse when they had filled their plates and settled down to eat.

When they had finished, Jesse used his napkin, pushed back his chair and said, "Let's be on our way. Jack's sister will be delighted to see me again, I'm sure," he said, smiling down at Cassie.

"I'll get you those pictures." Cassie was out of her chair and on her way as she spoke. At the desk, Wendy handed her the packet as Cassie asked, "Evelyn taking a break?"

"Yeah, she was feeling a bit done in. Should be back here before too long, though." Cassie hurried back to the dining room, handed the envelope to Gillis saying, "Just pick out the ones you want." As he looked, she said to Jesse, "You should have been here for that revue. It was really very well done. Those actors are professionals, I'll have to say that for them."

"That could throw a spanner in the works as far as this investigation is concerned, then," Jesse commented. "If our culprit is among them, he or she may be able to cover any tracks quite well with a nice little performance."

Gillis had selected the photographs he wanted to take with him, making sure he had pictures of as many of the actors, the residents and the staff as he could account for and the men set out for their visit to Amelia Pitts.

Twenty-six

The afternoon sun did little to warm the landscape as Jesse and Gillis, with Bernard in tow, arrived at the coffee shop in Cherry Lake, ushering in a flow of cold air as they entered. Jesse and Gillis moved up to the counter while Bernard assumed his watchful position near the door. The same woman Jesse had seen on his previous visit was again behind the counter, looking as if time had stood still between his visits.

"You here again? Did you ever talk to your Aunt Olivia? No, I don't imagine you did, though. Lorelei told me they took somebody out from Olivia's house on a stretcher. Had 'em so wrapped up she couldn't see who it was, but since Olivia lives by herself, I expect it was her. If you haven't seen her you might try the hospitals," she said to Jesse. "Lorelei said there was some man poking around there the other day. Reckon that was you."

"Probably so. Mrs. Pitts, this is Deputy Gillis from Hartsville. Perry, this is Amelia Pitts. You've met her brother, Jack Dothard."

Gillis acknowledged the introduction with a nod in her direction. "Mrs. Pitts. You don't look much like your brother. That's Bernard over by the door. He drove us over here," Gillis said, wondering what Jesse thought he was doing, acting so clever and stealing his thunder. Well, to give him his due, he had set the scene up well.

Amelia cast guarded looks at them. "How do you know my name? How do you know I'm Jack's sister?"

"Oh, Jack and I have spent a little time together," said Jesse. "He's told me about everything...you know." He tilted his head back, indicating some place or time not specified and grinned conspiratorially at the woman, who relaxed and smiled back at him.

"Stop calling me Mrs. Pitts," said the woman. "Just call me Amelia," she said, holding out her hand for Gillis to shake.

"Amelia," Jesse began, "who is this Lorelei you mentioned before?"

"Olivia's next door neighbor. You must have seen her around up there."

Jesse stared at her. "The only woman I've come in contact with up there could never be named Lorelei."

"That's her, then. That's not her real name. We all call her that because she is so god-awfully, shall we say, unappealing."

"Jesse, you can interrogate her, if it comes down to that."

"Not even if you deputize me, Officer Gillis."

Perry, feeling the ice was about as cracked as it would get, said, "Mrs. Pitts, is it true that Jack Dothard is your brother?" establishing his authority beyond question.

Fear made her eyes grow wary and distant again. She hesitated a moment then nodded.

"Then it is my duty to tell you that your brother is at this moment under house arrest in Hartsville in connection with what might be a serious crime. Of course, there are others we'll need to talk to as well, and some we still need to identify." He drew out the photographs and spread them on the counter.

"First though, Amelia," he changed tactics so smoothly she didn't notice, "I'd like a cup of your famous coffee, and one for Jesse here, and Bernard of course. Pour one for yourself if you'd like. Then I'd appreciate it if you'd just look at these pictures and see if there is a face you've seen before."

The coffee was served, then the pictures scooped up and taken nearer the light. A loud nervous cackle escaped her as she pointed to one of the snapshots. "That looks kinda like a lot of people I know," she said, showing them the likeness of Bottom, complete with donkey's head. Jesse cringed, dreading the fun and games he feared would come before they got the answers to their questions. After comments about Regan's hair being a wig, Puck being a real fairy, and several other inane observations, she said, "None of them look like anybody I know. Sorry. Who are these people, anyway?" she said, flipping back through the pictures.

Jesse said, "We have a troupe of Shakespearean actors at the hotel in Hartsville right now. These pictures are from a little revue they produced for the local residents who are snowbound up there." When she had finished with the stack of photos she tapped them on edge on the counter, and Jesse took them from her and replaced them in their envelope, putting the envelope in his inside coat pocket. Soon they thanked her for her help and said goodbye.

They were quiet on their way back to Hartsville, where they stopped at the jail for Gillis to check for any messages, found none, and then began the slippery climb back up to the hotel.

There was a lot that Gillis wanted to say to Jesse, but although Bernard had been present as driver during much of the investigation, he had heard nothing about Jesse's connection to the case. Gillis wanted it to stay that way for now, because when they had approached the van on leaving the coffee shop, Gillis had, for the first time, paid attention to the car itself.

The vehicle they now rode in, the one that had carried them over every mile they had traveled for the past several days, was well worn, dented, scratched and otherwise damaged. It could so easily be the one that had struck Jamey down. It could be just as Cassie had suggested. Jamey had taken Bernard's place, his job, at the hotel, leaving Bernard without steady employment, and he, Bernard, had stayed on in Hartsville at least partly because of Wendy. There could have been a lot of bad blood between these two over the job and over the girl that no one knew about. A double motive, so to speak. And yet, Bernard was so very helpful! Was he perhaps too helpful? Was he doing this just so he could keep aware of how the investigation was going? If so, he, Gillis, would have to approach this carefully in order to catch the culprit before he fled. He determined to question Bernard privately as soon as they reached the hotel.

But as it turned out, his plans were changed.

Twenty-seven

When Gillis and Jesse were gone, Cassie went back to her room and sat in the overstuffed chair for a long time, again deep in thought. She had confided in Meg about everything involved with this case so far, and although it would be nice to get Meg's point of view in the light of what had transpired earlier down at the jail, she could not violate Jesse's confidence.

Her thoughts turned then to the words Jesse had spoken before he left the room earlier. Again she saw the color of his eyes and the depth of something behind them. Something akin to....

Stop it, she told herself. *You can't have these thoughts about another man yet. Matt's death is still unresolved, and you must keep your mind on him.* Then, with her hands in her lap, she touched the forefingers and the thumbs of each hand together, forming a diamond shape, and gazed into the opening as she centered her thoughts. She had learned that technique years ago and found that it helped her concentrate when her mind would start to drift away from some nursing lecture she was supposed to be hearing or the problem she was trying to solve.

At last, having no idea how much time had passed, she was almost certain she had solved at least part of the riddle of the car in the jail's parking lot and began to devise a plan by which she could find out for sure if she was right. At last she settled on one plan of action; one that seemed to be both safe and effective.

Without disturbing Meg, she put on her warmest clothing and went downstairs. When she passed the receptionist's desk, Wendy, seeing Evelyn coming down the stairs, gathered up her coat and purse, saying to Cassie, "Where are you off to, all wrapped up for the North Pole?"

Cassie slowed only a moment. "Just thought I'd go out and see how the snow people are faring. A breath or two of that cold, fresh air might be just what I need to clear out the cobwebs." She hoped Wendy didn't offer to join her, as she wanted to be alone for this part of her plan. She hurried through the foyer and pulled the door shut behind her as she stepped outside.

The melting snow was dripping down from the roof forming icicles, but the cold was still bone deep. She walked along the veranda from end to end, gazing out across the expanse of snow-covered lawn. At the west end she left the veranda and began to walk toward the end of the building. Reaching the corner, she continued along the length of the west wing, around something that looked like an incinerator, then past a small greenhouse, until she found herself on the rear lawn of the hotel.

Not having found what she was looking for yet, she strolled along the lawn, pausing from time to time to gaze out across the valley toward the Christ figure in the distance, unhurriedly for the sake of any eyes that might be watching. Even in the warm clothing she had put on, she was beginning to feel the cold on her feet as snow had crept over the tops of her boots when she came through one of the heavier drifts. She passed the snowman and his little family and paused to restore their shapes, patting on small clumps of snow.

She didn't hesitate as she passed the woodworking shop where she had found the dowels and the furniture, but at the carriage house she opened the door just a crack to peek inside. The players must all be inside the hotel napping, she decided, for the building was empty and cold.

Moving on around the end of the east wing, she finally found what she wanted to see. A tall scraggly hedge stood ahead of her, and beyond that she glimpsed a small, secluded parking lot. There were only a few cars parked there, all of familiar makes and models that she could probably remember long enough to write them down later. She scolded herself for not bringing along pen and paper, then consoled herself with the thought that it would not have been wise anyway. If someone saw her taking notes of the automobiles parked here, they would certainly become suspicious.

There was an old black Cadillac, which she assumed would belong to Evelyn. A tan Chevrolet pickup truck with a camper shell which Ike would probably use to transport furniture stood beside a little blue Gremlin, almost covered by snow, indicating that it hadn't been moved since the snow began. Beyond the Gremlin sat a red Volkswagen beetle with its rear compartment cover open. Cassie remembered that a Volkswagen's engine is in the rear compartment, and surmised that the car was not in running condition.

She didn't bother trying to remember the license plate numbers. Numbers were anathema to her, had always been, and anyway, Gillis already had them. Her intention now was just to help him a little bit, perhaps move things along faster.

From somewhere behind her she heard a door closing, and moved back a few steps to see if anyone had come out, wondering if whoever it was had followed her. Wendy was walking in the snow, looking around as if searching for something or someone. *Drat!* thought Cassie, but maybe some good could come of this anyway. She might learn just a bit more, if she was careful. Cassie kept walking, angling off toward the kitchen door. "I see you've been relieved at the desk. I'm just going to look for a cup of cocoa. Want to join me?"

"Sure. What are you doing out here in the snow, anyway?" Wendy said.

"It's like I told you, just getting a breath of fresh air. I've walked almost all the way around the hotel and was just looking at all those cars parked over there. Is that the staff parking lot?"

"Yes, we park back there most of the time. We like to leave the front parking spaces open for hotel guests."

"I like that big old black Caddy. Who drives it?" Cassie asked, feigning nonchalance.

"That's Evelyn's."

"I'll bet the truck is Ike's, isn't it?"

"Yes. American men seem to love their trucks, don't they?"

"They surely do. And let's see. The little blue one. Is that yours?"

203

"No, that one is Ben's. He doesn't drive it much, though. He uses Ike's truck to pick up things from the market, those things that are not delivered. When he goes out for fun, he usually walks. He loves the outdoors. He loves to cook, but he says that being shut in the kitchen all the time is the very worst thing about his job. Likes to walk, does our Ben."

"Then the Volkswagen is yours? Why is the engine cover open? Or did you know it is open?"

"That one is—was—Jamey's, bless him. It hadn't run in several days. He was having some sort of problem with it and was waiting until he could get some new part for it. Guess he left it open."

"Oh. That's why he rode into town with you then, isn't it? He must have had plans for somebody to meet him somewhere."

"Maybe. I wouldn't know."

"Where do you park your car, then?" Cassie asked, at last getting to the question she had wanted to ask first, but she felt she had to work up to it. When Wendy didn't answer she changed her question. "Did you leave it in town for some reason?" She heard her own words come back to her, and thought, uh-oh! Have I been too obvious? Did I say too much?

But Wendy was no longer interested in talking about the cars. "I came out to get something from Ike's shop. Want to come in with me and see what all's there? It's interesting, if you like woodworking. And antiques." She took the lock from the hasp and opened the door. Stepping up into the shop she turned back and reached for Cassie's hand.

Cassie wasn't sure what happened next. She was aware, though, that she missed her footing and fell face forward into the shop, her previously injured leg striking sharply against the threshold, tearing a deep gash in the skin along the front of her leg, her kneecap taking the weight of her body as it pitched forward. Sickening pain paralyzed and blinded her for a long moment and consciousness almost left her. When the pain subsided a little, she realized Wendy had either lifted or pulled her into the shop, and she was lying on her back. Wendy was folding a tarp, which she placed under Cassie's head as a pillow.

"You fell. And you've hurt yourself." She knelt beside Cassie and began palpating the leg. "I don't know if it's broken or not. Here. Let me do this. We learned it in First Aid class at school." She took a roll of electrical tape from one of the work tables and began splinting Cassie's injured leg to the good one, as she continued talking in a comforting, purring tone. The words were lost on Cassie's pain-wracked consciousness until Wendy muttered, "People who want to hurt me always seem to end up getting hurt themselves. Strange, isn't it?"

Cassie at last heard the menace that lay in the voice behind Wendy's words. "What do you mean? Who are you talking about?"

"I told you. Mr. Wright, of course. The old man I told you about, when I was just a child. He hurt me badly, but he paid for it in the end."

"Wright? Janet Wright! *You're* Janet Wright, aren't you? That's your car in Gillis' parking lot!"

Wendy laughed. "You might say that. But you'd be wrong. There's a lot more to it than that."

Pain shot through Cassie like an electrical current as Wendy made one last adjustment with the tape and released her hold on the injured leg, and she cried out in spite of her efforts not to. When the splinting was done, she lay back and closed her eyes, willing the pain away.

It was only when the girl began taping her wrists together that Cassie realized Wendy wasn't trying to help her at all, but was in fact binding her. "What are you doing? What's wrong with you!"

She struggled against the force of Wendy's grip until Wendy leveled a commanding look at her and said, "Would you like for me to make sure your leg is broken? Be still!"

Cassie stopped struggling. She was weak and nauseated from the pain in her knee and leg, and the realization that she was now also at the mercy of a deranged person was overwhelming.

Wendy was talking again. "He was out in the field one day on his tractor. It turned over and pinned him underneath. Oh, he was begging me to help him when that tractor was on top of him, but I couldn't think of any way to help him. It reminded me of the way I'd cry when he was on top of me. Going to find someone else to help him would have taken too long, and it wouldn't have saved him anyway. I was happy to know I'd never have to help him again. It was almost healing, watching him die. Watching him squirm and scream in pain was sort of a payback to me. But I got my due out of him that day."

"What do you mean? How?" Keep talking, Cassie said to herself. Someone will come.

"After he died I went searching for his money, found several thousand pounds in a box with some old letters, and along with it I found the birth certificate of a little girl named Janet Wright. I had seen her grave out by the field. She was born the same year I was, but she only lived two weeks. She deserved a longer life than that, I thought, so I became her. That way we could both have a better life. That day I stopped being Wendy and began being Janet Wright."

Cassie's blood ran cold at the sound of Wendy's words. The girl was not only completely mad; her madness held a murderous tendency. She also knew that she might never get a chance to either help her or bring her to justice, or to protect anyone else from the tortured, sick mind, let alone help herself. The pain in her leg was intense, and fear was a mouse gnawing at her innards. It wouldn't take very long for her to die of exposure out here in this frigid building, weak with pain and unable to move about. Every time she struggled, Wendy hurt the injured leg again, and Cassie didn't doubt that she would break it if she had to.

"And Olivia paid, too," Wendy was saying. "Oh, but wait. You don't know about her, do you? Olivia is my mother. And Jamey's mother, too." Cassie's mind reeled with that revelation, but she kept quiet, listening as well as she could. "Yes, I found her, all right. She abandoned me when I was a toddler so she could follow an American airman over here."

She took a bottle of tablets out of a pocket. "Here, take some of these, they will take away some of the pain. You seemed to care about me when I told you part of my story the other night. You deserve to hear the rest. You've been good to me, after all. Someone I might call a friend. Up to now, anyway." Cassie swallowed the pills gratefully, not knowing or caring how many there were, as long as they took away the pain.

Wendy sat down beside her now, looking directly into her eyes as she had in the little lounge where they had drunk their cocoa, the same expression on her face.

"There were some old letters in that box of Mr. Wright's. They were postmarked from Bury St. Edmunds. When I read them I knew they were from my mother and I began to remember some other things then, things I had seen and things I had heard. In every one of them she had asked about Gillian. I knew that was me. The Wrights called me Wendy because they already had a child named Gillian, you see. I remembered reading in those letters about a beautiful country place, a happy place somewhere. I kept the letters and finally found that house. I made up my mind that I was going to live there, and I did. I got hired on as cook's helper, then worked my way on up till I was helping the estate manager with the books. I never told anyone who I was, but I learned everything there is to know about that estate. My estate. It will be mine now."

Cassie's only hope, she knew, was to keep the woman talking and pray that someone would hear them, find them.

"How do you know there aren't any other heirs?"

"There is one other, actually, but he doesn't care anything about the place. Jesse Lankford."

Cassie, already cold, now felt a new surge of ice in her veins.

"Oh, I've always known about him. If he ever shows up, I'll work a deal with him to buy him out. If he won't sell, well then…. But don't you worry about that, dear."

"How did you find your mother?"

"Oh, that was easy. Household staff talk and gossip. They love to tell family secrets, especially to new girls. It didn't take long for me to learn about the wayward daughter, who I knew was my mother, even learned about where she was. She was right there in Cherry Lake all the time, drinking herself into stupors and mooning after the worthless dog that fathered me."

Cassie didn't have to ask his name. She already knew who that man was. Jack Dothard.

Wendy continued. "When I had enough money saved up to see me through for six months, I came here. I bought myself a car and it didn't take long at all to find where my mother lived."

"Was she glad to see you?" asked Cassie, squirming. The pain was beginning to ease a bit.

Wendy snorted at Cassie's apparent ignorance. "She had no idea who I was, did she? I didn't use the name of Janet Wright, because she would have remembered that. And I certainly wasn't going to use my real name, Gillian. She'd be suspicious then, wouldn't she? So I just became Wendy Foster. She had made me a foster child, after all. I rented an apartment, and managed to make sure she got to know me in the course of her daily routine. I watched and found out where she shopped, where she got her booze, every place she was likely to go, and I went there too. And I made sure she heard me using the accent she would be sure to recognize. After we'd had a few conversations, I started going to visit her, and then one day she asked me to come and stay with her. She said her son had just moved over to Hartsville to work, and she was lonely.

"I lived there with her for a month and she never knew who I was until right at the end. You should have seen her face when I told her. Gillian Howe. That was my name when I was born. Gillian Howe was a very fortunate little girl. For a while, anyway."

"What did she say when she found out who you are?"

Wendy's face clouded and her eyes filled with tears that went unshed. "Not much. Didn't have a chance to. She had told me before, though, that she had another child besides Jamey, but that it didn't matter any more, that Jamey was the only one who mattered now. She said if his dad—our dad—found out about it, that she had given one of his children away, she'd lose him. So I searched until I found my birth certificate. It was in a trunk in her attic. Then when she caught me going through the trunk I pushed her down and locked her in the attic, but she will be able to get out someway. And she won't tell, because then she'd lose Jack, when he found out she'd given away his first child, wouldn't she? Not much of a loss, that."

Through the fog that was beginning to settle in on her as the pills took hold, Cassie thought, I must keep her talking. Someone will come. "What happened to Jamey?"

"He wanted to go see his mother, but I wasn't ready for that to happen. She might still be locked in the attic. But if she was able to get out, she might just tell him about me, and I didn't want him to know about that before I left this place. And I am leaving, as soon as I get my car loaded." She stirred, making herself more comfortable.

"Anyway, I offered to drive him, and fixed up a bottle of wine and took it along. There were a lot of pills crushed up and dissolved in it, but he couldn't tell the difference. The pills just gave the wine a flowery taste, and he was such a kid he didn't know what wine is supposed to taste like. I drove around for a while, running errands here and there on the way to Cherry Lake. It was slow going because

208

of the snow, and I just took my time. The roads were getting impassible anyway.

"He drank almost the whole bottle before he went to sleep. I turned around then and started back here. He roused up once and started raving, getting violent. I just hit him on the head with the empty bottle and then stopped the car and pushed him out. It was real late by then." She was quiet for just a moment, then said, "I sort of regret that now. He was a good kid. I didn't mean for him to die. I just didn't want him going to see his mother before I had a chance to get far away from here. It won't be long now, anyway. I have my birth certificate. I am somebody now. I have an identity of my own. And Gillian Howe is once again a very fortunate little girl."

Cassie noticed her own speech slurring as she asked, "Why would your mother not be able to get out of the attic?"

"She fell. I think she was hurt. I wonder if she hurt as much as I had."

"Was it you who locked me out on the balcony?"

"Yes. Olivia had told me about Jesse, and she said she had told 'them' about me. I figured she was talking about Jesse. I looked in his room first to see if there was anything in there about me. You almost caught me in there, but I slipped back later and watched you. I saw you coming out of his room with some papers in your hand. Then I moved some things into the room next to yours on the other side from Meg's, and watched you from there every chance I got. When you went out on the balcony that night I locked you out so I could search your room. You were pretty smart to break that glass. I thought you'd be out there for a long time, but I heard the glass breaking and never got another chance to look when I thought it would be safe. Now it doesn't matter."

Cassie, if she had a response, kept it to herself. She knew now what Wendy had in store for her, and resigned herself to hope and to prayer that someone, someone, would come and help her. She was too deep now in the drug's effects to think up any more questions. She barely heard Wendy saying, "You'll probably have pneumonia before the pills wear off. I hope you don't die of exposure first. They'll find you just in time, with any luck." The coldness was an unbearable pain, and consciousness faded as Wendy moved toward the door. In the last second of consciousness, from an ever increasing distance, she heard Wendy say, "Goodbye, Cassie. You were a good friend until you started to meddle. You'll sleep for hours and by the time they find you, I will be on a plane to some other place. I have lots of time before I go back to England to claim what's really mine. Goodbye."

Cassie heard the door close. Before the lock snapped shut on the other side, she was deep in a drug-induced sleep.

Twenty-eight

As Bernard turned the car up onto the mountain road leading to the hotel, Gillis sat looking out the window in deep thought, until Jesse shouted, "Stop! There's someone out there running in the woods. Looks like a woman! We have to stop her." He was out of the car as it stopped, skidding a little bit as it did so. Gillis hit the ground on the run, and together they closed in on the fleeing figure.

"Stop! What's the matter? We can help you!" Gillis called, but the figure turned and began running in the opposite direction. "Stop!" he called again. "This is the police." An outcropping of rock forced the fleeing person to veer back in their direction. Bernard, who had left his vehicle and run along an intercepting path in anticipation of just such a maneuver, had little trouble in apprehending the woman.

The other two were there in very short order. "God!" exclaimed Bernard. "Gillis, it's only Wendy. I thought it was some criminal trying to evade arrest," he said, releasing his hold on her. Gillis stood and stared at her. She made a sudden move as if to flee again, but Jesse took a firm hold on her arm. She struggled against him for a moment then became quite still, her eyes large with panic, darting from one face to the other.

"Why were you running like that?" Gillis asked.

"I was just, uh, I was going down to the supermarket parking lot to pick up my car. I had to leave it there when the snow started." Her eyes darted from one to the other.

"In the supermarket lot? That's between the supermarket and the jail," Gillis said, his face hard with realization. "You'd better come back to the hotel with us. The car can wait a bit longer," he said, taking her other arm and leading her back to the van. This time he sat in the back with Jesse, Wendy wedged between them.

At the hotel he sent for Nate and Ike, and when they arrived, asked for the keys to Ike's office so he could question Wendy, and then secure her there under Nate's watchful eye, confident she could not escape, while he, Gillis, checked out the situation. But when he began questioning her, Wendy said not a word. She sat mute, staring straight ahead as if she didn't hear a thing. "Wendy, I'm going to ask you for help in a murder investigation. If you do not cooperate, I will have to charge you with obstructing the law." He handed Nate his handcuffs, saying, "Use them if she tries to leave, but not unless she does." Then he began to question the others in the hotel.

Evelyn knew nothing of Wendy's behavior or, for that matter, Cassie's whereabouts. None of the people engaged in their activities in the lounge were aware that anything unusual had happened. Meg came down the stairs just as Gillis and Jesse started up them. "Is Cassie up there?" Gillis asked.

"No, I was just looking for her. She's not in her room."

After much searching and many questions, they still had not found her. No one had seen her in quite a while. There was no clue as to where she might be. Returning to Ike's office, he asked Nate and then Wendy where they had last seen Cassie. Nate hadn't seen her since their last meal. Wendy just stared straight ahead, seemingly oblivious to all of them.

Jesse immediately asked Meg to start searching the upstairs area of the hotel for any sign of her, and after explaining the situation, obtained a master key so that every guest room could be searched. There were no objections from the guests, at least those who knew that Cassie was missing. Gillis asked Evelyn to search through the staff area. He sent Bernard to the lower area where the actors were, to search and to solicit their help in locating Cassie. Ike was asked to lead them through every outside building and secluded area on the site.

He led them first to the greenhouse, and a cursory look told them it was empty. Ike walked ahead of them, moving on behind the hotel past the shop, until Gillis called him back. "Unlock this door Ike," he said. At the door of the shop, Raucous stood on her hind legs sniffing and scratching at a dark stain below the door, looking like a small white fury. As they drew even with her, she yowled and yowled at them.

"Aw, it ain't locked. Besides, there's nothing in there except wood work stuff. I work out here every night, never do lock it," Ike said, coming back to join them. Then he looked at the door and said, "But it's locked now. Wonder why?" He began searching for his keys.

"There's that cat of Meg's again," said Gillis. "There's something in that building and it could be Cassie. Hurry up. Let's go."

"Oh, it's just my shop. She wouldn't be in there. I must have locked it by mistake."

"Then unlock it, damn it! Let's see what's inside there. That cat isn't just looking for mice," came Gillis' sharp command.

Ike fumbled as he tried to insert the key in the lock.

"Just open it, man!" said Jesse. Ike finally pulled the door open, then stepped back as the other two men entered. What they saw brought dread to Gillis' eyes, but it brought fire to Jesse's. Cassie lay still and white on the floor, with no visible signs of life. Blood had oozed from the lacerated skin and formed a small puddle on the floor. Jesse said, "Ike, go get Doc! Now! Hurry!" and knelt beside the icy form, instantly listening for breath and feeling for a pulse. Relief surged through him like a live current when he felt a feeble flutter at her throat. Pulling his coat off, he spread it over her and found a tarp to place over that.

It seemed ages before Ike came back with Doc in tow. In just a few minutes they had fashioned a stretcher from a wide piece of wood and gently moved the frail figure onto it. They carried her to her room where, with Meg's help, they removed the tape and most of her outer clothing. Then the men fetched warm blankets and towels as Meg massaged the cold, limp arms and legs and Doc applied ointment to the wounds and to the irritated skin where the tape had bound her. Evelyn brought an urn of hot coffee and several cups. When at last they had her settled, Gillis left them, saying he was going downstairs to have a little chat with Wendy and Bernard.

When the others had done all they could, they began to drift away. Meg stayed, sitting in the wing chair. Jesse drew the other chair up beside the bed and watched as warmth and color began to return to Cassie's cold and injured body. At one point Jesse excused himself to go see what was keeping Gillis, but he was back by the time Cassie's eyes fluttered open for a brief moment. Meg was there with a cup of coffee laced with sugar and cream. Jesse lifted Cassie's shoulders as Meg held the cup to her lips. Cassie took a weak sip of the strong brew, then another and another, at last lying back, waking slowly, recalling reluctantly the events that had placed her in this situation.

When it had all come back to her, she raised a hand to her brow. "Oh, my God. I must tell Gillis. Where is Gillis?" she said, trying to rise to a sitting position but stopped by the fresh pain in her injured leg.

Doc came in to administer an injection for the pain, but Cassie refused. "Not until after I've talked to Gillis and Jesse. And Meg, too. And you too, Doc. Maybe you can explain some things."

"I'll get Gillis," said Jesse rising from his chair. "He was in Ike's office trying to question Wendy just a little while ago." He paused and said to Doc, "It's strange. She was just sitting there, staring straight ahead. It was as if she was somewhere else but her body is still here."

"Yes. That's a perfect description of it. Her mind has gone to a safe place, away from the trouble she is in right now."

Meg made sure there were chairs for everyone, then seated herself near the window and watched and listened. Her son had not yet been exonerated, after all, and it seemed as if the moment of truth was near.

Over the next hour Cassie related Wendy's confessions to them all, repeating as closely as possible the things Wendy had told her, beginning with the way she had left the hotel with Jamey, and how she prevented him from going to visit his mother. They let her tell it the way she wanted to, speaking only when she elicited a response from them. Jesse kept her hand in his, and if asked why, he would have said he was holding it to give her reassurance and to enable himself to monitor the state of her nerves. That is what he would have said, but the others in the room would not have believed it to be entirely true.

Their eyes never left Cassie's face as she began to tell about her exploration of the parking lot. She told them that Wendy had confessed to stealing the birth certificate of the baby Janet Wright after watching the horrid old man die in agony, about her keeping that identity through the years, until she arrived at Cherry Lake, where she became Wendy Foster. She related how Wendy had found the letters that led her to America and Olivia, and how she had found the birth certificate that would confirm her identity as Olivia's firstborn, Gillian Howe. And that she intended now to get what was hers, the estate in England, Jesse's home.

She told how Wendy had drugged Jamey, then pushed him from the car into the snow, where he lay unconscious until he died. As she related how Wendy had pushed Olivia down and left her injured, she said, "I don't think she even knows Olivia is dead. She said she didn't mean for any of them to die, she just didn't want them to stop her doing what she intended to do. She even told me that someone would probably find me soon, but not before she was well away."

"I don't know how I could have been so deceived by someone as deranged as she is," she concluded, tears welling up in her downcast eyes.

Doc began to explain. "You weren't taken in at all, Cassie. Wendy was being exactly herself all the time. In her sick mind, she just felt no responsibility for any of the things that had happened as a result of her behavior. Her own early trauma had obviously caused her to dissociate herself from the results of her actions. To her it was all a matter of survival." He looked away, his gaze moving toward the door. "I'm not a psychiatrist, but that's a pretty well defined phenomenon. And now, with all that has happened this afternoon, she is in an almost catatonic state. She is definitely living in a separate reality from the rest of us. I should probably go and see about her again."

He moved about a bit, then continued, "If she had you fooled, she fooled me more. I have been treating her for depression with certain MAO inhibitors and tricyclic antidepressants, and I feel like those are the things she put in the wine that she gave to Jamey. Wine and those medications just do not mix. I've talked to her about it before, but she wouldn't hear me." He hushed suddenly, as if examining his own role in this chain of events.

Meg's head snapped around then. "MAO? Did you say MAO?" She laughed lightly, and said, "Cassie, that's what I heard him say that I thought sounded like mayonnaise, or the Mayo Clinic. Remember?"

Cassie did remember. "I should have made the connection then, but of course we had no clue that Wendy was so troubled." She smiled at her friend as Doc left the room to see to Wendy.

Meg refilled Cassie's cup and placed the steaming hot drink in Cassie's hand. Before she had finished the drink, Nate appeared at the door. "Knock, knock. How is the patient?"

"Feeling better now, I think," said Gillis. "You can probably say hello to her without doing too much harm."

"Good. Why is it, Cassie, that you are the one to dive headlong into danger whenever it comes near?"

"Just need a little excitement in my life I guess, Nate. But don't put that in your paper, will you? I need a little break from excitement right now."

"If you insist. But I do need your help with something. I'm setting up the story about the performances the other night, and need to know the names of some of the people. Do you feel up to looking at the pictures and telling me who is in which?"

"Of course. Let me see." She reached for the envelope and Jesse handed it to her. She withdrew the photos. "Here's the one called Regan, with the harp, and Heather, who sings with her. You know them, of course. You can get their last names from Evelyn. She'll have them at the desk on the registration forms. And there's Raucous. You can get her last name from Meg. Oh, and here's Bernard. He makes a lovely large fairy, doesn't he?" They laughed, Gillis somewhat uncomfortably. "And these are the Morris Dancers. There's Kitty, and there's Heather. I don't know that one. This is the boy who played Puck, and of course that's Wendy there in the long white wig."

Gillis was on his feet, and Jesse was quickly on his at the other side of the bed. "Where?" they demanded simultaneously.

"Right there, in the middle. See? You might not recognize her, with that wig. That and the costume make her look different."

"We aren't the only ones who didn't recognize her. That Mrs. Pitts didn't recognize her either. She's the one who was visiting Olivia, you know."

"Yes, I know. All too well, now, thank you very much," said Cassie, smoothing the covers over her lap.

Gillis sat nearest Cassie's head, leaning forward with his elbows on his knees, his hands interlocked to support his chin as he looked into Cassie's eyes. "How did you happen to be in that shop with Wendy?"

She thought about that, looking into space, telling the story as she recalled the sequence of events. "I had been out looking at the cars, trying to figure out which one belongs to whom. Wendy came out, and I asked her about the ones that were there, but there wasn't one that she claimed. I knew she had supposedly left with Jamey in her car that afternoon, so she must have one. I wanted to ask her about the one in your parking lot, but I just asked if she had left hers in town for some reason. I guess that's all it took to give me away though. I already knew too much, and when I asked about the car it scared her."

"When did you suspect the car in my parking lot belonged to Wendy?" asked Gillis.

"Not until I read something...," she looked at Jesse for his nod of approval then went on, "Jesse's letter. Anyway, I got out there and she told me who the cars belonged to. I just had no idea she would do what she did," her voice trembling with tears as she recalled the hurt, the betrayal.

"It's all right, Cassie," Jesse said, lightly rubbing the back of her hand, the one he had been holding again since he sat down.

"I've been feeling like a dope ever since we left Cherry Lake," Gillis said, looking at Jesse. "Still do, because I had looked at the cars in the parking lot at the hotel and when I didn't find any sign of a hit-and-run, I put off checking the registrations to see who owned them.

"Then, when we were getting into Bernard's van at the coffee shop to come back here, it dawned on me that there is hardly a place on that thing that isn't dented or banged up someway, and I began to suspect him. I even had a scenario all figured out for how it could have happened. Motive, means and method."

"Did you question him about it?"

"No. When we got back here, we found this," he waved a hand in Cassie's direction. "It scares me, though, to think how easy it would be to charge the wrong person with a crime, even with our criteria. Scares me and makes me feel sort of dumb."

"Your criteria is all you have to go on when you're looking for facts," said Cassie. "I had a different set of criteria that I just simply overlooked. Wendy told me about all those traumatic experiences at the first of the week, and with my training I should have realized they would have had a powerful psychological effect on her. But it never entered my mind."

"Well, that's enough self recrimination from both of us. Let's get back to the facts. What happened next?"

"Where was I? Oh, yes. When we got even with the shop, she said she had come out to get something from there, and asked if I wanted to come in and look around at the antiques and stuff. I was already interested in that part, so I just went right on in. At least I started in. Somehow I managed to fall in the doorway and hit my kneecap. You know how that hurts. I almost passed out. Before I knew what was happening, she had pulled me inside and she was saying something about splinting the injured leg to the other one. By the time I realized what she was really doing, it was too late. The rest you know."

After Gillis left to try questioning Wendy again, Jesse said, "The snow is melting now, and the roads are pretty clear. We'll probably be able to go home soon, but Cassie, you're going to need someone to help you for a while." He would have said more but Meg interrupted.

"That's no problem. Raucous and I will be there with her until she is back on her feet."

"What about Ben? Won't he be needing you now, too?"

Meg looked at him, surprised, and hopeful. "I guess he might. I really don't know. Maybe," she paused, and Jesse spoke into the silence.

"Tell you what. You can stay with Cassie at night, I'll drive you back and forth, don't worry about that, and I'll stay with her in the daytime. That won't be any problem at all. It'll be a lot like being in one big house, since we live so near each other."

Meg thought for only a moment. "Okay. For a few days, until we're sure Ben is okay with this. Then I'll just come and stay as long as I'm needed."

Jesse hesitated for a minute before he asked, "What do you suppose Jack will do? I mean, he's lost more than any of us, and we haven't even given him a thought, really. Where is he, anyway? I haven't seen him since we got Cassie up here."

"You haven't seen him since he and Ike hightailed it out of here right after you and Gillis found Cassie. They didn't know I saw them, much less heard them, but Ike told Jack they needed to lie low for a while, needed to go somewhere private and talk, decide what they were going to do about the 'goods', as Ike put it. They got in his truck and lit out."

Jesse leaned back, straightening his back with his fingers splayed on his knees. He was quiet for a thoughtful moment, gazing at his hands. "Well, a lot of the responsibility for all this is on his head, so we will just wait and see what happens about the antiques business, what Jack decides to do in the future. He hasn't shown much concern for the people he has hurt. He may just need to face that. And he doesn't seem to have a very strong bond with Ben, certainly not with you, Meg, but he does still have a sister in Cherry Lake who is always ready to stand by him."

Cassie had been quiet and thoughtful during their conversation but now she expressed some of her thoughts aloud. "You know, I wonder if we'd ever got all those young people together at one time, if we'd have seen any resemblances. I know how much Ben looks like you, Meg, and I know, at least I realize now, that the picture of Jamey sort of resembled you, Jesse."

"And I noticed Wendy's resemblance to Olivia the minute I saw her, but at the time I didn't even know Olivia had another child, so I didn't mention it," Jesse said. "But that first day in the dining room, I knew her accent and the expressions she used were too genuinely East Anglia to have been learned by rote. She grew up with some of those things. At the time it didn't seem too important, because a lot of the actors are true Brits."

"The thing is," Cassie continued, bringing the conversation back to the children, "they all have the same father, but none of them look like him. One dead, one with a severe psychosis." She paused for just a second before adding, "At least there is one who seems to be made of good stuff. You're very blessed in that boy, Meg."

"Don't I know that? And you know what? I've been grieving because he is growing up and away from me, but now, after all this, you know how I feel about that? I feel like I can encourage him to go on and become everything he is capable of being."

Doc came in, looking tired and disappointed. Meg asked, "Did you get her to talk?"

"No," he said, "her mind has gone, as the old folks used to say. I don't know where it went, but it is not with her body." Then he spoke to Cassie. "How do you feel now? Any pain?"

"No, not right now. I think I'm going to be all right. Thank you so much."

"You'll need to come by the clinic and let me get some x-rays when you leave the hotel. Bernard can take us by there on the way home. I'm sure he won't mind. You've got a mighty bad bruise there. And there may be a fracture of the kneecap. Meanwhile, stay off of it, all right?"

"Yes, I don't think I could walk if I tried right now. That kneecap thing, that was the most painful. It completely wiped me out. I never knew a blow right there could hurt so much!"

"Well, you know now. In the future you should try to be a little more considerate of that leg," Doc said, giving her a big wink while he patted her shoulder.

"All right. I don't really think there is any place I want to go at this particular time except home, anyway." She looked up and found Jesse gazing into space with concern smouldering in his eyes and wondered what was bothering him now—if possibly there was some new complication she hadn't yet heard about.

Twenty—nine

Sunday, January 19, 1985

Melting snow was a steady drip off the eaves of the hotel as Bernard boarded group after group of people to return them to their homes. The Shakespeareans went first, eager to get back to their own habitat.

When the mayor and his family passed through the lounge on their way to the van, Amy pulled away from her father's hand and came to where Cassie was resting on a couch. The little girl laid a folded paper on Cassie's lap, explaining, "I made this for you. I'm sorry you got hurt. Thank you for the snowman. I won't forget how to make them. Maybe we can make another one sometime. Good-bye, Cassie."

Cassie, having looked at the picture the child had given her, reached out and drew her into a strong embrace. "Good-bye, Amy. I won't forget our snowman either, because I'll always have this to remind me. Thank you. It is a beautiful water color. And you are a beautiful girl. I'll see you after I get well, I promise." The mayor took Amy's hand and led her away, smiling at Cassie as he joined his wife at the door. They left and boarded the van along with one or two of the commissioners and their wives.

The older residents of the village were not quite so eager to get back to their homes. They had been enjoying the pleasure of being cared for and of seeing their lifelong friends again, but they went anyway, with promises to get together more often than they had in the past.

At last Bernard had delivered his first group up Mountain Road. These were the ones who lived nearest the hotel and the town. His last load of passengers included Cassie, stretched out on the seat behind Bernard and Jesse, with Meg, Doc and Nell on the back seat. Gillis had gone back to the station and retrieved his vehicle, stating he would be up later to get an official statement from Cassie. Raucous and Porsche rode in the very rear of the van in their respective carriers.

At the clinic Bernard carried Cassie in, and Doc x-rayed her injured leg, discovering a fragment of chipped bone at her kneecap. He made an appointment for her with an orthopedic doctor in Murphree in one week, hoping the snow would be gone by then. He splinted her leg, fitted her with crutches and handed her a small vial of pain pills. Then they were on their way home.

As soon as they started the ride up the mountain, a lively conversation began between the two animals in the back of the van, the wires of their carriers keeping them safely separated from each other. Raucous, her infinite curiosity sparked by this previously-heard but never-before-touched animal beside her, began with mewing sounds that gradually increased to trilling vibrations, and from there to clearly demarcated meows in normal cat language. There was no response from the arrogant Porsche. Raucous, apparently not accustomed to being snubbed, finally reached a tentative paw through the wires of her cage toward the near-hairless feline in the other cage. Porsche hissed. Raucous was not amused. A low growl began in the depths of her cat soul and reverberated long, as her hair seemed to grow about three inches longer, standing straight out, her tail swelling like a feather duster and standing straight up. There was then much horrible hissing between the cages, and though she tried dramatically, Porsche could not in any way make her hair look nearly as frightening or impressive as Raucous', but my, oh my, the howl that finally erupted from that cat's genetically powerful vocal chords!

The human passengers in the van could only listen and wonder at what was being said between the two, and give thanks that it wasn't directed toward them. Once, Nell turned to speak soothingly to Porsche, but she was coldly ignored by the furious beast and soon turned back to the humans for companionship.

At last, they arrived at Cassie's door. Bernard, Jesse and Nell carried in the luggage and the still angry Raucous. Doc and Meg helped Cassie, now wearing a splint and hobbling along on crutches, make her painful way into the house. When Cassie was settled into bed, they prepared to continue on their way to deliver the other travelers home. As they were leaving, Doc drew Nell into the curve of his arm and said, "I guess this is as good a time as any to invite you all to the wedding. We're going to be married—when, Honey?"

Nell had the grace to blush. She was unaccustomed to being addressed by pet names, especially in public, but she quickly stifled any objection and smiled up into Doc's proud face. "How about in June, Dear? Maybe the first weekend in June."

"Sounds good to me." He looked at the others. "Hope you can all make it. In fact, Jesse, I'd like you to be my best man, if you will."

"Of course," Jesse said.

Nell looked from Cassie to Meg, and back again, and said nothing. Neither woman paid the slightest heed to her. Meg was already making tea and looking for something to feed her patient as Doc and Nell closed the door behind them. After they had gone Cassie said, "This week is going to make several wonderful chapters in my history of Hartsville."

While Meg was preparing the food, Jesse pulled a chair up to Cassie's bed and sat down leaning forward with his elbows on his knees. For perhaps the first time ever, he was about to take hold of his life. It may be a mistake, but he had to do it. After a few moments he spoke so that only she could hear his words. "I'm glad you're going to be okay. While I was gone you kept popping into my mind and I found myself wondering what you were doing at those exact moments. I guess I was worried about you, but I can't be sure. It's not something I usually do, worry about people."

She returned his look, understanding all that lay behind his words, and suddenly realized that she no longer needed or wanted to postpone life, waiting for something that might never happen. "I know what you mean. I kept finding myself wondering when you'd be back, wondering what was going on to keep you away, wondering if you were all right. I don't know why either. Maybe we've just been neighbors so long that we've developed some sort of bond, having a certain amount of neighborly concern for one another but not enough to get our attention, what with each of us knowing the other was right next door most of the time."

With his left eyebrow raised, he smiled at her in a most knowing way. "Yes, maybe so." He stood, preparing to leave.

She couldn't let him go without thanking him. "Jesse, when I was going through that ordeal at the hotel, I was really frightened. When I came to, I was still scared until I saw you, and then I knew that everything would be all right. I can't tell you how much I appreciate that. Not just your help or your friendship, but *you*, for being the genuine person you are."

"I understand," he said, and leaning over her bed, placed a fleeting kiss on her forehead. "I couldn't have said it better. For now." Pausing at the door he said, "I'll be going back to England soon. There's a lot to be taken care of there. But not until you are well, of course. You may want to go with me." He walked out of her room, pausing to give her a long look and a smile before he left.

Cassie touched the place where his kiss had fallen, and knew she was going to need to have a long talk with Matt's ghost. Well, one day soon anyway, after she was back on her feet, and all this confusion and turmoil had settled down.

Meg opened the door of Raucous' cage and placed a saucer of warm milk just outside it. The whiteness within gathered itself into the shape of a cat and cautiously emerged into the warmth and the tempting aromas of Cassie's kitchen. Purring her appreciation to Meg, she began to lap up the milk, which left no trace on her whiskers.

Across the road the lights went on in Jesse's house and before long smoke drifted from his chimney as he set the fire to crackling in the grate. When he had the kettle whistling, he brewed a bold cup of Typhoo tea and settled down to gaze into the fire which reflected the glow that warmed his heart. "Ahhh," he sighed. "Home. And peace." He rested his gaze on the embroidered sampler that hung above the mantle, the little cross-stitched blessing that was the only thing he had brought with him that was his mother's: 'East, West, Home's Best'.

Down the mountain at the Sheriff's Department, Deputy Gillis dialed the Corona Hotel to tell Evelyn that her assistant was presently on her way to a locked ward in a distant hospital and would not be back to work in the foreseeable future. And too, he would tell her that Ike and Jack Dothard had not been located, but he would keep trying.

Up the mountain at the Corona Hotel the phone rang on and on, ignored by Evelyn, Ben and Bernard as they sat in the little lounge by their own fire with their own private thoughts, and gathered their wits about them before planning how best to arrange the hotel's return to business as usual.

Porsche shivered in her sleep and dreamed of one day owning a fluffy white fur coat.

Raucous seemed only to smile. She found it lovely being Meg Dothard's cat.

The End